MOHAMED'S SONG

To Joanne

Sing a new Song

KEITH R. CLEMONS

GEORGE COLTON
PUBLISHING

Most GEORGE COLTON PUBLISHING products are available at special quantity discounts for bulk purchase for sales promotions, premiums, fund-raising, and educational needs. For details, email: GeorgeColton@att.net

Published by George Colton Publishing LLC
Mohamed's song / Keith R. Clemons. -- 1st ed.
Library of Congress Control Number: 2014903945
ISBN 978-0-9916129-1-8

Quotations from the Bible are taken from the King James Version with language updates for clarification.

Quotations from the Quran are taken from *The Quran Translation*, 7th edition, translated by Abdullah Yusef Ali (Elmhurst, NY: Tahrike Tarsile Quran, Inc., 2001).

The characters portrayed in this book are fictitious unless they are historical figures explicitly named. Otherwise, any resemblance to actual people, whether living or dead, is coincidental.

Also by Keith R. Clemons

Stretching Heaven

Mohamed's Moon

Angel in the Alley
Honorable Mention - Word Guild 2008

These Little Ones
Best Contemporary Fiction - Word Guild 2007

Above the Stars
Best Contemporary Fiction - Word Guild 2005
Honorable Mention - IPPY Awards 2005

If I Should Die
Best Contemporary Fiction - Word Guild 2004

Songs

The Love of God - Frederick M. Lehman - 1917

My Jesus I Love Thee - William R. Featherstom - 1864

Doxology (Awake my Soul) - Thomas Ken - 1674

He paid a debt He did not owe - Anonymous

To my wife Kathryn, my daughter Melody, and
my sister Kathleen, who employed their talents in
the design, layout, and critique of this manuscript.

And to all the readers of Mohamed's Moon
who came to me saying they would like a sequel.
It is for you I have written this book. Enjoy!

Soli Deo Gloria — To God alone the glory!

Could we with ink the ocean fill
And were the skies of parchment made
Were every stalk on earth a quill
And every man a scribe by trade,

To write the love of God above
Would drain the ocean dry
Nor could the scroll contain the whole
Though stretched from sky to sky.

From, *The Love of God* by Frederick M. Lehman

PROLOGUE

...along the road I saw a light from heaven, brighter than the sun, shining around me... — Acts 26:13

IT HAD BEGUN as a spark—the sun glinting off a piece of broken glass in the alley—and spread from there until it consumed the sky. Amin found himself standing in a circle of light, though it wasn't light really, that description was too narrow, it was more like the brilliance of a thousand prisms reflecting the radiance of the sun. His body tingled as the pellets of color danced across his face.

He raised his hand to block the light, but it engulfed him, drawing him in. He reached for it, wanting to be embraced, but something held him back. It felt like the light, or whatever it was, was trying to communicate, but with words he couldn't understand. It was a language of intrinsic beauty, notes, yawls, and vibrations; a sound so pure he was certain only ears tuned to the frequency of heaven could comprehend its meaning.

He yearned to be touched by the light. He wanted to reach out and hold it. It wasn't just producing warmth, it was providing something else. It was generating pure energy in the form of something he recognized because it was what he felt when he sat next to Sabah, only magnified a thousand times over—it was love.

Sabah stepped outside searching for her husband, but the street was empty. Her hand slid up to touch the wall, the rough block heated by the sun feeling warm under her fingers. She made her way down the lane toward the alley, tapping a plastic water bottle with her foot sending it skittering across the pavement. Her skin tingled. She turned the corner and was brought up short by what she saw—*Amin?*

Her husband stood in the alley with his hands raised like he was fending something off, but...what? Whatever it was, she couldn't see it. His lips were moving. He was trying to speak but no words came from his mouth. His body appeared to be quaking.

Something heavy, like a soft weight, began pressing down on Sabah's shoulders, pushing her back. She staggered, bumping into the wall and with her hands pressed flat against the brick, stepped to the side fingering her way along. It seemed to take forever to complete the two or three steps it took to bring her safely around the corner again.

Seconds passed with the beating of her heart. She tugged at her scarf, pulling it in front of her face thinking if she hid inside her *hijab*, she wouldn't be seen.

Her husband was whimpering, the sound of his voice echoing in the alley strained as he begged the specter for mercy. Finally she heard a *whummmp*, like a sail caught in a sudden gust of wind, and the heaviness lifted.

She crept forward peeking around the corner. Her husband was collapsed in the lane. A plume of dust wafted around his head. She raised her hand to her mouth—and gasped.

CHAPTER 1

Be not forgetful to entertain strangers: for thereby some have entertained angels unawares. — *Hebrews 13:1-2*

THE SOUND jolted Mohamed from his sleep. He lay unmoving, eyes open, waiting for the noise to stop. It continued unabated, relentless as a woodpecker attacking larvae in a palm tree—*tap, tap, tap, tap, tap.* His eyes were staring into the blackness above him, his heart pounding. He tossed his blanket aside and sat up rolling his feet over the edge of the mattress.

Layla stirred, snuggling the covers under her chin. "What time is it?" She brought her arm out to look at her watch and tucked her pillow around her face. Her words were muffled. "See if it can't wait until morning."

Mohamed nodded. He reached for his pants, pulling them on, and slipped into his shirt, shuffling into the living room drawn by the faint light emanating from the window. He raised the corner of the curtain and peeked outside. Two people were standing on the porch, a man and a woman, looking blue in the moon's pale glow. The man folded his arms in front of him, nervously glancing over his shoulder. Mohamed let the curtain slide back into place.

His heart quickened. He reached for the door, pulling it open.

The man stood in front of him, shivering. His eyes went to the woman beside him, and then checked the dirt road up and down as though searching for someone lurking in the shadows. He brought his head around to face Mohamed.

"Yes, what is it?"

"Please, can we come inside? We don't want to be seen."

Mohamed sighed and stood back, letting the young couple enter and then stepped onto the porch to scan the road himself. His eyes probed the darkness. Down the lane the worker's quarters stood in the moonlight like a brick of white cheese, but all was calm. He closed the door and turned to face his guests.

"So, what brings you to my door at this late hour?"

The man's furtive eyes flicked back and forth, scanning the interior of the house. "I was told to come," he whispered. "I had this…this thing, like someone was speaking to me who wasn't really there. Whoever, or whatever, it was told me to come to you. You are *Masehia*, are you not? I think it was Isa. He showed me the scars in his hands. That's…that's all I know. But I am a Muslim, right? You understand?"

Mohamed stepped around his visitors and went to turn on a lamp. The room filled with light.

The man wore a button down shirt and blue denims and looked to be in his early twenties without beard or mustache, though the stubble on his cheeks suggested he hadn't shaved in at least twenty-four hours. He had thick eyebrows and dark hair which he combed straight back. His nose was flat, setting his eyes wide apart, and his mouth was red and knotted giving him the appearance of someone chewing a radish. It was warm outside, but not enough to account for the beads of sweat on his forehead. His hands were trembling. Mohamed couldn't see the woman's face. She was hiding behind her *Hijab*.

"I'm not afraid so much for myself as for Sabah," he glanced at his companion and then back at Mohamed, "I told her about my experience. I think she understands. I have decided to follow the man, Isa, but she has not yet decided for herself. If she joins me, her father will kill her for dishonoring the family.

Mohamed drew in a deep breath and let it out slow—*If you extend your soul to the hungry and satisfy the afflicted soul, then your light shall dawn in the darkness, and your darkness shall be as the noonday...* Layla would not like what he was about to do.

"*Al hamdullah*," he said. He extended his hand to the right, "There's a spare bedroom down the hall. I can put you up for the night. Tomorrow we'll see if we can't find someplace safe for you to stay."

CHAPTER 2

And he said unto them, follow me, and I will make you fishers of men.
— Matthew 4:18-20

MOHAMED WIPED the dust from his feet and crawled back into bed. He let his breath out slowly and tried to relax, lacing his fingers behind his head as he stared at the ceiling.

Layla was right. If they continued taking people in, they'd attract suspicion. He was putting those he loved in danger. But what was he supposed to do? The ceiling stared back at him, bereft of answers.

He rolled onto his side with his arm under his pillow, closing his eyes. He wished he were a prophet, someone who could see into the future, but his future was revealed only after the fact.

Layla squirmed, dragging the blanket off him as she pulled it over her shoulder. "Did you send them away?" she mumbled.

Mohamed didn't answer. She was only half awake, and she wouldn't like what he was thinking anyway—*she hadn't been there...*

A thin light fogged the horizon, dense and gray, but the city was asleep. Looking around, Mohamed could make out the shadow of several towering minarets. Soon the imams would be calling men to prayer. The town would awaken then.

Something on the side of a cinderblock wall caught his mother's attention. It was a cross painted on the side of a building.

They approached the door. His mother sipped in her breath and began to knock. He pulled his hand free of her grip, his eyes only half open. He felt heavy. He wanted to lie down and go to sleep. His mother grabbed his arm propping him up as she continued pounding.

When the door finally opened, a man stood there, yawwwning. He curled his shoulders in, shivering in the cold, then folded his arms in front of him.

"Please, can you help me? I am Christian but for a short time only. My family must not hear of this. I need a place to stay."

The man hesitated, searching for the right words. "I'm sorry, there's no room for you here," he said.

"But I am Christian. Do not Christians help other Christians?"

"Go home. There's nothing I can do. It is against the law to convert. Keep Isa in your heart but keep Him to yourself. To do otherwise will only bring pain."

"But...but I can't...I"

"You must. Do you think you are the only one? Only last month a girl came to me saying Isa had appeared to her. I urged her not to speak of it, but she would not listen. Last week they found her body. Her throat had been cut. If not for your own sake, do it for your son. I beg you, keep your conversion a secret."

"But what can I do? I have nowhere to go."

Mohamed rolled onto his back, staring into the black void of his conscious. He brought the luminous dial of his watch up to check the time—just after midnight. He closed his eyes again. A nervous energy coursed through his veins, his temples throbbing with the beating of his heart. He fluffed his pillow but try as he might, he couldn't get comfortable. He tossed the covers aside and sat up, looking back over his shoulder. Layla was asleep.

The night air coming through the open window was cool on his skin. He slipped into his shirt and pants and went outside.

The moon's blue light cast the cane in shadows as Mohamed made his way to the river. His *felucca*, barely visible in the thin light, was keeled to the side resting on the shore. He kicked off his sandals and stepped into the water, the silt swirling up around his bare feet. Taking hold of the gunwale, he reached over and set his Bible in the hull, then moved to the front and placed his shoulder under the bow, lifting as he slid the small boat back into the water. The Nile was moving slowly, highlighted by the moon peeking through the clouds. The boat turned into the current as he walked it out into the water and climbed inside.

The sail was tied to the spar. He loosed it, using the rope to draw it to the top of the mast. The lateen unfurled and billowed out, catching the breeze. He swung the boom around, turning the rudder, letting the wind carry him into the presence of God.

Mohamed lowered himself and sat down, allowing his *felucca* to drift with the current. Leaning against the mast, he scooped up his Bible flipping it open to the Gospel of John, the part where Christ first called His disciples.

He could relate to a guy like Peter, a crude fisherman with calloused hands, told to let down his nets in the shallows where the fish didn't congregate. He'd been fishing all night and hadn't caught a thing, but he did what Jesus said and instantly his net found so many fish, he couldn't haul them in. Then Jesus looked at Peter and said He would make him a fisher of men.

The wind whipped the sail, furling the canvas. God had spoken those very same words to him, though perhaps not in an audible voice, but definitely in the quiet of his heart.

And now here he was, out on the Nile worried about how many fish he might actually catch. The little boat he was in, with its triangular sail and coarse rigging—hemp ropes, steel rings and wood rudder—probably bore a striking resemblance to the one in which Jesus stood. The hull rocked back and forth; the lateen creaked; the current lapped against the bow. And he, like Peter, was indeed a fisher of men.

Mohamed closed the book. *I will make you a fisher of men.* That commission would send Peter into the temple to be beaten, cause him to be imprisoned, and ultimately cost him his life. Being a fisherman for Christ wasn't without cost. He stood and repositioned the rudder, swung the boom around, and with the sail popping in the wind, headed back to shore.

CHAPTER 3

Rejoicing in hope, patient in tribulation, continuing in prayer, distributing to the necessity of saints, given to hospitality.
— Romans 12:12-13

DAWN CAME with a call to pray ringing from the minaret on outskirts of the farm. Men rose and with their prayer rugs rolled under their arms, began the trek to the mosque. Standing at the open window, Mohamed watched as they plodded down the half mile dirt track to the main road, the shape of their bodies obscured by the morning fog, their long *galabias* glowing pink in the diffused red light of the sun. They were the labor force, men who had worked for his uncle Sayyid most of their lives, and now continued in service to his mother.

He turned to look at his wife. He envied her and her ability to sleep. He wished he could stay in bed and lose himself in the scent of her hair as he held her close, but the evening had been fraught with uncertainty and it needed it be addressed.

Sounds were coming from the kitchen, the women scurrying about preparing the morning meal. Layla looked to be resting soundly. He decided not to disturb her. He slipped out of the room to see if his guests were awake.

The service porch bustled with activity, the smell of dark Egyptian coffee permeating the air. Zainab sat at the dining room table with a cup in her hands.

"Good morning, my son. Did you rest well?"

"Morning, Mother. No, actually, I didn't." He leaned in to kiss her cheek and, walking around to the other side of the table, sat opposite her.

He lowered his voice. "We had visitors last night; a young couple. I know we're getting too many, but I had to let them in. The man said he'd received a vision of Christ, just as I once did, and Christ sent him here. I couldn't say no."

Zainab's eyes went to the door. "They were sent?" She looked at Mohamed again, addressing him by the name he used in public. "It's okay, Matthew. We're not going to turn anyone away."

"Nor can we ignore the danger it puts you in."

Zainab took a slow sip of her coffee. "What can they do to an old woman like me?" she said.

Sami, the oldest of the family servants, appeared holding a cup and saucer which he set in front of Mohamed. He trundled back to the kitchen swishing in his *galabia*, his bony knees arching outward as he returned with a coffee pot in hand. "Good morning, Haj Matthew," he said, bowing slightly as he filled the cup.

"Morning, Sami. Thank you, that's enough," Mohamed waved his hand though the cup was only half full. "Could you let the kitchen help know there will be two more joining us for breakfast."

"Ah, have friends come to visit?"

"No, just two new employees. I've put them up in the spare bedroom. Please see to their needs when you get the chance.

Sami's brown face wrinkled. He set the coffee pot down and rubbed his hands together, and when he spoke his lips flapped over toothless gums. "But Haj Matthew, we do not have any more jobs. Was I not speaking with the foreman just yesterday? He said he does not know what to do with all the people you bring. He says the workers are beginning to grumble. They think you are going to replace them."

"It's okay Sami. Leave Uthman to me. You just see that our guests are comfortable."

Zainab eased her chair back and stood. "Well we wouldn't want our visitors to think we're ignoring them. Come, we're being inhospitable. They're probably wondering if it's alright to join us for breakfast. Let's go make them feel welcome."

Zainab's mint green *hijab* rustled as she led her son down the hall. The morning shadows were lifting but the walls still held shades of gray, though it was light enough to see.

As soon as Mohamed was sure Sami could no longer hear, he leaned in close and whispered. "One more thing, Mother. The man received the vision, his wife did not. I suspect she's only here because he refused to leave her behind. You might want to be careful what you say. I get the feeling she's not overjoyed with his decision."

They stopped just outside the door. The couple kept their voices breathy in an obvious attempt to keep from being heard, but it was obvious they were having a spat.

Mohamed knocked lightly, bringing an end to the fight. Their heads snapped up as Mohamed and his mother entered. "Sorry to intrude, but we noticed you were awake. I thought it might be nice if we introduced ourselves." He placed a hand against his chest. "I'm Matthew Mulberry..."

Mohamed sipped in his breath. The deception was necessary. He couldn't let people know his real name. He was supposed to be dead. The Brotherhood counted him a martyr—though it was his twin who actually died. Matthew sacrificed himself so that he and Layla could live—*greater love hath no man than he lay down his life for a friend*—He'd taken his brother's name, not just because it allowed him to enter the country as a Christian, but to honor his brother and in some small way, keep his name alive.

"…and this is my mother, Zainab," he said, tipping his head to the side. "Unfortunately, my wife is still asleep, but you'll get a chance to meet her later. And you are?"

The young man looked flustered. He jumped up and turned to his wife taking her hand to lift her from the bed. The girl brought her scarf around to cover her face. "My name is Amin, and this is Sabah, my wife of one year," he said.

Zainab raised her chin and nodded slowly. "Sabah, Amin, I want you to know you're welcome here. My house is yours for as long as you wish to stay."

An awkward silence followed. Zainab waited for Amin to respond, but he seemed reluctant to speak.

The room was simple, furnished with a bed and an armoire. A few framed photographs graced the walls. The largest print showed a soccer player with his foot arched over his head having just launched a ball off the tip of his toe.

"You're the first married couple we've had as guests." Zainab continued, glancing over at her son. "Matthew told me about the appearance. She reached out and took Sabah's hand, bringing her around until they faced each other, but the young woman avoided her eyes.

"You're a very brave girl, Sabah. I admire your willingness to follow your husband. Most would not. I pray God gives you a peace about the decision you've made."

She turned to Amin. "This room once belonged to my other son, Mohamed. He went to America to study law but met with an unfortunate accident and…" Zainab swallowed, trying to distil her emotions, "…and did not return. Matthew," she said, glancing at Mohamed, "was taken to the United States as an infant and adopted by an American family. That's why our family name is El Taher, but Matthew's is Mulberry. Still, he is my son by birth, if not in name. I hope this is not too confusing."

She brought her eyes to rest on Sabah again. "I trust you will be comfortable. I ask only that you refrain from discussing your husband's experience with anyone. This is a very sensitive subject. I'm sure you understand the need for discretion." Zainab smiled, her eyes shifting to Amin who was studying the picture on the wall. "Amin, Matthew will try to find suitable work for you to do. Are you currently employed?"

Amin pulled his head back, his expression puzzled.

Zainab's eyes went to the photograph. "They were twins," she said. "I know it looks like Matthew, but that's actually Mohamed, his twin brother. They were separated at birth. They only got the chance to meet a few months before Mohamed died."

Amin nodded. "Most recently I was employed by the Ministry of Water Resources and Irrigation. "I was a student engineer, but it was only a summer job. I'm still enrolled in graduate studies at the University of Cairo."

"Cairo, that's a long way. You have family there?"

The boy glanced at his wife. "No, my family is gone. I'm originally from Tanis, but when my parents died. I sold the shop they owned and moved to Cairo. That's where I met Sabah. She is from there. We are staying with her family."

Zainab went to open the blinds, allowing the sun to stream through the louvers.

"But I don't think I will be returning to school," he continued. "I had been reading the Christian Bible as part of a project for one of my teachers and the things this man Isa Jesus said, they touched me. And then I saw the vision, and it was so beautiful, perhaps the most beautiful thing I have ever seen, and that's why we are here."

"It's not likely you'll find work on the outside," Mohamed said, "not unless you keep quiet about having seen Jesus."

The young woman glanced at her husband, her eyes moist and red. "What is to become of us, Amin?"

15

CHAPTER 4

He took also of the seed of the land, and planted it in a fruitful field; he placed it by great waters... — *Ezekiel 17:5*

MOHAMED AND AMIN stepped outside, blinded by the morning sun. They had sat through breakfast, but no one seemed particularly interested in eating. Layla was still asleep, Zainab had already eaten, Amin and Sabah sat quietly picking at their food, and Mohamed fidgeted, anxious about telling Uthman that he'd hired another new employee. Breaking the silence, he finally said, "Why don't you ladies stay and get to know each other while I show Amin around?"

They stepped outside, cupping their hands over their eyes to shield them from the glare. A waist-high rock wall surrounded the house separating it from the fields where laborers in their white *galabias* toiled, tilling the soil and carrying buckets of water to irrigate the crops. Mohamed led Amin through the gate at the end of the flagstone path and turned right heading toward the river.

The land his uncle once owned was as fertile as any in the Nile valley. They passed row upon row of beets and turnips fanning out like the rays of a green sun. Laborers were out in the fields wearing soiled white *galabias* as they stooped over sacks and sickles tending to the crops, their feet breaking up clods as they stepped through the pasty mud.

The Nile meandered off in the distance glittering like a belt of green sequins as they strolled down a long dirt road bordered by palm trees on both sides. The air was musty, mixed with the humus of the marsh.

Mohamed felt odd walking to the river without a ball at his feet. He'd taken this road a thousand times in his youth, and always with a soccer ball spinning in front of him practicing moves that would one day make him a star, but that was a lifetime ago.

"All you see once belonged to my uncle," he said, his arm sweeping out to take in the vast fields of sugarcane, beans, and cotton.

Amin nodded, his head bobbing aggressively. "It seems he was a very great man to have accomplished so much. I should like to have met him."

"No, unfortunately he was vicious and cruel, and committed to destroying the gospel I now profess."

They approached a barefoot man attacking the ground with a hoe. "I'll be introducing you to a few of the farm workers, some of which, like you, have left Islam for Christianity. We've taken in about a half dozen recent converts, but, to reiterate what my mother said, you must not speak of your faith openly. You'll learn who the Christians are over time. We also employ about sixty laborers who previously worked for my uncle and hold to his ways. We must be careful not to let them know what we're doing. The man I'm about to introduce you to is a Christian."

The worker wore a long white *galabia* stained with sweat and soil. He looked up. His neatly trimmed beard was the color of asphalt with a white stripe down the center, his nose was long and slightly hooked, and his eyes, though small, seemed to glimmer beneath the tangle of his brows.

"Good morning, Masud. I see you're up bright and early. How are you doing?"

The man drew a sleeve across his forehead. "We had a problem this morning, Haj Matthew. One of our sluices broke and flooded two acres. But this we have fixed and the field has been drained and is now dry, though I'm not sure we'll be able to salvage the crop."

Mohamed lips pressed into a flat line as he nodded. He turned to the man standing beside him. "Masud, I'd like you to meet Amin. He and his wife will be staying with us for a while. Amin has been studying water management at the university in Cairo. Maybe he can offer some advice." He leaned in, lowering his voice. "Amin recently met our Lord, but hasn't as yet had any formal training. Maybe you can take him under your wing."

"It would be my pleasure, Haj Matthew."

Amin's face broke into a broad grin. "I am a very good water engineer for the Ministry of Water Resources and Irrigation. Yes, I am a good engineer. I am at your service."

"We could have used you this morning," Masud said. "The system we use was constructed many generations ago. I have only been here a short while and already I have seen it collapse twice."

"Can I see where this problem is? Perhaps I can make a recommendation."

Masud looked at Mohamed. "Of course. That is, if Haj Matthew does not object."

"No, not at all. You two go ahead," Mohamed said.

Layla made her way down the path, taking the long way around to avoid being seen by her husband. She wasn't angry, perturbed maybe, but not angry. He should have thought to awaken her. She didn't like getting up early, she wasn't a morning person, but she didn't like being left in the dark either. Inviting strangers to stay overnight was a big decision, too big to learn about it second hand. He should have sought her opinion.

She didn't even get the chance to meet them. The woman had gone back to her room after breakfast, and the man was out somewhere wandering around with her husband. What if they weren't who they said? Mohamed was taking too many chances. Losing Matthew had been enough. She wasn't prepared to lose her husband, too. She grimaced, feeling the pain as though it were yesterday...

"I know how this must look, Layla, but please, hear me out. Not everything is as it appears. That grave over there has my name on it, but Matthew's the one buried there. I...I had them use my first initial on the headstone...it's the same as Matthew's...and El Taher is our family name, so it's accurate." Mohamed turned his head, staring out the window. "In some ways it is me, at least the old me. I feel like a very real part of me has died, but here I am, and Matthew's gone and I can't bring him back. He brought his hand up drawing a cross on the fogged glass with a finger, then paused to swallow the lump in his throat.

Layla's eyes widened, the color deepening in her cheeks. She leaned forward, staring hard at Mohamed's face. "What are you saying? You can't mean . . . "

Mohamed brought his head around. "Yes, I do. It was Matthew who was killed when that bomb exploded, not me"—his eyes welled and began to overflow—"I got called back to Egypt and...and something happened...and I met your Jesus, and then I knew I had to stop them, and...and Matthew got involved and we... But now the FBI wants me to assume his identity. They plan to propagate the myth that I, Mohamed El Taher, was the one killed, not my brother. He's the hero, Layla, not me. I don't even know who I am anymore."

Mohamed tried to relate the story, including his uncle's death and how he'd found his mother alive, but Layla, though she was nodding, heard only the words, "I met your Jesus." Her eyes were like floodgates bursting open, her heart stammering within her chest. She pulled her purse up into her lap, scrambling for the letter she'd received from Matthew several days before.

Dearest Layla,

Please forgive me if I've seemed a bit distant lately. I've had a lot on my mind. I know you haven't said it, and would probably deny it if I confronted you, but I know it's my brother you love, not me.

When you're with him, the light shines the way it once did when you were with me, but now when we're alone, the shadows grow ever longer. I know you never meant to hurt me, and I love you for that. Layla, I love everything about you and I probably always will, but I have to let you go.

That was the moment where everything came together and she was able to see for the first time what really happened. Matthew had given his life to save both her's and Mohamed's.

But then Mohamed had said he was going back to Egypt and in spite of her desire to complete her medical degree, and all her misgivings about returning, she'd determined if God was calling Mohamed to serve Him there, then that was where she had to be.

She scrunched her lips into a pout. She was acting childish. She should be helping the young woman get settled, not throwing a pity party for herself. She picked up her pace, heading back to the house.

Muffled sobs came from the other side of the door. Layla reached up and knocked softly. "Sabah? My name is Layla. I'm the wife of Matthew. May I come in?"

She waited but when she didn't hear a response, leaned in, opening the door slightly. The woman sat on the edge of the bed with her head bowed, her face hidden by her *hijab*. Layla went over and sat down beside her.

"Sabah, I'm Layla," she said.

The girl trembled. She brought her head up, tears streaming down her cheeks. "What is to become of us?"

Layla reached her arm around the girl's shoulder and gave her a gentle squeeze. "What do you want to become of you?" she responded.

"I don't know what you mean."

"I mean, what do *you* want? I understand you're here because your husband has decided to convert from Islam to Christianity. But that's a personal decision. What about you?"

"My husband saw a vision." She brought her hand up, wiping her eyes. Her body shuddered again. "I love my husband, but this...this thing he saw has changed him, and it's changed everything."

The woman began swaying, then stopped to look at Layla. Her small nose was wet. Her face was round, her lips full, and her eyes dark as chocolate. In the world of American fashion she would have been considered plump, but it was baby fat and it made her skin appear smooth and soft.

Layla glanced around the room looking for a box of tissues but there were none. Sabah wiped her nose on her wrist.

"I wish I could have seen it," she said, her voice faltering, "the vision, I mean. Then maybe I could understand." She shuddered again bringing her hands up to rub her arms. "When my father finds out, he'll come after us. He'll probably kill Amin, and maybe even me. I love my husband. He's the kindest, most gentle man I've ever known."

"Your father won't be able to find you. You'll be safe as long as you're here."

Sabah nodded. "I had to come. I didn't know what else to do? I...I want to be with Amin, but I don't understand what he's going through. I'm confused."

"You have to give it time, Sabah. God will work it out."

Chapter 5

The waters compassed me about, even to the soul: the depth closed me round about, the weeds were wrapped about my head.

— *Jonah 2:5*

MOHAMED SAUNTERED down the path, heading toward the river. The date palms were listless, their fronds hanging limp in the absence of a breeze. He took a deep breath, squaring his shoulders, imbibing air filled with the sweet humus of the marsh. Seagulls waiting to steal the remains of the fisherman's catch, screeched in the distance. He raised his hand, waving, as he crossed to the other side of the road.

"*Salam*, Masud, *Keef halak?*"

"*Al-Ḥamdolillah.* I'm fine, thanks be to God."

"Where is Amin, the man I left you with?"

"Ah, Haj Matthew, I was showing him how we grow the crops, but I'm afraid he was not very impressed. He saw all we are doing and began muttering to himself. He was asking how such an obviously prosperous farm could be so outdated. He was saying we need to bring in modern irrigation, sprinkler systems, he called them. I tried to explain that Haj Sayyid was against all such modernization. But he was not to be deterred. He ran off toward the river." Masud raised a hand pointing toward the water. "That's the last I saw of him."

Mohamed nodded. "Maybe's he's right."

"But I am told Sayyid…"

"Sayyid is dead, Masud, and so is the old way of doing things. You say he's down by the river?"

"This is where I left him, yes, but he is like a child running this way and that. He could be anywhere by now. I told him I must get back to my work and he said to go on without him."

"I think he's anxious to show me what he can do. But this is good. He has a wife, so they will be staying with us in the big house until we can make other arrangements. It's important he receives training in his new faith. I trust you will welcome him into your study."

"*Na'am,* yes, of course. Have him come to our quarters after the others have gone to bed. I will be happy to personally instruct him, myself."

Mohamed took his friend's hand, gripping it tightly. "*Shokran,* thank you, I knew I could count on you."

The sun, low on the horizon, glittered on the water. Mohamed held a hand over his eyes as he scanned the shore. Seagulls circled a felucca downriver, a crocodile meandered upstream eyeing a white egret that took to flight before becoming the reptile's dinner. He didn't see Amin.

He stood on the riverbank kicking the tuffs of grass at his feet. Doing a pirouette, he danced around a small rock like it was a soccer ball, pushing it forward, skating along with the stone in front of him. There was no wind, only the open vacuum of blue, he drew his foot back and bringing it under the stone, swept it far out over the water till it plopped with a *kerplunk. Not bad for being out of practice.*

He straightened himself, squinting at the sun sparkling on the water while taking in a lungful of the marsh, the air rife with the smell of river reeds and moss. A silhouette moved, hard to make out against the glare. It appeared his new friend was standing waist deep in the Nile. *What's he up to?*

Amin saw him coming and raised his hand to wave, but the water was now up to his chest and the current strong. He lost his footing and slipped, disappearing into the flow.

Mohamed waited expecting Amin to bob to the surface but seconds passed and the man remained submerged. Rushing over, Mohamed scanned the deep green of the river but it was thick as grass. He couldn't see a thing. The man had disappeared. He raced up and down the shore, his heart thumping in his chest. "Amin? Amin!" A second later he caught a flicker of movement and a head broke the surface. Amin was caught in the current downstream. His hands were flailing as he sputtered up water. "*Heeellp,* I do not swim."

Mohamed ran along the river stumbling over rocks and tuffs of grass. Not all memories of the Nile were good.

On the day he learned of his mother's death, he'd come down to the river and jumped in, hoping to drown himself. The waters had received him with open arms, sucking him down into the deep like Jonah waiting for a fish. The murky green swirled overhead, a liquid sun floating above. The weight of the water held him glued to the bottom, but at the last second he'd decided he wanted to live. He'd pushed up and broke the surface, flailing just the way Amin was doing now. God had saved him with a soccer ball, one he'd kicked into the water just before he went in. He'd clung to the ball like a life preserver until he reached an oxbow in the river and, ebbing into the shallows, crawled to shore. But there was no soccer ball for Amin. And Mohamed couldn't save him. He didn't know how to swim, either.

Amin's arms flailed out. "Help!" he screamed. He was struggling to stay afloat but his head kept going under.

"God, help me!" Mohamed sloshed through the water, the sinuous grasses pawing his ankles holding him back.

This was foolishness. The river had always been his nemesis, even as a child. It was Layla who delighted in splashing through the reeds along the shallows. He preferred the shore. Where was that crocodile?

He plowed on, tugging at the undergrowth until he broke through, and kept going, using his hands like paddles to pull him ever forward, the water now soaking up around his chest. He'd lost sight of Amin. He tried standing on his toes and looking around. *Ah, there.* They were almost even, but Amin was a few feet further out. He had to act fast. He took three labored steps and lunged forward reaching out as Amin swept by. Their hands touched, but he couldn't hold on. The water engulfed him and he found himself being drawn into the current along with Amin. The Nile moved slowly, thousands of tons of water pulled along by the force of gravity. The current sucked him down. He looked up and saw the sun shining on the surface, just as he had as a child. The pressure in his lungs was building as he tried to hold his breath. God had saved him before, God would save him again.

His foot took purchase of the bottom and he pushed up, breaking the surface again, gasping for air. Something struck the side of his head. It was Amin's foot, pumping wildly. Mohamed grabbed the man's leg to prevent being kicked again but Amin felt the pull and panicked jerking all the more violently. Mohamed wrapped his arms around the smaller man and pulled him in until they were bound together. Amin was still thrashing the water.

Mohamed fought to hold on, "Stop kicking, I'm trying to help," but Amin twisted and squirmed and flailed his arms until he broke free. He slipped under again, out of Mohamed's reach.

He felt a tug on his leg and quickly gulped in air mixed with water as he was pulled down, his clothes twisting around his body. A moment later he bumped into Amin. They'd reached the bottom. It couldn't have been more than ten feet deep. A stream of air bubbles escaped Amin's lungs and bobbed to the surface. His hands were waving about like a tree caught in a breeze. His hair swirled around his face.

Mohamed took hold of Amin's hand and used it to pull himself down. He spun around, planting his feet in the silt of the riverbed and, with his arms wrapped around Amin's waist, thrust forward, not in the direction of the surface, but toward the shore. The water surged around him. His lungs were on fire. He crashed to his knees, no longer able hold his breath. He needed to find air fast or he'd end up like Amin, breathing water. He let go and pushed off the bottom. A second later his head broke the surface, the air exploding from his lungs.

Water surged around him. He gasped, took a quick breath, and went under again. The water became murky as though something was disturbing the silt, dusting it up in clouds of gray. He tried to feel for Amin but his hands remained empty. *No, God. No! You didn't bring him here for this!*

His hands continued their search and found a rope, taut, but he couldn't see where it led. He grasped on and began pulling himself hand-over-hand until his head broke the surface alongside a boat. Someone grabbed him by the collar, and pulled him up over the gunwale. Mohamed collapsed and rolled onto his back sputtering and coughing and spitting up water.

"Are there any more of you?"

Mohamed looked up through liquid eyes. The blurry image of a man stood over him. A mast with a lowered sail creaked in the wind. He shook his head and struggled to sit, *Aaakuff, kuff, kuff,* coughing up water. He wiped his lips on his wet sleeve and lifting his head, tried to focus on the man's face. "Any more?"

The man pointed to the stern of the vessel. "We brought that one up in our net."

A second man was leaning over Amin pushing down on his chest. Amin spit up water and then began coughing and groaning as he rolled onto his side, spewing more water from his lungs.

CHAPTER 6

For it is better, if it is God's will, that ye suffer for well doing, than for doing evil. — 1 Peter 3:17

UTHMAN STOOD at the door with an absurdly large turban balanced on his head like a piece of white cauliflower. The sun at his back made his white muslin *galabia* glow with a fringe of light. He had his arms crossed, his beard nearly touching the ground, his face dark and menacing.

"What is going on here?" he growled.

Layla glanced up. She had been summoned to deliver a baby for a mother who was experiencing complications. She was trying to pick up where her father left off. *So far so good.* In the few months they'd been there, she had stitched gaping wounds, set broken bones, dug out ingrown nails, and treated colds and stomach flu. Maybe she wasn't a fully licensed physician, but she knew enough to help.

She continued dusting the baby's bottom, the white powder billowing up in front of her nose. She had seen the man before. He managed the labor force, a man of influence, but what was he doing here? These weren't communal dwellings. The women servants, those who cleaned house, worked in the kitchen, and did laundry, were housed separate from the men. For a man to enter here was forbidden, the only exception being Marwan, the child's father, who had to be there for the occasion.

Marwan, spun around, spreading his hands in greeting, though the effort seemed forced and the joy he'd expressed only a moment before quickly faded. "Ah, welcome my friend," he said beckoning the man with a wave of his hand. "Come, come, you must see for yourself." His voice quivered as he spoke. He turned back toward his wife.

Uthman looked past Marwan but didn't step into the room. "I heard Habibah had delivered a child," he said. "I came to give my blessing, but you insult me. Why is this woman not wearing her *hijab?* Is this not the Christian who stays in Haja Zainab's house? Why does this infidel defile a servant of Muhammad?"

Marwan's head bobbed like a cork on water. "Yes, yes, but she is the only doctor, is she not? And a good one. The infant was turned the wrong way. Her feet wanted to come out first and my wife was in great pain and we were in danger of losing the child. But as you can see, all is well. The doctor has delivered unto us a beautiful girl."

The baby started crying, *waaahhhhhhhhh, uh-huh uh-huh!* as if to emphasize the point.

"Are there no midwives? Where is Habibah's mother? Could you not find someone else?"

Layla's stomach tightened. They were talking about her in the third person, like she wasn't even there. She handed the little girl back her mother and began gathering her things.

Marwan was rubbing the thumb of one hand into the palm of the other. "But, there was no time. The child wanted to be birthed and the doctor lives right here. *Al hamdullah,* Allah has blessed us with a beautiful daughter. Come, see for yourself." He extended his arm toward his wife.

"If Allah had blessed you, you would have had a son!" The eyes of the man narrowed as they shifted to Layla.

She ignored him, leaning in to sweep a moist lock of hair off her patient's face. "Just feed the baby and keep her clean and warm. Everything will be fine." She stood holding a blood pressure monitor to her chest and moved toward the door, but the man blocked her way. *Help me Lord.* She took in a breath and let it go, gazing into the man's eyes with more confidence than she felt. "I am the wife of Matthew Mulberry, son of Zainab El Taher. If you want to continue working here, I suggest you let me pass."

The man grunted, but stood aside.

Layla squeezed by, stepping into the late evening sun before releasing her breath. She paced across the yard without looking back. *It's starting all over again,* she thought. *This is exactly why I didn't want to return. They would rather see their loved ones die than let me help.*

The palms guarding the El Taher estate were shadows against the azure sky. Beyond them the sun's flickering embers dropped below the horizon taking with them the intense heat. Mohamed glanced over and caught Amin shivering. They carried their shoes as they made their way home. Water dripped from their noses and chins. Their shirts clung tightly to their shoulders.

Mohamed's cuffs soaked up dirt. He nodded with an, "un-huh," as Amin recounted what he'd seen while buried underwater.

Amin's jaw quivered. "It was incredible. I have never seen such light, so many colors, you understand? The city shone like gold, but not because of the sun, I did not see a sun, I saw only light. I know this sounds crazy, but I can't remember breathing, or the beating of my heart. I thought, maybe I'm dead, maybe this is paradise, and then I saw Isa reaching out to receive me. I knew it was Him because I saw the scars in His hands, you see. I think He wanted me to come with Him but I argued. I said I wanted my wife to come too. That's when I felt this beating on my chest and I threw up all this water and found myself on this boat with you."

Mohamed kept his eyes on the path, pursing his lips. He couldn't deny the appearance of Jesus. Each of the recent converts had shared a similar experience, as had he. The part that made him uncomfortable was that this man had been a follower of Christ less than a week and he had already seen Isa twice! He brushed his arms, wringing water out of his shirt. "What were you doing in the river? It seems like a foolish thing to do if you can't swim."

"Ah, I was checking the depth. I notice you still water your fields using sluices. This not only erodes the soil, it is time consuming." Amin shivered, wrapping himself in his arms. His jaw quivered as he spoke. "If we were to stretch a number of pipes out into the river we could use pumps to bring the water up and maybe even get a sprinkler system to water the crops."

Mohamed nodded, a bead of water dripping from his chin. "With the number of acres we have, a project like that could take years. Would it be something you'd be interested in doing?"

Amin's smile was broad, his white teeth glowing in the dusky light. "This was something I was going to suggest myself, so yes, I am glad to be at your service, yes."

"*Hummm,* I've been looking for an excuse to separate Christians. I need to keep them out of Uthman's way. Maybe I can assign them to help you, and make everyone happy."

They approached the house. Light glowed from the dining room. Layla, Zainab, and Sabah, were seated around the table. Mohamed and Amin followed the waist high wall until they reached the corner at the end of the driveway and turned left, walking up the side of the house to enter through the service porch. The servants preparing the evening meal stopped and looked up. One grabbed a towel and dropped to her knees wiping their muddy tracks. Water still dripped from their clothes.

"Matthew, what on earth?" Layla and his mother were sitting on either side of Sabah, but all three jumped up at the sight of the deluged men.

"Amin, what are you doing? Stop! Remove those wet things at once," Sabah scolded. "We are guests here."

Both men began peeling off their shirts. Mohamed nodded at Layla. "I'll explain, but first I think Amin needs a shower."

"What about you?"

Mohamed looked down and raised his foot scraping mud from between his toes. The servant with the towel started gathering the wet clothes into a basket. Mohamed and Amin handed her their shirts and she scurried away. "I'll take a shower too, but our guest must be first."

Sabah took her husband's hand. "You should be ashamed."

"I just had the most incredible experience," he said, as she led him away.

"What does he mean by that?" Layla asked, watching them disappear around the corner.

"He means he was blessed with another appearance of Isa."

Layla nodded. "Matthew, we need to talk," she said. Her voice was terse, keeping him from objecting. She spun around and led him down the hall to his uncle's old bedroom, closing the door. The room had been redecorated by his mother. She'd taken down the tapestries with verses from the Qur'an, along with his uncle's prize collection of swords, and replaced them with works of art. Zainab seemed to favor contemporary artist Sayed Saad El Din. Mohamed found himself drawn to the paintings. One called, "Kites," reminded him of games he'd played with Layla, building paper kites from newspapers and letting them soar on the autumn breeze. But he felt an even stronger connection to the one called, "Hope." The oil on canvas showed people on the river in a boat reaching their hands toward the moon. He could relate to the image. He'd sailed on the Nile at night with the moon's reflection on the water, and Isa had appeared. There was certainly hope in that.

But if the room felt different, it was more from the absence of fear than the change of décor. There was a time when entering this space made his heart tremor. He would hold his breath and sneak by the door hoping his uncle wouldn't call out his name.

He sat down beside Layla. So much had changed, though art and bric-a-brac aside, the main fixtures, couches, tables, chairs and beds, were the same. Indeed, the bed on which he and Layla sat was the same bed upon which Sayyid had wasted away, and ultimately breathed his last.

His hand swept a bedspread made of fine Egyptian cotton. The one that covered his uncle when he died had been embroidered with the *Shahadah*: There is no God but Allah and Muhammad is his messenger. This one had a pastel floral print.

"Matthew, I was accosted by one of the farm workers today," Layla said.

Mohamed's head jerked around. "What? Who? Are you hurt? What happened?"

"Settle down. I'm okay. I don't know the man's name, and it's not important, but he called me an infidel. It scared me, Matthew. It made me think of when we were children. I felt like I did the day they drove my family from the village."

Mohamed's cheeks puffed, expelling his breath. Layla's eyes, normally dark and alluring, were now clouded with questions. Her wavy hair hung down on her shoulders, her cheekbones dusted with just a hint of rouge, and her lips glossed in pink. He reached over and took her hand reassuringly.

"We have to give it time Layla. People don't know us yet. It takes time to build their trust."

"My father gave it time. He spent seven years ministering here and what did it get us? They drove us out and burned our house. If we hadn't left when we did, we would have been killed. All we wanted to do was help."

Mohamed skewed his head to the side. "That man is no different than I was, Layla. There was a time when I would have said the same thing. He just doesn't know any better." He looked at the door making sure it was closed.

Layla slipped her hand from Mohamed's and brought it to her neck, sweeping the hair off her shoulder. She closed her eyes for a moment, and then opened them to look at Mohamed. "Do you think we should leave?"

"Leave?"

"Go back to the States. We can always serve God there."

Mohamed paused, searching Layla's eyes. "*Habbity,* you know I love you. If you're really afraid, then say the word and we'll start packing. But I think you may be overreacting. You're the one always singing that song. Remember, how does it go? 'Have I not commanded you be strong and courageous, do not be terrified, do not be afraid, for the Lord your God will go with you wherever you go.'"

He puckered his lips, squinting. "I thought you agreed that God had called us here. I mean, He sent Amin right to our door, and now I have a project I want him to work on, which I'm hoping will provide an opportunity to teach him more about Christ. And Sabah? I think she questions what kind of God would make her father want to kill her and her husband. Our ministry is just getting started. I think we're safe here, Layla."

"Are we?" Layla shook her head. "This farm can't continue to harbor new believers. It's bound to get back to the wrong people eventually. It only takes one match to start a fire."

"So you think we should leave."

"Maybe...No, not really. I don't know."

"Because if you do, say so now. I'm working on a plan to increase the number of people we shelter, but I don't want to start making promises I can't keep."

Layla looked at her husband. "It's not that I don't want to. It's just, I felt so much safer in the United States. I'm trying to fit in but every time I step outside I feel like I'm being watched."

"Maybe it's because you are. You're new here, Layla. You're still a curiosity, but they'll get over it. Here, give me your hand. Let's pray."

CHAPTER 7

For no other foundation can anyone lay other than that which is laid, which is Jesus Christ. — 1 Corinthians 3:11-13

THE SEAGULLS, flying low on the horizon, were silhouetted by a rose colored dawn. Amin turned and looked out over the water, watching a fishing crew laboring to haul in their nets, the mesh squirming with the morning's catch. Two weeks ago, he'd been that catch, brought out of the liquid abyss from death unto life. He looked down at his diagram trying to read by the light of dawn. He'd done all the calculations, and as far as he could determine, this was the best location. He folded his sketch and tucked it away in his pocket.

It had been two weeks of discovery as his newly acquired brothers surrounded him and explained things in the Bible he'd read but didn't understand. Studying the Christian Scriptures to refute them was like reading while wearing a blindfold. He couldn't see what they revealed. That day in the water, when God had hauled him from the depths, he'd been forced to consider the brevity of life. He didn't know how much time he had, short or long, but he was determined to learn as much as he could.

Every night, as soon as Sabah was asleep, he'd sneak back into the men's quarters where he would stay until midnight, huddled in a corner with the small computer in his lap. The men trying to sleep in their bunks must have been disturbed by the light of the screen glowing around them, but they never complained. They rolled over and left him alone as he poured over the on-line Arabic translation of the *Injil*. They seemed to understand his obsession.

If only God would open Sabah's eyes. He tried to share what he learned each night, and she always listened, but she was wearing the same blinders he once wore. Isa Christ had come to free men from the bondage of sin; men didn't have to sacrifice themselves, Christ was their sacrifice; paradise was granted to all who believed, things so simple, and yet she couldn't seem to understand. *Oh God, help her to see You.*

He looked around at the vast fields of crops, vegetation stretching as far as his eye could see. A sprinkler system would work fine for turnips and beans, but tall growth, like corn and sugar cane would block the spray. He'd have to find a way to channel water to these areas.

He was a student, not a full fledged engineer. He had never built a distribution system such as the one he proposed. He knew the mechanics, in theory, but knowledge and experience were two different things. He'd spent the past few weeks on the internet reading about similar projects, sourcing suppliers, ordering materials, and drawing up plans.

His Christian brothers were waiting. It was time to begin the work in earnest. The air was cool, but the day grew brighter and the shadows shorter as the sun rose over the plain. Soon it would be too hot to work. They had risen while the sun was a sliver on the horizon and followed him out to the site with shovels and hoes braced on their shoulders. It was imperative they accomplish as much as possible before the sun became a fireball in the sky.

The pile of pipes looked like a handful of straws dropped on the ground. He felt their eyes on him, waiting for him to start. He stooped over and picked up a length, pulling it with him to a sawhorse. Unsnapping a measuring tape from his belt, he extended the rule, then paused. A man rolled up beside him riding a small wooden cart pulled by a donkey.

Amin's heart picked up speed, thumping loudly in his chest. He'd never met the foreman before, though he had seen him from a distance, always with his turban looking like a wad of dough stuck to his head.

Uthman brought the donkey to a halt, easing back on the reins. Hunched over the way he was, it was hard to tell he was over six feet tall. His head looked like a fig with a long nose and bushy eyebrows, and his turban was disproportionately large, a distortion emphasized by the fact that his face was so narrow. His long *galabia* hung down around his feet—big feet, and big hands, too—and his beard looked like it had never seen a razor. It hung from his chin in unkempt strands of gray. Uthman's eyes closed slightly. "What do you plan to do with all this?" he said.

Amin raised his measuring tape, pushing the button to make the ruler snap back into its casing. His heart was pitter-pattering but he smiled broadly. "It will be used to bring water in to irrigate the crops so your men don't have to work so hard. We will dig trenches and…"

"You wish to take our jobs. You think you can run this farm by machines so Haja Zainab will no longer need us."

Amin took a step back, his smile fading. "No, no. I just want to make things easier for you. All day long I see your men fitting the locks into place to redirect the flow of water. With this," Amin turned to look over his shoulder at the haphazard stack of pipes, "you can water the whole farm just by turning a few knobs and opening a few valves. This will give them more time to do other things. This is better, I think."

Uthman grunted, his beard waving back and forth as he shook his head. "It is time for the cane harvest, not time to play foolish games. We cannot have you slowing us down. It would be best if you do not get in our way." He squinted at Amin as though seeing him for the first time. "Why do I not know you?" He stopped and looked around. "Why do I not know any of you? Do you not observe *fajr*. Do you not pray?"

Amin's fellow workers, leaning on their shovels, stiffened, exchanging furtive glances.

Amin swallowed, shifting his weight. He was supposed to be discreet, but... "Yes, I pray, but not at *fajr*. I can't speak for the others, but I've chosen a different path."

Uthman's nostrils flared. His throat made a guttural sound as he turned to spit over his shoulder. "Then it is as we have heard. You are all disbelievers. You bring a curse on this place."

"I think we bless it, as I hope this watering system will prove, but I assure you, we will not get in your way."

Bahhhh! Uthman whipped his donkey, causing the animal to bolt. The tiny cart creaked as the donkey broke into a trot.

Amin released his breath, feeling chilled in spite of the warming sun. He turned around, looking at his brothers, and raised his hand, flicking his fingers to shoo them back to work. "Enough standing around; there is much to do," he said, but his voice faltered and his hands were visibly shaking. Was the man upset about his religion, or that his work might eliminate a few unnecessary jobs?

CHAPTER 8

Wherefore, if God so clothes the grass of the field, which today is, and tomorrow is cast into the oven, shall he not much more clothe you, O ye of little faith? — Matthew 6:28-30

THE SUN was well beyond the horizon, the sky a purple haze. Uthman stood at the entrance to the men's quarters, shrouded in light from the door. The building was long and narrow with bunks on both sides of a center aisle and a latrine at either end. He began tugging on his beard, shaking his head.

"What is wrong, my brother?"

Uthman looked down, his lips taut. His eyes were narrow, glaring at the shorter man standing beside him. "What is wrong? Do you not see that infidel heading for the house of Haja El Taher?"

The man didn't answer. He kept his eyes fixed on the shimmering twilight. In the fields, crickets droned under a blanket of stars.

"He is a disbeliever," Uthman continued. He folded his arms and brought his shoulders back to lean against the door's frame. "Haj Sayyid would never have allowed such a man to cross his threshold. More than fifty years I myself have worked for the El Taher family and have never eaten at their table, yet this blasphemer and his wife are asked to live in their house. This man brings dishonor to the El Taher name."

The second man shook his head, folding his arms to mimic Uthman's displeasure. "My cousin Salma works in the kitchen. She thinks Haja Zainab is of this persuasion as well. She has heard her say many things she does not understand."

"*Bahhh,* this is exactly what I fear. What do we really know of this woman? Was she not discovered only after Sayyid was received into Paradise? No one knows where she came from, only that she showed up after he died claiming to be his wife. Now she rules his house. I heard he put her out because she was unfaithful."

The shorter man looked up, nodding. "Salma says there are stories from newspapers framed and hung on the walls. They tell of her two sons, neither of which came from the seed of Haj Sayyid. Mohamed El Taher we know. He grew up here and died in the service of Allah, but this other one, Matthew, was raised in America. It is said Haja Zainab sent him there to learn the Christian way?"

Uthman's lips twisted into a knot. "I must know more of this. Have your cousin open her ears and let me know what she hears. In the meantime, this one who lives like a king while we sleep with the rats has already admitted to his blasphemy. This must not go unpunished."

Amin stood at the entrance to the kitchen, his clothes caked with mud.

"You are early, my husband. *Al hamdullah.*" Sabah jumped up from the couch in the parlor and went to meet him at the door. "It is good to see you. I was just saying to Haja Zainab how wonderful it would be if you could join us for the evening meal, and here you are, but look at you, you're filthy."

Amin reached out for Sabah but she rebuffed him, pushing him away.

"Not until you clean yourself. Get out of those clothes. I will see they are washed so you can wear them again tomorrow." Salma, the only worker in the kitchen to wear a full burka stopped what she was doing, looking annoyed at the dirt Amin was tracking in.

Mohamed entered the kitchen his hair damp from his shower. "Hey, Amin, I'm glad you're here? Whoa, what happened to you? You look like you went for another swim."

Amin began peeling off his damp mud-soaked shirt. "We ran into a problem. We were digging a trench to the river but we hit a rock and when we tried to dig around it, we found it was too large. It looks like we'll have to drill through it, or blast it out of the way. Unfortunately, we didn't have what we needed, and it was too late to start such a job, so I sent the men home. We'll look at it again tomorrow and decide what to do."

Mohamed nodded, then glanced at the kitchen crew who promptly returned to the task of bringing out spoons and bowls and reheating the *torley*. *Aysh*, long thin loaves of bread, were laid out on the counter. "We'll be eating in a few minutes. Go take your shower and join us."

Mohamed hefted a spoonful of the leftover *torley* onto his plate. It was the same lamb casserole the staff had prepared for lunch, but it was customary to serve whatever remained of the midday meal for dinner.

The conversation was light and warm. Zainab and Layla poked fun at Mohamed's black silk shirt, the expensive Armani he'd brought back from the States. They teased him for looking like an American tourist, but he didn't care as long as it kept Layla laughing. Around the table, everyone had smiles—even Sabah, who shed the look of timidity she'd worn since the day she arrived.

"If he had a few gold chains he'd look like an American gigolo. Would you like another bun?" Zainab said, passing a plate across the table to Layla.

"No, thank you. I think he looks more like a Chicago gangster. I would like a little more *torley*."

As for Mohamed, he was ready to change the subject. He was wearing the shirt because it was the only thing he had that was clean. The Taymurs had left with only the clothes on their backs. It was time to do some shopping. He rolled his wrist around to look at his watch, *eight o'clock*, an early dinner by Egyptian standards. "So, aside from today's problem, how's the project going?" he said, passing a plate of greens to Amin.

Amin took the platter and scooped a small portion of lettuce and raisins onto his dish and passed the plate to his wife. "Overall, it is going very well. I just want to say thank you again for giving me this opportunity. I'm learning so much."

"Learning? I put you in charge so you could show the others what to do. I thought you were the teacher."

Amin shoveled a spoonful of lamb into his mouth and began talking with his mouth full. "Yes, with respect to the laying of pipes and the irrigation of your property, I am. But I speak of things more important. Your friend Masud has been teaching me the things of Christ."

Mohamed glanced up sharply, shaking his head. He brought a finger to his lips.

"Sorry." Amin leaned closer and began to whisper. "I am amazed at all he knows, and he himself has only been a Christian for a year. And the laptop computer you allow the men to use has so much information." He paused and glanced over at his wife who'd pulled back from the conversation. "But I no longer sneak into their quarters at night. I'm much too tired."

Mohamed looked at Sabah but her eyes darted away, ever reticent. The topic made her uncomfortable. Layla had befriended her, they could converse for hours, but no matter how many times Layla tried to explain what Amin had experienced, Sabah always ended up shaking her head and saying, "but I don't understand." Only time would tell if she ever would.

"Have you two thought of having children," Zainab said, passing a bowl of bread to Amin.

"Yes but, as you can imagine, we're a bit unsettled right now. But we think about it all the time."

44

"Good, but sometimes it's better to do than to think. I'm still waiting for my own children to bless me with twins."

Mohamed shook his head, his smile mixed with reproof, but it was a smile nonetheless. "We're trying, Mother, but you can't rush these things."

"Good. Just don't wait until your fountain dries up."

"Mother!"

"*What?* What did I say?"

Mohamed watched Layla pick up her spoon and twirl it in her fingers, smiling sheepishly as she dug into her casserole. She wasn't sold on his new idea, she'd voiced her concerns adamantly, but she'd conceded. It was all the license he needed.

He leaned in close to Amin, lowering his voice. "As you can see, there's not much privacy in this house. Layla and I need a place of our own, and so will you and Sabah. I plan to go to Minya tomorrow. You both need clothes, so I'm going to let the ladies go shopping while I meet with a few pastors. I want to let them know if they come across any new converts, they can send them here."

He brought his head up and resumed his normal tone, feeling a little self conscious in the silky shirt that set him apart from the others. He flicked away a bit of onion that had fallen to his lap. "While you're laying pipes I plan to build a row of three or four apartments where couples can live. My foreman is concerned that we're hiring people but don't have enough jobs, but now with your project I have the ability to keep a number of people employed, and if we start building apartments, I can hire even more."

CHAPTER 9

For I was hungry, and you gave me no meat, I was thirsty, and you gave me no drink, I was a stranger, and you did not take me in.
— *Matthew 25: 42-43*

MINYA—cement cube buildings and steel girded towers, rising out of the dessert like sandcastles on the beach. Mohamed squeezed through traffic on the outskirts of town, a sultry white haze filling the sky. His shirt, the black Armani he'd worn the day before, stuck to his skin. He tugged at a button, pulling the material away from his chest, letting the air circulate.

A barefoot girl, standing on the sidewalk, washed her family's clothes and dishes in a tub of stagnant green water. Shirts and pants hung from a rope over her head, and plates and cups were stacked on wood crates, dripping wet. Children chased each other through the streets dogging cars. Vendors sold fruits, vegetables and eggs from board displays with peeling paint. Awnings meant to provide shade for the produce were ripped and torn, or hanging limply without purpose. And flies were everywhere.

Mohamed had a theory, though it was nothing he could prove. He'd only lived in the States a few years, but it was long enough to see how North America enjoyed more blessings than Africa. There were rich people in Egypt, but they were comparably few, while the poor were everywhere. In the United States it seemed the majority lived in abundance, and the poor, chiefly relegated to the ghettos, were few and far between. Was it because America, as a whole, worshiped a different God? God had brought the nation of Israel to a land flowing with milk and honey. Under David and Solomon, they were blessed. God's word, as revealed by Moses, said as long as they followed His precepts, He would bring them sun and rain and a bountiful harvest, but Israel had turned its back on God and the nation had fallen into ruin. Now it appeared America was on the same path and instead of seeing the sun and rain of prosperity, they were receiving droughts and floods and economic decline. It all seemed to depend on worshiping and remaining faithful to the right God. The souls he saw standing at the curb hawking melons, needed Jesus. And if the entire country worshiped Jesus, perhaps Egypt might know God's blessing.

He pulled to the side, stopping in front of a cart filled with maize. The girls would have to do their shopping at the *Wast El-Balad* mercantile. By its name, it should have been in the city's center, but downtown was still a good distance away, and the churches he wanted to visit were here on the outskirts.

He caught Layla staring out the window. Her expression was flat. He ducked his head, eyeing the drab storefront. The canopy was ripped and the pockmarked walls encrusted with dirt, but it was still a shopping spree, and she'd been given carte blanche. He'd hoped for a bit more enthusiasm.

"Well, here we are," he said, trying to generate excitement. "You've got the money my mother gave you. You ladies can buy anything you like, just make sure you don't forget us men. We need clothes too." He brought his wrist around to look at his watch. "I'll only be a few hours. Let's say we meet back here around two?"

The door popped open letting in the heat along with the smell of rotted fruit. Litter and stagnant water lined the street. Layla pulled herself from the car looking like she was being asked to scrub floors. She ducked her head back inside. "Be back at two, no later!" She slammed the door.

Mohamed cringed, then turned to wave, but Layla and Sabah had already disappeared into the store. He squeezed into traffic, the horn of the car behind him blaring as he cut in line.

The interior of the Greek Orthodox Church was dark, which was probably as much to keep it cool as to save on electricity. The bearded priest, in his long black cassock and small round hat, led Mohamed past rows of empty pews down the center aisle toward the front of the building. A large crucifix hung on the wall over a pulpit that stood on a raised dais. They passed several stations with candles flickering in small glass vases, the air thick with the pungent smell of incense. The only other light came from several small holes in the roof, and a row of stained glass windows.

Father Botros ushered Mohamed into his office and closed the door. The room was better lit, but only because the window was uncovered. He raised his palm offering Mohamed a chair and circled around behind a large wood desk where he took a seat. Folding his hands over his ink blotter, he stared at Mohamed, blinking a few times. His eyebrows were long and unkempt and his beard a mat of gray.

"Now, what can I do for you, my son?" The lips bulging from the priest's beard were chapped and grey, and the skin at the bottom of his eyes sagged revealing the pink inside of his eyelids, making him look weary. He blinked again. In the stream of light that fell across his shoulders, his face looked ashen white.

"First, thank you for taking time to see me," Mohamed said. "You have a beautiful church, quite majestic."

The priest nodded, his head bobbing up and down. "It would be if they'd allow us to make repairs. The roof leaks, but the bureaucracy in this town keeps us from getting it fixed. Every time I submit a request, I get turned down." He placed his hands on the desk, his palms pressed against the wood with fingers splayed. "But that's just the way it is."

"You need more Christians on the counsel."

"And a cold day in hell."

"But what if we *could* get men who were formerly Muslins elected to places of power, wouldn't that help?"

"If there were such men, perhaps, but as I said, hell will freeze over first."

"But what if we could? That's why I'm here, to ask if you'd be willing to help Muslims who want to know more about Christ."

The cleric rocked back in his chair, folding his hands over his stomach. *Hummm*, he sighed deeply, slowly shaking his head. "I'm sorry, there is nothing I can do. We don't receive Muslim conversions. There's too much at stake. It's one thing to have a church with a leaky roof, and another to have no church at all."

Mohamed nodded, his lips drawing tight. He leaned forward placing his elbows on his knees with his fingers interlaced. "But what do you do when someone comes to you professing Christ?"

"Do? Why we do nothing. I cannot help them. It is against the law for a Muslim to become a Christian. Any help I give would only lead to my arrest. Where would the true followers of Christ be if they closed my church and put me in jail? When a Muslim is so bold as to seek Christ, he falls into the hands of God, and may God have mercy on his soul."

"But how are they going to learn about what it means to follow Christ if there's no one to shepherd them? Wouldn't you at least give them a Bible?"

The priest released one of his hands, flopping it palm upward on the desk, his long fingernails chipped and yellow. "But don't you see, that's precisely the point. If I offer to help one or two Muslims and I'm thrown in jail, or worse, killed, I won't be able to shepherd them, or anyone else, so the many will suffer because of the few. Besides, it is a moot point. No one ever comes here seeking shelter. But if they did, I would do as you said. I would try to find a Bible for them to read. Then I would tell them to go home and keep their conversion a secret. God can teach them from His word.

There's no point in telling others. No one else will listen, and they can't learn about Christ from inside a jail, or in their grave."

Mohamed clenched his teeth, his cheeks hard in thought...

Zainab hesitated for a moment looking back over her shoulder. Another church, another attempt to find shelter. She held her breath and raised her hand, and with her fist clenched, pounded on the door three times. She let a minute pass, then raised her hand and knocked again. This time she heard a muffled voice from the other side.

"Yes, yes, be patient. I'm coming. I'm coming." The door opened letting a thin curtain of light escape. "What do you want?"

"Momken te'sa'edni?" Can you help me? I'm looking for a doctor from the Adjulah family. He is my friend. We need to find him."

"I'm sorry, I do not know this man. Come back in the morning. Maybe I can ask around." The door started to close but Zainab raised her hand holding it open. "Please, you must help us."

The man on the other side paused, his cheeks sucking in, his face growing stiff. "What is so important you must knock on my door before the sun rises and wake everyone?"

Zainab turned around looking into the darkness and pulled her son in cupping his ear with her hand. "Please, I am Christian. The doctor is the one who told me of Isa. He told me of this place. I know he is here. Please. They burned his house. I know they will come for me."

The door closed again leaving a crack through which she could only see one of the man's eyes and part of his nose but even in the dim light she could tell he was shaking his head. "I'm sorry, there's nothing I can do." The door shut with a thud...

"You don't remember me, do you?"

"Pardon?"

"You said no one ever comes here seeking shelter? There have been those who have come. I was just a boy when my mother decided to follow Christ. She was fleeing from my uncle who would have destroyed her faith. If you think back, it was about fifteen years ago. A mother with her young son woke you in the middle of the night asking for shelter, but you sent them away. I was that boy."

The priest smiled thinly and leaned forward, clasping his hands on his desk. "See then, you have proved my point. You fell into the hands of God. I couldn't help you, but He obviously did, for look, here you are alive and well."

Mohamed sipped in his breath. His Adam's apple slid up and down his throat clearing the bile in his mouth. Sometimes Christianity was hard. "Yes, it's true. God did help me. But because we were offered no shelter, my mother fell into the hands of my Uncle who confined and brutally raped her for twelve years. That was the price she paid, because no one would take us in. I pray this will never happen again. Please, at least do me one favor." Mohamed reached two fingers into his shirt pocket and removed a slip of paper. "This is my telephone number. If anyone ever does come to you seeking help, send them to me."

Mohamed walked out into the light, squinting until he could see. He had to be careful. He'd just revealed—without using his real name—that he'd been there before. In the eyes of the world, Mohamed El Taher was dead. He was supposed to be Matthew Mulberry, as his passport said.

The Mercedes shimmered in the sun. The car was ostentatious but it was the one his uncle had owned and left to his mother, who didn't drive, who had passed it on to him. He reached for the door, checking his watch, mindful of his promise not to leave Layla and Sabah standing at the curb.

He swung the door open letting the hot air escape before climbing inside. His shirt was already damp. He wanted to preserve his composure as much as possible for his next meeting. This man, too, had turned them away. *Please God, if you want me to do this I'm going to need your help.*

He started the engine, cranking up the air as he pulled into the street dodging traffic. The whole tolerance thing was a sham. Egypt, like so many other Arab nations, did not prohibit Christianity. Those who were born into Christian families were given cards saying they were Christian, and those born into Islam, were given cards says they were Muslim. A Christian was free to remain a Christian and attend whatever church they chose, as long as they didn't proselytize. A Christian was also free to leave their faith and become a Muslim, but a Muslim could not become a Christian. To leave Islam was considered blasphemy and, according to Shari law, blasphemy was a crime punishable by death.

Mohamed parked in front of the building, another place his mother sought shelter on her ill-fated attempt to escape Sayyid's grasp. The pastor had not slammed the door in their faces, but neither had he helped. He'd simply allowed them to spend the night in a shed at the back of the church.

Mohamed knocked on the door, wondering if the same pastor was still there.

The door opened. It was him, older and greyer, but the same build and face. "Yes, can I help you?"

Even the same words spoken so many years ago. "My name is Matthew Mulberry I phoned earlier asking for a few moments of your time."

The pastor nodded. "Yes, yes, please come in." The man turned and walked back through the room, so different from the church he'd just left. It was an open space, filled with the light that poured from the windows along the wall. Instead of pews, the sanctuary was crammed with metal folding chairs, and the pulpit at the front was smallish, and plain, with a simple cross affixed to its façade. There were no candles burning, nor did the smell of incense fill the air.

They continued on, crossing a linoleum floor with places so worn you could see through to the cement foundation. Mohamed followed the pastor into a small study barely large enough for a desk and two chairs. A half dozen well worn books were stacked on the floor, probably the pastor's entire library.

"Please, sit down," the man said. He squeezed around to the other side and took a seat, leaning forward with his hands folded in front of him. "You said you wanted to discuss how to help Muslims that convert to Christ."

"Yes, I did. How's your wife?"

The man squinted, shaking his head. "My wife passed on more than five years ago. Cancer," he said with a shrug. "Did you know her?"

Mohamed leaned back, trying to relax. "I'm sorry. No, we never actually met, but I was here about fifteen years ago. My mother and I came to your door in the middle of the night. You let us sleep in the shed around the back. Your wife was here that night. That's why I asked."

Light began to dawn in the pastor's eyes. He pushed himself up and struggled to squeeze around his desk again.

Mohamed scooted his chair back. The man was hovering over him. He stood, feeling awkward.

The pastor placed his hands on Mohamed's shoulders, looking him in the eye. "It is you. Praise God! Thank you, thank you, thank you for coming. You don't know how often I have prayed for you since that night. When I saw you and your mother getting into the back of that car, I feared the worst. But I pleaded with God that no harm would come to you. Praise the Lord!"

The man embraced Mohamed, tears brimming in his eyes. "I can't believe the Lord has brought you here. How is your mother?" he said, standing back again.

"She is well. The man who took us away was my uncle, but he's gone now and my mother and I are safe, so I guess everything turned out alright in the end. That's kind of why I'm here."

"I felt so bad about what happened; I promised the Lord if He'd forgive me I'd never turn anyone away again. But I also prayed you would forgive me, too. Will you forgive a foolish old man who in his youth, thought saving his own skin was more important than that of saving someone else?"

Mohamed stared at the man. "It's not necessary. We were grateful for the shelter you provided, but if it's forgiveness you want, you have it. Please, let's put this behind us."

"Thank you. What I did was wrong, but at least one good thing came of it. I no longer turn Muslims away. We have established a network of families who take them in. Of course it's always done in secret. The people we shelter would be in great danger if they were caught."

Mohamed's heart picked up speed. *Unbelievable.* "How do you keep them concealed?"

"That's the difficult part. We tell them they must remain inside. We know if they're discovered they could be killed, but what else can we do?"

Mohamed smiled. "I just might be able to help with that."

The ladies stood at the curb where Mohamed left them, sweltering in the sun. He knew he was in trouble. It was two-thirty. He'd made them wait a half hour on a street that smelled of sewage and offered little in the way of shade. As he pulled to the curb, he bolstered himself for the rebuke he would surely receive.

Layla was wearing a new outfit—*that's good, at least she found something.* He couldn't see her feet, surrounded as they were by a half dozen shopping bags, but he wouldn't be surprised to find she had new shoes to match. Sabah, on the other hand, still wore her drab brown *hijab.*

Layla tried to open the back door but the handle snapped out of her fingers. Mohamed quickly released the electronic lock. Layla tossed her bags onto the seat. Mohamed caught Sabah's eye in the rearview mirror as she climbed in and sat down. She didn't say anything, but she was smiling. Her almond cheeks were round as a chipmunk's and her eyes were shiny and bright.

Layla hopped into the front seat and scooted over, leaning in to kiss her husband's cheek.

"Hey, that's nice. You both look happy. How'd you girls make out?"

"It was wonderful. I can't remember when I've had so much fun. Sabah kept me in stitches every minute. She's really quite a comic when you get to know her."

Mohamed checked his mirror again. The back seat was piled with bags stuffed like balloons about to pop. "You got all that at the *Wast El-Balad*?"

"No, we didn't get anything there. As soon as you left we called a cab. There are several nice stores downtown. And we were fortunate enough to get a driver who knew just where to take us. I tried to get poor Sabah to buy something pretty," she turned around resting her elbow on the back of the seat to look at her friend, "but she's not ready for western fashions." She winked, and spun back around to face the front. "Maybe someday. She did try on a couple of things. And we found a few nice *hijab* outfits she liked, so she does have something new to wear."

Mohamed looked over his shoulder at Sabah. "So she's a comic, is she? That's something I'd like to see."

CHAPTER 10

Yes, the time will come when the one who kills you will think he has done God a favor. — John 16:2

THE AFTERNOON sun sparkled on the Nile like jewels dropped from an airplane. Amin looked out over the river admiring its beauty and power. He would tame its hydraulic force. He would harness its energy and use it to irrigate the entire plantation.

Out in the fields, sun browned men in long white *galabias* traipsed back and forth carrying buckets of water to irrigate the plants. It was archaic. Wood locks channeled the water through a series of sluices that ran throughout the property, but bringing the water up to fill the sluices had to be done by hand, and watering the plants had to be done one bucket at a time.

He leaned against a sawhorse, wiping a sleeve across his brow. How pleased they would be once they realized it just took the turning of a knob and several acres could be watered all at once. He envisioned the sprinklers spinning around, their misty tails reflecting the sun in a rainbow of color.

They already had one trench dug and were laying in the pipes. Yellow sparks flew from a welder's torch at his feet. The man in the trench below him stopped and raised his visor.

"All done," he said, "they can start filling it in now."

Amin grabbed his level from the sawhorse and stepped down into the hole to examine the weld. He and his crew had rested through the hottest part of the day, but now they were hard at it again, and the sun, beating down on their backs, was not proving to be their friend. He laid his level against the side of the pipe, watching the bubble rise. "It angles perfectly," he said. "Well done." The pipe, braced by a series of struts, ran under a temporary wooden bridge as it angled away from the river.

Amin pulled himself out of the hole, followed by the man with the welder's torch. "Help me get this length filled in, will you, Masud? We need to start digging at the other end. It will save us from having to build another bridge if we can reuse this one."

"It is good progress we make, I think," Masud said, removing his welder's mask.

Men standing at both ends of the bridge hoisted their shovels and began tossing dirt into the channel.

Already they had pipe buried along the edge of one field. They would have to wait to run the rest, the harvest was on and they'd been warned about getting in the way.

The rock that had brought a halt to their progress had been easier to remove than anticipated. Sami, the oldest of Haja Zainab's *khadem*, had overheard Amin asking Mohamed where they might find dynamite for blasting. Begging their forgiveness for interrupting, he had showed them to a locked room behind one of the barns, and with a key taken from Sayyid's old desk, had opened it.

Sami reached up and pulled a beaded chain, snapping on the light. The dirt floor was strewn with bits of newspaper, straw and hardened mud. Several car batteries and wood crates filled with salt sat on two tables layered with grime, along with dozens of enamel coated steel containers, bottles of bleach, and a small butane stove. It was a lab for making plastic explosives. Mohamed had spun around and walked outside with his hand to his mouth, suppressing memories of men standing in his uncle's living room with small pipes strapped to their chests—men being fitted to die for God.

Amin stayed and collected several slabs of the plastic explosive. A few well placed lumps and—*kerrrrrrpow*—the rock was no more.

He slid his shovel into a pile, tossing more dirt into the trench. It was hot grimy work, but it felt good to be in charge of something so important. He paused to wipe sweat from his brow and caught a glimpse of Uthman approaching, riding his donkey cart and surrounded by a band of workers. The donkey's hooves kicked up dust as they clip-clopped up the path. Uthman pulled back on the reins bringing the animal to a halt. He sat for a moment watching the men work.

"Your bridge will not hold the weight of our loaded carts," he said, indicating the makeshift construction they'd erected to allow farm workers to cross while they were laying pipe under the road.

Amin leaned on his shovel and smiled. "I assure you it will. That is the very reason for which it was built."

Uthman guffawed. "We shall see, but may Allah protect you if one of my oxen stumbles and has to be destroyed." He turned eyeing the rest of Amin's crew now standing with their shovels at their sides.

"I need these men in the field today," he said. "We have to get the cane in before the juice dries. I need everyone's help. You men drop your shovels and follow Ziyad. He will show where there is work to be done."

"You can't do that. Haj Matthew has assigned these men to me. I need them to get this pipe laid." Amin moved to the center of the bridge, stomping it with his foot. "You don't trust this, fine, we'll fill the hole and move it out of the way."

Uthman leaned over and spat on the ground. "Ostaz Matthew does not own this farm. These men are on the payroll of Haja Zainab. They were hired to work for me. I am in charge of all farm labor, and I say they are needed elsewhere. I'll return them to you, but not until after the cane harvest. That is the only thing of importance right now. Now, you men, go!" he said, pointing down the road with his finger.

The man Uthman called Ziyad walked across the bridge and kept going, looking back only to make sure Amin's crew followed.

The men standing around the pile of dirt gazed at each other. One-by-one they dropped their shovels and fell in line. Only Masud wavered.

"You too. I need everyone working in the fields. This man can fill the hole by himself. It won't take him long."

Masud hesitated, the perspiration on his brow more pronounced than a moment before. "He's right, Amin, Haj Matthew doesn't own..." but he didn't finish the sentence. He turned and stepped down from the mound of dirt, traipsing off after the others.

Amin turned and called after him. "It is okay, Masud, I will straighten this out with Haj Matthew tonight when he returns." He watched as the band of men was led away. Ziyad veered off the road into a tall stand of cane, and they followed, disappearing out of sight. Amin turned to face Uthman again. The foremen and his cohorts stayed on the other side, stalling. They had no reason not to trust the bridge.

Uthman tilted his head back. "So tell me, you who defy the Almighty, is your God able to give you strength to finish this job alone?" There were snickers from the men standing around the donkey cart.

"There is only one God. It doesn't matter if you call Him Allah or anything else. And it is to God that all men must account for their sin."

"You have spoken well. And would you not also agree that his greatest Prophet is Muhammad?"

Sweat rolled down Amin's cheek. He wiped his face on his sleeve, his heart thumping in his chest. "Jesus said, I AM the Way, the Truth, and the Life, no man comes to the father but by me. This is what I now believe."

Uthman stiffened, his lips compressed and turning white. "See, what did I tell you? We need no further proof." He raised himself and climbed down from his cart. "The blasphemy comes from his own mouth." He stepped onto the bridge, meeting Amin halfway. "You must think me unfair," he said.

Amin tried to swallow but his mouth was dry. His heart pounded so hard it hurt.

"But I am a reasonable man." Uthman shrugged and continued on until he reached the other side. He stooped to pick up a shovel. "I will help you fill in this hole."

Amin watched, feeling like he should run, but his feet were glued to the ground.

"Do not just stand there. I said I would help, but I have no intention of doing the work by myself." Uthman shoved his spade into a mound of dirt to emphasize the point.

Amin's grip tightened around the handle of his shovel. He scooped a pile of dirt and tossed it into the trench.

Uthman did the same and a few seconds later they were working in concert, spade for spade filling in the channel.

Uthman paused and stepped back, mopping his brow. Amin turned to compliment his coworker. He saw only a blur as the shovel came crashing down on his head.

Amin found himself surrounded by light. He reached for it but his arms waved vainly in the air. The light could be felt, but it couldn't be touched. It was like the color of a million prisms dancing in front of his eyes. He heard a sound. He could remember hearing it once before like the light was trying to communicate; only this time he understood. The voice spoke in a language of intrinsic beauty, a sound pure as transparent liquid, like the sound of rippling water. "Well done, good and faithful servant, enter into the joy of your Lord." He saw something like arms reaching for him, and hands bearing scars, and then everything faded to into a brilliant white light—so bright, soooo brrrrriight!

Amin's body slumped, keeling forward as it fell into the ditch.

"Bury him. They will think he finished filling in the hole and left. His own men will testify how he was angered by my pulling them off the job. Let them assume he thought I was being unfair and decided to quit. It is time to put things back the way they were."

CHAPTER 11

Oh come, let us sing to the Lord! Let us shout joyfully to the Rock of our salvation. — Psalm 95:1

THE ROOM was bathed in bands of yellow light that streamed through the window picking up flecks of cosmic dust. Layla hummed as she and Sabah stood at the table peeling oranges for an afternoon snack. Sabah reached for a date.

"Where does this song come from?"

"What song?"

"The song you always sing. You have a beautiful voice, Layla, but where does your song come from?"

"I don't have just one song. There are many. Which song do you mean?"

"Any of them."

"From God. He put the songs in my heart."

"I don't understand. God is too far away to speak songs to you."

"No, God is everywhere. He's right in this room. He's even closer. He's in my heart. Bring your food and we'll go sit down. Maybe I can explain."

A fly circled the women seated on the couch, buzzing and landing again each time they shooed it away. Sabah fanned her fingers in front of her face, keeping the pest off her cheek. She wore a yellow *abaya,* the new one she'd purchased during their shopping spree. She reached around and scratched the back of her neck. "But what do you mean you have a personal relationship with God? God is too big to know. He is not like us. We cannot *know* Him."

A fan in the corner of the room oscillated back and forth keeping the warn air circulating. The fly landed on a dish of dried fruit, but skittered away when Sabah reached for a slice of dried apricot.

Layla sat beside Sabah with a Bible in her lap trying to explain the nature of God. She poked at her maroon blouse tucking it into the waist of her skirt and leaned in to scoop up a handful of sunflower seeds, shooing the fly away again.

The question was a difficult one to answer. It took faith to believe in that which could not be seen. Skeptics always said, "Show me a miracle, and I'll believe," but God said, "Believe, and I'll show you a miracle."

"That's precisely the point, Sabah, God is too big to know. That's why he had to become man." She nibbled on her seeds for a few seconds before continuing the thought. "He had to become like us so that we could know him. Even Islam believes the prophets were called by God to reveal who He is, but it was never enough. All they could do was tell us about Him, not help us know him."

The fly landed on a page of her open Bible providing a momentary distraction. Layla started to wave it off but instead held the Bible up for Sabah to see. "We can't know or understand God any more than this fly, or an ant, or a worm, can understand the mind of a human.

"In order for us to know God, He had to become a man." She brought her Bible down and the fly darted away. "Just like if I wanted to show a fly what a human is like, I would have to become a fly, while still retaining my human nature so I could explain to other flies what humans are like. That's the wonder of Christ."

Sabah shook her head. "Forgive me," she said, "but I do not think God is interested in flies."

"But he is interested in us."

"But we are too big to fit into the body of a fly. And God is too big to become a man, so this is clearly impossible."

Layla folded her hands over her Bible. Sabah's round face was smooth as a cherub's, her naturally red lips smiling decorously. Her questions were sincere, not hostile. "It may be difficult to understand, Sabah, but it's certainly not impossible, because nothing is impossible for God. I know you believe that. And it's not like God left the kingdom of heaven to come here. What He did was put a part of Himself, the uniqueness of His person, His divine nature and power, into human form so that we could see what God is like and know Him. I was raised a Christian, so I confess I don't know Islam as well as I should, but I do know Muslims believe that men sin."

"Oh, yes, very much. I fear I do things every day of which Allah does not approve." Sabah looked down folding her hands in her lap. "I fear perhaps I should not be here, may Allah grant me mercy." Then she looked up. "I see you as a sister, a dear friend, and I don't question that you mean well, but I also know Allah is displeased when we listen to things that make us question him."

The late evening sun poured through the living room window, highlighting Sabah's face—a gentle face that refused to perspire even though her *abaya* covered her body like a blanket. Layla tugged at the sleeves of her blouse, letting the air cool her wrists. "But will Allah let you into paradise if you sin?"

"Perhaps, at least I hope so. I am a good Muslim. I have practiced the five pillars from my youth...well, except that I have not made a Hajj to Mecca, but I plan to very soon." Sabah brought her hand up and began counting on her fingertips. "I repeat the Shahadah, and I try to pray five times a day, and I give alms to the poor, and I fast wherever possible. If I do enough good things, then maybe Allah all merciful will overlook my little sins."

Layla nodded as she reached for a date. "All those are good things, Sabah. But there's nothing unique about them, because every other religion on earth requires pretty much the same thing. It doesn't matter if you're Hindi, Buddhist, Muslim or Jewish, all religions teach that you must do good to earn God's favor."

The pesky fly was back. It tried to land on her date but she shooed it away. "Only Christianity stands alone. Christianity acknowledges that everyone sins but it also recognizes that no matter how much good we do, it will never be enough because we can't be perfect. I'm sure you'd agree that only God is perfect. You and I can never be good enough to enter into God's presence on our own." She bit the end of the date. "But God knew this so He made a way out. He allowed a part of Himself to become man, to experience every pain and temptation we feel, but because his nature was divine He was able to avoid sinning, and then as a perfect sacrifice, He was able to give Himself to die in our place and take upon Himself the punishment we deserve."

Sabah shook her head. "This is too much for me to understand. I don't know how my husband does it. He seems so different, so sure, but I sit here and feel foolish because I know Allah cannot lie, and this is not his way. Maybe if I saw Jesus the way Amin did, then maybe I would believe…"

Layla sighed, shaking her head. "He could, Sabah, and maybe He will, but what's more important is…" her eyes lifted as her husband came through the door… "that you recognize what He did for Amin was real, and that He can do the same thing for you. All you have to do is believe."

Mohamed stopped, waiting for a chance to interrupt. The women paused looking up. The air from the fan flicked his hair. He pursed his lips and took a breath, letting it out quickly. "I'm looking for Amin. Have you seen him?"

Sabah shook her head, her smile fading as she glanced out the window. Layla followed her gaze. It was growing dark. The palms across the road were silhouettes against a slate blue sky. Sabah turned her attention back to Mohamed. "No, he is so excited about his work I have not seen much of him the past few days."

Mohamed nodded. "He's probably still down by the river. I'll go see if I can find him." He spun around and with his sandals slapping the tile floor, exited the front door.

Mohamed approached the Nile. To the south, the water appeared flat and purple, like a deflated cobra. He turned looking back over his shoulder. Stars in the eastern sky were blinking. He could see the yellow lights of the house shining in the distance. The air was musty, constricting his breath.

He passed workers coming in from the fields, most of them on the opposite side of the road. He didn't stop to acknowledge them. He didn't know them by name. He turned his head away, trusting the darkness to keep him from being recognized.

By the time he reached the construction site, it was getting hard to see. He walked onto the bridge and looked over the edge, reviewing the progress they'd made. The piles that had stood on both sides of the causeway were gone and the ground under the bridge looked level. He continued on tamping the dirt with his foot, his sandal sinking into the loose soil. The hole was filled, but the dirt wasn't compressed the way it needed to be before carts could cross.

"Has Amin told you what happened today?"

He jerked up, swinging his head around. It was Masud. He stood to the side of a trestle, a reaper's knife in his hand. His white *galabia* was soiled from the day's work.

Mohamed wiped his hands on his pants. "No. Actually, I was just looking for him. Isn't he with you?"

"No, but this is something we need to speak about," Masud said, lifting his chin toward the trench. "We were not able to work with Amin today. The man, Uthman, he said we were to work in the fields. Amin was the only one Uthman allowed to stay, so he had to work alone. The rest of us have been cutting cane." He raised the knife as though offering proof.

"Must be a mistake. He wanted *all* of you in the fields?"

"Yes, all but Amin, who he left here to fill the trench."

Mohamed shook his head. "Uthman's just trying to goad me. Hiring people used to be his job. He doesn't like it when I interfere. I'll have a talk with him about it. So, you don't know where Amin is?"

"No. But I see he has replaced the dirt in the channel. I doubt there was anything more he could do by himself. He's probably back at the house waiting for you. I think he was very upset."

"I just came from the house and he wasn't there. He could be out surveying the site. I'll take a look around. *Shokran.* Thank you, Masud, and don't worry. I'll straighten this out. I want you and the others on *this* project."

Mohamed's sandals were wet and heavy, filled with the silt of the river as he approached the house. He'd slogged the watercourse back and forth the entire length of the property, but hadn't found Amin. He'd even searched the shoals and marshes, praying his new friend hadn't been caught up and swept away, though he was sure, after what happened last time, he wouldn't be so foolish as to try wading out into the water again.

He wanted to believe Amin would be inside, but he didn't see him through the living room window. A deep foreboding settled in his gut. He slipped out of his sandals and entered through the kitchen just as dinner was being put on the table.

Layla walked over and kissed her husband. "*Masaa el kheer,* Matthew," she said. "It's good you're back. Clean your feet and sit down. We were waiting."

Mohamed wiped his bare foot on his pant cuff, dislodging the remaining loose dirt, then turned and entered the dining area where he found Zainab and Sabah already seated. He pulled back a chair and held it for his wife and sat down beside her at the table. The kitchen help followed him in carrying a silver platter of fish.

"Did Amin show up?" he said, looking at Sabah. He took the plate handed to him. The broiled red snapper was served whole with head, fins, and bones intact.

Sabah shook her head, scooping two fillets onto her dish with a spoon. "I hoped he'd be with you."

"No. Apparently there was some kind of confusion. I guess our foreman pulled the workers off the irrigation job and made them cut cane."

"Why would he do that?" Zainab queried. She reached for another platter filled with sliced breads and meats, took some, and passed it on.

"I don't know but I plan to speak with him about it. I only put six men on the irrigation project and I want them to stay there. If he's falling behind, we'll hire more help, but I doubt it's that. He said I was hiring too many men. He didn't think we had enough work to keep them busy."

"Then where is Amin?" Sabah asked. "All the workers have come in from the fields. Did you not see him?"

Mohamed filled his mouth with a filet and chewed, savoring the briny taste. "*Ummmm, that's good.*" He pulled a bone from his teeth and looked at Sabah. "Apparently, your husband was the only one Uthman let stay on the project, and all he could do was finish one section. It looks like he completed the job early and left. I searched around, but I didn't see him. He must be in the men's quarters. I imagine he's talking with his crew, trying to create a solution to the problem on his own. He's probably lost track of time. I'll go over after dinner and chase him home."

CHAPTER 12

For He Himself has said, "I will never leave you nor forsake you."
— *Hebrews 13:5*

MOHAMED MADE his way up the drive. The evening had drawn a curtain over the desert leaving the bristling cane beneath a blanket of stars, but the barns and living quarters were alive with light. He avoided the long narrow building that housed the workers, heading instead for the garage that was once used for storage. One of the first arguments Uthman used against hiring new employees was that there weren't enough beds. In response, Mohamed had the storage facility emptied and a dozen beds installed along with a latrine. Light poured through the open window.

Mohamed paused just outside. There was excitement in the air as the men jabbered back and forth. They were huddled around the laptop, listening to an Arabic speaking pastor in Canada explaining the Bible on YouTube. He smiled and continued on, turning the corner to enter through the door.

Masud was sitting on the cement floor with his back against his bunk and his knees up. He held the computer in his lap and, looking up over its lid, acknowledged Mohamed with a nod, then turned his attention back to the others seated around him. A fan at the far end of the room was whirring.

Mohamed crossed the floor to close the shutters. "You men need to be more careful. Anyone outside can look in and see what you're doing." He walked to the other side of the bunk, examining the face of each man one at a time. Their eyes withered like scolded puppies. Four men sat in the group and—he looked behind him—one, Nour, was curled up on his bed—*five*, but there was no Amin.

Masud passed the computer to the man on his left who eagerly accepted it. He pushed himself up and stepped out of the circle to speak with Mohamed. "It is my fault," he said. "It's the heat. The open window lets in cool air."

"I know, but…"

"No, you are right. We need to be more careful."

They continued moving until they were at the far end of the room where they could talk in private. "Ah, Haj Matthew, did you speak with the foreman?" Masud queried.

Mohamed brought his hand up, scratching his chin, and dropped it again. "No, we just finished with our evening meal, but it can wait until morning. I don't want to confront him in front of his men or do anything that might cause him to lose face. Have you already eaten?"

As if on cue, the man with the computer suddenly snapped it shut and slipped it under the bed. All eyes turned to the door as two women entered. They swept by quietly, carrying shallow pans of food that were stacked one upon another. *Abayas* draped their bodies and their heads were covered with *khimars*, a show of modesty reflecting Muslim tradition.

They went to the end of the room and began laying out the pans on a table with folding legs. One of the ladies took a glass pitcher and went back outside. The other removed several dishes and plastic cups from one of the pans. She unfurled a napkin to reveal half a dozen spoons which she placed on the table.

The second woman returned with the pitcher, now filled with water from the hose in Sami's garden, and set it down. The ladies grabbed the hems of their *Abayas* and scurried out the door as quickly as they'd come.

The group rose in unison and clamored around the table filling their plates.

Masud stepped away from Mohamed to join the others. He took a dish and lobbed on a stack of fish and cold meats, the same meal Mohamed had enjoyed a few minutes earlier, though perhaps not as nicely presented.

Masud used his fingers to push a fillet into his mouth and turned to face Mohamed again. "I have a question for you, Matthew," he said. His cheeks bulging as he licked his fingers, his teeth still chomping on the mouthful of fish. He swallowed. "If Jesus was going to die and He and the Father knew it all along, why didn't He just die at the beginning, right after the first sin. That way He could have paid for that sin, and all those of everyone else to come?" He held out his plate, offering to share his dinner with Mohamed.

Mohamed waved him off. "That's a good question. I think it has something to do with God wanting to prove men aren't good enough to make it on their own. I think that's why they needed to make sacrifices."

"But why do that? Would not His own sacrifice have been enough?"

"Probably, I mean God can do anything, but I think He wanted men to know how lost they are without Him. My brother once told me that the Quran reads like the Old Testament. Men of Moses' day were trying to do good to earn God's favor, just like faithful Muslims do today. The problem is no one's good enough to meet God's standard because He's perfect, and we humans commit some kind of sin nearly every day. The sacrifices were supposed to show us we're deserving of death but God, because He loves us, substituted animals in our place. You do that for a couple thousand years and you're bound to figure out God doesn't take sin lightly. But then God sent Jesus to become the ultimate sacrifice."

Masud nodded. He picked up a few olives and popped them into his mouth.

"It took me awhile to accept the idea, but I believe my brother was right. I guess we'll know soon enough."

"What do you mean?"

"Jesus is coming soon, so we can ask Him."

Masud spit the olive pits onto his plate and looked up grinning. "Yes, I have heard this also. The teacher we listen to on the computer, he says this. As Arabs, we have fought much with Israel. I always believed it was wrong for the Jews to run our brothers off their land. But our teacher says the Jew's return to Israel proves we are living in the last days."

Mohamed skewed his head to the side, nodding.

The other men were beginning to gather around, each holding a plate of food. Nour set his dish down and used the back of his hand to wipe his mouth and then wiped his hands on his pants. "This is something with which I do not agree. Ishmael, the true son of Ibrahim, lived in the land while the Prophet Moses was still wandering in the desert. This land, all of it, belongs to Ishmael's sons. The Jews stole it then, even as they have done now."

Mohamed hesitated. It was a touchy subject. In some respects, the man was right. The Jews had returned from all parts of the world to displace the Palestinian people. "Yes," he nodded, "but God has allowed this. It is not for us to challenge the will of God."

Nour's eyes narrowed, his eyebrows furrowing in. "You were brought up in America so you cannot see. The United States wants us to love Israel while millions of Palestinians are starving because the Jews have stolen their homes and driven them from their land." He paused, his eyes blinking as though clearing his mind. "I may be a Christian, I know God has revealed Himself to me, but I cannot love the United States anymore than I do the Jews. America has invaded us with its immorality. It has exploited us. It intimidates us with its military and it manipulates us with its American dollars. And Israel is just America's little sister. She wants to grow up to be just like her, a superpower in the Middle East dominating our politics and resources."

Mohamed wanted to tell the man he *did* understand. He wasn't raised in the United States. He was born and raised in Egypt where he'd heard his uncle continually complain about the same thing. He'd watched young men strap on explosives and give their lives to liberate Palestine from its oppressors, but he choked back the thought. Revealing his identity, even to a fellow believer, could be dangerous. And continuing down this path would only lead to further argument. Old prejudices die hard. "Even if you took Israel out of the equation," he said, "we would still know we're in the last days. The Bible speaks about the formation of a world government, and a global economy, and even a world religion led by a false messiah."

"That won't happen. Jews and Christians and Muslims will never agree to worship the same God."

"I wouldn't be so sure. A lot of people view all religions as the same. Coming from a predominantly Muslim country it's hard to see, but in the western world, a lot of people accept the idea that everyone's just trying to reach God in their own way, which is setting the stage for a false messiah. Who knows, the way Islam is overspreading the globe, it may be the world religion. Maybe the one they call the Antichrist is the twelfth imam foretold by Shi'ite scholars."

"Ah, see, there goes your argument. Jews would never accept an Arab Messiah."

"But what if he's half Jew and half Arab? Maybe he could bring both groups together. The Jews are looking for their Messiah too, one who will bring peace.

Nour held a piece of bread to his mouth, nodding. Mohamed wasn't sure he really understood. In fact, all the men crowding around him looked confused. Mohamed scanned the room one more time. "Have any of you seen Amin?"

Masud took a fish bone from his plate and set the dish aside. "You still haven't found him?"

"No, I thought he might be over here using the computer."

Masud shook his head, using the sharp bone to pick his teeth.

Mohamed pursed his lips, dreading the idea of finding Amin's body washed up on the shore. He turned to say goodnight but Nour had another challenge. It was too late to debate eschatology but he'd opened the door and it wasn't fair to leave the men with unanswered questions.

... 🌙 ...

It was after midnight when Mohamed finally entered the house. The lights were out. It appeared everyone was already in bed.

He slipped quietly into the bedroom trying not to wake Layla. He wanted to get his Bible and do a little further reading. Having gone through the scriptures front to back several times, he was becoming familiar with their stories and teachings but prophecy was a bit harder to understand, especially those not yet fulfilled. He needed to be certain he'd answered the questions posed by the men correctly.

"Is that you, *Habibty?*" Layla stirred. She rolled over tucking a blanket under her chin. "*Hummmm*, did you find Amin?"

"No. He didn't come back to the house?"

"Unh uh." Layla sighed. "I think Sabah is worried."

"So am I. If he doesn't show up by morning, I'll gather the workers and go looking for him; but it's probably nothing. Maybe he hitched a ride to Asyut for supplies." Mohamed leaned over and gave his wife a kiss, stroking her cheek with his finger, and then stood. "Anyway, it's too late to do anything about it tonight."

He slipped quietly down the hall to the living room. The space was dark, causing him to bump into the sofa, its legs screeching on the hard ceramic tiles. His fingers used the curve along the back as a guide until he reached the lamp and turned it on. Light flooded the room. He settled himself on the couch easing back into the cushions. The Bible in his lap fell open to the book of Acts. He picked it up and began to read.

"Please, I don't mean to disturb you, but I can't sleep."

Mohamed glanced up to see Sabah standing just outside the lamp's cone of light. Her hair was braided behind her. She was wearing one of his mother's robes.

"Did you find my husband?"

Her eyes were tense, filled with anxiety...or was it something else? "No, no one's seen him." He slipped his finger into his Bible, closing it while holding his place. "Did you want to talk?"

Sabah shook her head. "This is terrible," she said.

"I wouldn't worry. He's got to be around somewhere. I was just saying to Layla, he probably went into town for supplies."

"But he would be back by now."

"Perhaps. Maybe they didn't have what he needed in Asyut. Maybe he went all the way to Cairo. Who knows? I'm sure he'll be back. If he doesn't show up by morning, we'll get a crew together and go search for him."

"But I very much need to see him. I have something to say. I was praying, you see. I asked this God of yours to show Himself. I said, 'if you're the true God, like my husband believes, show Yourself to me the way You did to him,' and I suddenly felt this presence like someone was standing behind me. I didn't dare turn around and look, but the hair on the back of my neck and arms tingled, and I felt my body shudder and I knew it must be God, and I was afraid. Then I heard a voice say. 'Do not fear. You will not be alone.' And then the presence left, and I was crying but I did not know why. What can this mean? I want to ask my husband, but he has not come back, and in spite of what I heard, I have never felt so all alone."

CHAPTER 13

For we wrestle not against flesh and blood, but against principalities, against powers, against the rulers of the darkness of this world, against spiritual wickedness in high places. — Ephesians 6:10-12

MOHAMED TOSSED his blanket aside, swinging his legs around to sit on the edge of the bed. The room was still in shadows but a pale glow in the window heralded the coming of dawn. He hadn't been able to sleep. He'd shared scriptures of comfort with Sabah, prayed with her, and sent her to bed hoping she'd find rest, but he hadn't found any for himself. Every time the shutter creaked his eyes popped open. He'd listened with his ears tuned to the stillness of the night hoping to hear Amin's footsteps, but the hours passed with only the sound of rustling leaves and the hooting of a desert owl.

Mohamed stood and slipped quietly to the window. A faint ribbon of blue burnished the horizon. Soon the sun would crest, shedding its crimson light on the Nile—the very waters Amin was trying to harness. He felt a chill and rubbed his arms.

The devout had already begun their morning march to the Mosque. In a few minutes, the imam would begin chanting the azan calling them to *fajr*. It wouldn't take long. Prayers had to be made before dawn and the light was steadily increasing. He had to catch them on their way back, before they put their prayer rugs away and returned to work in the fields.

He went to the armoire and removed his clothes, denims and a blue work shirt, laying them on the bed. Layla rolled over and opened her eyes, sleepily, and closed them again. "*Hummm,* it's too early. Come back to bed," she mumbled, pulling the blanket under her chin.

"Far as I know, Amin didn't make it home last night." Mohamed spoke in English as he always did when discussing things he wanted to keep private. He pulled on his pants, buckling them around his waist, and slipped into his shirt. "I have to question the men and find out if anyone knows anything."

Layla pushed her hands out from under the blanket, stretched and *yaaawnned.* "I guess I better get up. Sabah probably needs me."

Mohamed tucked in his shirt. "I spoke to Sabah last night," he said, tucking his shirt in. "The poor girl couldn't sleep, but it gave me a chance to talk to her, and she made a profession of faith…"

"*Really?*" Layla propped herself up on her elbows.

"Yes, really, at least if her confession was sincere. We read a few scriptures together, but it would be good if you were there for her this morning. I doubt she slept any better than I did."

Layla tossed the covers aside and sat up, combing her long hair through her fingers. "I'll see what I can do." The noise of pans clattering echoed down the hall. "Sounds like the kitchen's alive. Must be time for breakfast."

Mohamed buttoned his cuff as he leaned in to kiss his wife's cheek, but she wrapped her arms around his neck and stood, kissing him on the mouth instead. He embraced her, holding her tight enough to feel the warmth of her body.

"I'm worried," she said, "and not just for Sabah. You be careful out there. I don't want you to disappear."

"I won't. I Promise."

He moved down the hall, slipping quietly by his old bedroom so as not to disturb Sabah. He could hear the clamor of food preparation, the subdued voices and rattle of silver coming from the next room. He rounded the corner and saw light coming from the kitchen. The servants were bustling about. A cast iron frying pan sizzled on the stove with a cube of white cheese turning golden brown in a hot bath of olive oil. Fluffs of scrambled eggs were cooking in another pan. A woman stood at the counter slicing cucumbers and tomatoes, while someone else laid scones of bread on a tray.

He entered the fray, slipping his arms into his jacket. It would be incredibly hot later on, but the morning air was cool.

"*Sabah el kheer,* Ostaz Matthew. *Kaifa haloka.*" Good morning, Mr. Matthew. How are you? Sami stood there, his toothless mouth grinning, his bald head shining in the light.

"*Ana bekhair, shokran,*" I'm fine, thank you. Mohamed nodded, acknowledging his mother's *khadem.*

He turned and made his way through the kitchen, twisting to avoid bumping into a girl in a black burka carrying a platter of meats. He reached for the door but was brought up short by his mother's voice.

"Matthew, is that you?"

He spun around, stepping into the dining room. His mother was seated at the table with her hands wrapped around a cup of tea. Across from her sat Sabah, her eyes puffy and red.

"*Sabah el kheer.*" He glanced at Sabah. He didn't have to ask if she'd slept well. It was obvious she hadn't.

"Amin is still missing," Zainab said. "Sabah's been up all night."

Mohamed exhaled, his breath coming out in a grunt. "I'm on my way to question the workers. I'll find out if anyone knows anything. But if I come up empty, I'll form a search party."

"He's dead," Sabah said. "I can feel it." She was wearing the same pale pink robe she'd had on earlier and her hair was still in a braid. Her eyes were wet and red.

Mohamed shook his head, his eyebrows furrowing. "Don't write him off just yet. We haven't even started looking.

"She has reason to feel the way she does, Matthew."

Mohamed glanced at his mother.

"Sabah encountered Jesus last night. He told her she would never be alone. Sounds like He was preparing her for something to come. It's possible Amin fell into the river again. He might have drowned."

Mohamed shook his head tersely, glaring at his mother. "Yes, I thought about that, but I doubt he'd be so foolish as to go near the water again."

Their heads turned as Layla entered the room. She was wearing one of the outfits she'd bought during their shopping spree: a navy pullover dress with a white blouse. Her hair was freshly combed and a brush of pink glossed her lips.

Mohamed smiled and leaned in to kiss her on the cheek. "I've got to go." He straightened himself. "And don't worry if I'm not home until late. I intend to find Amin if it takes all day."

"Don't forget your promise," she said.

Mohamed stood in the road waiting for the men to return from their pilgrimage to the mosque. There was a thin line of clouds on the northern horizon but the sun was creeping up unobstructed in the east. In the far distance, he could see his workers trudging back from their morning prayers, just tiny dots, too far away to recognize faces. Each day they made the same ritualistic *hajj* in search of God's favor. It didn't have to be so hard. If only they knew Jesus. Perhaps one day they would. Only God knew.

He was watching the sun inflate like a giant yellow balloon, but turned at the clomping of hoofs. Uthman was trotting toward him, his buggy whip waving in his hand. He couldn't see the man's face, silhouetted as it was by the sun, but only Uthman drove a donkey cart. It was a privilege he allotted himself as foremen. The rest of the men were still a good distance behind. *Good.* He'd wanted a chance to consult with the man in private. He stepped into the donkey's path and raised his hand obliging Uthman to draw back on the reins.

"A word, Uthman, if you don't mind." The dust swirled up, covering Mohamed in a cloud. He waved it away, coughing. He could see the man's expression through the diffused gray. It was hard and narrow, a face from Easter Island, carved in stone.

"You are fortunate I have control of this animal, Ostaz Matthew. You could have been killed." Uthman laid his carriage whip across his lap and stared at Mohamed stoically, his beard pulling the corners of his mouth into a frown. A breeze whipped at the turban that billowed like a cloud over his head.

Mohamed dusted the front of his shirt. Uthman should refer to him as, Haj, a title of authority, not Ostaz, but he chose to let it pass. "I hear you pulled my men off the irrigation project."

"The cane needs to be gathered. You left me shorthanded and we were starting to fall behind. I need their help to catch up."

Mohamed shook his head. "I thought you said I was hiring too many men. You said there wasn't enough work to keep them busy?"

"That was when the cane was immature. Now is the time of harvest."

Mohamed took the donkey by the bridle, stroking the side of the animal's neck. "You have a good position here, Uthman. I recommend you don't abuse it. Answer this question. Would you have done such a thing if my uncle had put these men to work on a project he had wanted done?"

Uthman grinned, his lips pinched together like oily sardines. He shook his head. "Your uncle left me in charge. He trusted me to make decisions about who to hire, and where they should be used, and I know he would not have wasted time on something so foolish." He raised his hand, pointing at the construction site. "Getting machines to do what Allah gave men strong hands for, is an affront. How do you think my men feel when they see you building something that could replace their jobs?"

"I expect the men to do as I ask as long as they work for me, and that includes you, Uthman."

"May I respectfully remind you, that we *don't* work for you. As far as I know, Haja Zainab is the owner of these lands, and she has left me in charge, just as your uncle did before her."

Mohamed exhaled, grunting. "So that's it. Fine, I shall see you receive instruction from her. I want this irrigation project to move forward unobstructed. You and your men are not to get in the way. In fact, I want you to assist whenever you're asked."

Uthman scowled. "And how do you propose to do that now that you've lost your engineer?"

Mohamed glanced up abruptly. Letting go of the donkey's bridle, he stepped to the side. "What do you know of that? I don't recall saying my engineer was missing?"

Uthman pulled on the reins, backing the donkey up. "I heard it from the men. Is it not true? Word is he finally realized he did not know what he was doing, and rather than admit this to you, he ran off. Now, if there's nothing else, I have work to do." He laid the reins to the side of the animal's neck and gave them a flick, turning away, but Mohamed lunged forward grabbing the bridle again, preventing Uthman from leaving. The two men glared at each other.

"I want you to assemble the men, all of them," Mohamed said. "I want you to gather them in front of the house where Zainab can speak to them. Let's not have any misunderstanding about what's expected of everyone."

CHAPTER 14

For there is nothing covered, that shall not be revealed, neither hid, that shall not be known. — Luke 12:2

SIXTY-FIVE WORKERS gathered on the lawn in front of the El Taher estate, milling in and out, anxious about possibly losing a day's pay. The clouds had rolled in, the dry lightning snapping and popping in the heated sky. Masud and the Christian brothers were huddled off by themselves, standing by the wall at the end of the drive, their faces filled with concern.

Towering over the assembly was Uthman, seated on his cart with whip in hand. He turned to see if they'd finished the count. Four men stood clustered around him like bodyguards, one of which held the donkey's bridle to keep the animal from bolting when lightning cracked the ground.

Mohamed stood on the porch waiting until everyone was accounted for. He received a nod. Apparently, only one man was missing, and he was reported to be sick. He turned and went back into the house, letting the screen door slam, and a few moments later reappeared with his mother on his arm. Layla and Sabah followed them out.

The men grew silent at the appearance of Haja Zainab. She was the wife of the late Sayyid, heir to all he once possessed. She was owed their respect.

She stood, dressed in a *hijab* of mint green chiffon, looking regal with her gray hair pinned up and khimar covering her head. Gazing out across the faces to make sure she had their undivided attention, she slipped her arm out from Mohamed's and leaned forward placing her hands on the porch-rail.

"I'm told there are questions about the authority of my son," she said. "Some of you may not even have had the chance to meet him. This is my fault, a situation I now wish to correct."

Zainab straightened herself and reached out placing her hand on Mohamed's shoulder. "This is Matthew, brother of Mohamed El Taher, and nephew of Haj Sayyid. He is heir to all I own. You are to respect him as you respect me. His words are my words. If he asks you to do something, I expect you to do it. If this makes you uncomfortable, Matthew will see that you are paid any wages you are owed, and you may take your leave. Are there any questions?"

She let her arm drop and stood waiting a moment, folding her hands in front of her, but her eyes were fixed on Uthman. His face was hard, his lips pinched. It was obvious he wanted to protest, but wisely held back. "Good. I trust I won't hear of this again. Now, Matthew has something to say." She took a step back so Mohamed could address the men directly.

"Thank you mother." He looked out over the crowd. The clouds behind the men were rolling in and becoming thick. The air smelled like rain. "My first question is about the engineer I hired to oversee the irrigation project. He hasn't been seen since yesterday. Does anyone have any idea of where he might be? Anything you have might be helpful, even if you think it's unimportant. Did you overhear him talking about going somewhere? Or maybe you saw him in some remote part of the property. If you know anything that might help us find him, please tell me now."

He scanned the group but they stared at their feet refusing to answer. "So no one has seen my engineer since Uthman asked that his crew join in the harvest? Uthman, that makes you the last person to have seen him."

"He was not alone. He had others with him."

Mohamed glanced over and saw it was Masud.

Uthman also craned his head around to see who was speaking.

"Is that true? Okay, I want those who were with Uthman to stay behind. And I want the rest of you to form search parties. I want you to cross every inch of this property. And I want a truck to drive downriver for at least twenty kilometers checking every marsh and stand of reeds."

Heat rose off the ground meeting the cooler air above, the conditions perfect for a storm. Uthman guffawed. "With all due respect, we are in the middle of the harvest. We have to get the cane to the mill before it loses yield. We'll be lucky if this rain doesn't ruin us. We should be out gathering everything we can. Your so called engineer probably just realized he couldn't live up to his promise, and ran off to avoid being caught in a lie."

"He would not do that!" Sabah blurted out. She broke away from Layla and rushed to the edge of the railing. "He would not leave without telling me."

Uthman's eyes hardened. He leaned over and spat, wiping the dribble from his beard with long fingers. "If he was your husband, you should be glad he is gone. He committed blasphemy against Allah most high. It would not surprise me to find he was struck down by the hand of God." He looked around receiving nods and murmurs from those around him. "But I would not worry; he has probably just gone into Asyut. I'm sure once he sobers up he'll come to collect his wife and that will be the end of it."

The men standing around Uthman's cart chortled, but stopped when they saw Mohamed wasn't smiling. "Your judgment of the man's character is as lacking as your sensitivity to his wife, Uthman." Mohamed shifted his eyes to the Christian brothers. "Masud, I'm putting you in charge. I want you to organize the men and get them going. And hurry, it looks like it's going to rain. Uthman, you and those who were with you yesterday, stay behind for a minute."

The clouds were swelling overhead, flickers of phosphorescent green pulsating in the distance. The air was thick with the smell of wet straw. Masud began assigning men sections of the acreage to walk. He put ten men into a truck and sent it downriver instructing the driver to let one man out every two kilometers so that each could walk that distance along the shore looking for a body.

The scarves of the women began snapping in the wind. They tucked their wraps under their arms and went back inside. Mohamed had Uthman, along with the other four who remained, join him on the porch. He instructed the men not to talk among themselves and led Uthman into the dining room, seating him at the table while he took a chair on the opposite side. Rain began to spatter against the window.

"I want to hear exactly what happened when you spoke to Amin. "I need you to tell me everything you, or anyone else, said, and recount the order of events as best you can."

Uthman tucked his beard between his legs, his oversized turban balanced on his head like a toadstool. "All my life I have worked for this family," he said. "Even as a boy, before you were born, I was cutting my hands on the spines of the cotton bolls, yet for all my labors, this is the first time I have ever been invited into this house."

Mohamed shook his head. "That's another matter entirely, one which I know nothing about."

"Do you suspect me of doing something wrong?"

Mohamed leaned forward folding his hands on the table in front of him. "That has already been established. You had no right to stop a project I wanted done. Now please answer the question."

"I did nothing but ask for the assistance of a few workers. They followed Ziyad into the field while I stayed to test the strength of the bridge. Your man, Amin, was busy filling the trench when we left. That is the last I saw of him."

It did not surprise Mohamed to find each man's story the same. They had approached the crew and Uthman had asked the workers to stop laying pipe and go help with the harvest, but there was discrepancy regarding what happened after that. Uthman said he told Amin to continue working alone, that he could fill in the trench by himself, but one of the others said Uthman told Amin he would not be able to resume laying pipe until the harvest was in, and another said Amin had run off threatening to report Uthman to Zainab, and still another said Amin had threatened to quit.

There was only one left to interrogate. Mohamed stepped outside into a storm so heavy he had to put his arm over his head for protection as he ran splashing through the mud.

Egypt wasn't known for having the kind of monsoons common in Ethiopia and Sudan, but if ever there was a monsoon, this was it. The rain hammered the earth bouncing off the ground, forming small rivulets that turned into streams and became rivers in minutes, eroding the soil.

On the access road, under a bridge spanning a culvert that led to the river, the loose dirt covering Amin's body was being washed away one grain at a time. The flow had begun as a trickle, which quickly grew into a stream, and finally into a torrent as the water filled the trench, taking the path of least resistance on its way to the Nile. At first, only a small portion of Amin's sleeve was exposed, then as the flood thrashed its way to the river, a hand became visible, then a cheek...Amin's blood was crying out from the ground.

The room smelled rank, like a mixture of human waste and unwashed clothes. Mohamed walked up and down the long center aisle, his feet leaving tracks of mud on the cement floor. The beds were filthy. Grains of sand had accumulated in the creases of the unmade sheets, turning the white fabric a dingy brown. The servants were only required to launder the bedding once a week.

He stood on his toes, scanning the upper bunks, and stooped to examine the mattresses of the berth beneath. One of those he'd interviewed let it slip that the worker who didn't make it to the assembly, the one reported to be ill, was also there when Uthman brought the irrigation project to a halt.

The rain beat on the tin roof like a drum. He passed an open window, the smell of wet earth a relief from the fetid stench of the room. In one corner, a bucket collected rainwater from the dribble of an overhead leak. Sayyid should have used his money on maintenance. The building needed repair. Mohamed made a note to get things started as soon as possible.

He found the man he was looking for lying on a lower bunk near the end of the aisle. He was curled up in a fetal position, facing the wall. His arms were wrapped around his stomach, and when he groaned, he cinched his arms tighter.

Mohamed sat on the bunk behind the man, the springs creaking under his weight. He folded his hands and rested his forearms on his knees, waiting to be acknowledged, but either the man hadn't heard him, or was choosing to ignore his presence.

"I hear you're not feeling well," he said. "I hate to bother you, but the situation is urgent and I need your help. One of the men who works here, the engineer I hired to oversee my irrigation project, has disappeared. I'm told you were there when Uthman asked the other workers to leave the site, so you may have been one of the last people to see him."

The man rolled over to see who was speaking. His eyes were half mast, and his forehead dotted with perspiration. He moaned, gripping his belly with both hands. "Do you think Allah intends to kill me for what we did?"

"That depends. Allah is compassionate and merciful. Do you know the whereabouts of the man I seek?"

At first the man didn't answer. He closed his eyes. Then he cramped up again and curled into a ball. "Please, I didn't do anything. I only watched."

Mohamed clenched his teeth, leaning in close. "I need you to tell me exactly what you saw."

The man groaned, his face grimacing in pain as he clutched his stomach, but he nodded.

The rain pelted Mohamed as he splashed through the mud, running down the road. Visibility was near zero, the clouds and rain forming a gauzy curtain. He had to keep pushing his matted hair out of his eyes to see. His denims stuck to his skin, but he didn't care, he was determined to find Amin.

The group appeared out of the cloud like ghostly shadows. It was Masud and the Christian brothers. They stumbled forward, carrying something to keep it from dragging on the ground. Each man held an appendage; one had a hand, another a foot, all the way around.

Mohamed fell in line next to Masud. He swallowed, feeling his Adam's apple catch in his throat. "I...I see you found Amin."

Masud nodded, his beard a waterfall dripping from his chin.

They entered by the stone gate, their shoes leaving muddy tracks as they lay the disinterred body of Amin on the lawn. His face was streaked with dirt and his skin held a whitish-blue tinge. Only a few short days ago, Amin had nearly drowned but Jesus had spared him. Now he was gone. *Why, Lord? Why save his life—for this?*

A tear rolled down Mohamed's cheek—or maybe it was just the rain—no, it was warm, it had to be a tear. More followed. He looked up, allowing the downpour to wash his face. The clouds were metal gray, roiling up like wads of steel wool. Other workers were beginning to gather. Lightning pulsated to the north. The storm was a long way from over.

Sabah ran out onto the porch, followed by Layla. She put her hands to her cheeks. *"Oh no, no, noooooo!"* she cried, and ran back inside.

Chapter 15

Submit yourselves to every ordinance of man for the Lord's sake, whether it be to the king, as supreme, or unto governors, as unto them that are sent by him for the punishment of evildoers... — 1 Peter 2:13-14

MOHAMED WATCHED Layla disappear behind the screen door, letting it slam. The rain continued to pour, streaming off his chin. He examined the gathering crowd of workers, their numbers growing. Uthman was not among them. The man and his donkey were strangely absent. *Murderer!* His body trembled, trying to hold his rage in check. This was a matter for the police. He bounded up the steps but turned before entering the house. "Cover that body," he said.

"What do you want us to do with him?"

"Leave him there until I call the police."

He could hear Sabah's moans coming from the bedroom as he marched down the hall heading for the phone. The population of the rural community wasn't large enough to support a full police department. He would have to contend with a remote outpost manned by one or two officers and a few soldiers. He could only hope their investigation would be thorough. He stood dripping water on the floor as he dialed the number of the *noata el shorta.* and waited.

"*Salam*, can I help you?"

"Yes, there's been a murder. I need to speak with a detective."

"Hold, please." The phone went silent, probably answered by one of the soldiers. A few seconds later he heard a click, then a voice.

"Hossame."

"Yes, hello, my name is Matthew Mulberry. I'm at the El Taher estate and there's been a murder. I need someone out here as soon as possible, someone who can make an arrest."

"And why was this person killed?"

Mohamed shook his arms spraying water across the room; his clothes were soaked. He stretched his shoulders, his shirt binding across his back. "What does it matter? The man's dead. He was hit over the head with a shovel and his body dumped into a ditch and buried. Are you going to send someone, or not?"

There was a moment of silence and when the man spoke again, his voice was reservedly cool. "It's called motive, and it goes to degree. It might be a few hours, but I'll get there as soon as I can."

"I have a body on my front lawn starting to decompose."

"I'm sorry, but yours is not the only crime I have to investigate. And there's not much I can do in this rain."

Mohamed began pacing. "Fine, do what you can, but please hurry. I don't want anyone else getting hurt." He put the phone down and turned, leaning against the desk, then stood again to avoid getting the furniture wet. Sabah's grief filled the house.

Mohamed's cuffs made wet streaks on the tiles as he trudged down the hall. He pushed the door open a crack and stepped inside. Sabah held her face in her hands. Words wouldn't bring her husband back but he had to say something. "Sabah, I am so sorry..."

She looked up, her eyes raining tears, her mouth a wilted rose. "I told you this would happen. I told you." She began kneading the fabric of her *hijab*. "What kind of God would do this? He lied to me. He said I would not be alone." She closed her eyes and began sobbing again.

"Sabah, I…"

Layla wrapped her arms around Sabah and pulled her in close, humming softly. She glanced at her husband, shaking her head reproachfully.

Mohamed nodded. She needed time to grieve. He backed out the door, closing it behind him.

He started down the hall, his shoulders sagging under the weight of his responsibility. He'd told Amin and Sabah they'd be safe. He leaned against the door, breathing deeply to regain composure, then clenched his teeth and straightened himself. His wet clothes were glued to his skin. Uthman was going to pay. He pushed the screen door open. It creaked and banged against the wall as he stepped onto the porch.

Pools had formed on the lawn, stippled by the rain. Most of the men had left, fleeing to their quarters to escape the downpour, leaving behind a lawn dented with the imprints of their shoes. Only Amin's five Christian brothers remained. They had covered the body with a brown tarp but were now shuffling their feet with their arms folded looking cold and confused. Mohamed glanced over and caught Masud's eye.

"This man needs to be buried. Should we not make preparation?"

Mohamed looked down at the shroud that now covered the body of his friend. It almost looked like they'd already buried him, the mound marking the grave. He couldn't fault their impatience. Getting the body interred quickly was imperative, but they had to wait for the mabaneth. It wasn't like the corpse would bloat in the hot sun.

"No leave him there for now. I have a police investigator coming and he'll want to examine the body. You men can go back to your quarters and get dry. There's no point in standing outside in the rain." The men hesitated, shuffling uncomfortably for a moment, but one by one turned and began walking away. A few stragglers were still returning from the fields having found nothing. Their caps were dripping water and their *galabias*, looking transparent, stuck to their backs. He stepped off the porch to explain that his engineer had been found, and that they were to return to the bunkhouse. No one asked him what happened, as curiosity might compel them to do—*if they didn't already know.*

. . . ☽ . . .

The mabaneth, the official district police investigator, showed up two hours later. Mohamed, having showered and changed into dry clothes, greeted him at the door. He was a short man, maybe five-foot-six, with close cropped hair that resembled whiskers as his head turned in the gray afternoon light. His cream colored suit was frumpy and ill-fitted. And his striped tie, slung around an open collar, hung loose around his neck. He was accompanied by a pair of uniformed soldiers who stood behind him with their automatic weapons slung over their shoulders. The man handed Mohamed a soiled calling card with his name, "Hossame El-Din," and then took it back, placing it in his wallet again. Mohamed glanced over his shoulder at Zainab who was sitting on the couch.

"Excuse me Mother, I have to take care of this," he said. He turned and stepped out the door closing it behind him. The air was moist and smelled of humus. The crops in the field across the road were saturated with water, but the rain had stopped, at least for the most part, and the sun was finding occasion to peek through the clouds. Mohamed stepped off the porch followed by the three men. He stooped over to remove the tarp, but the mabaneth caught his arm.

"Please, this is my investigation now. You must not contaminate the evidence." The officer nodded and the soldiers each took a corner of the tarp pulling it back, letting the water run off the canvas in a stream. The blue tinged face of Amin, with eyes half open, stared up at them. The head was flatter and seemed wider, but that was just rigor mortis setting in. But what caught Mohamed's attention was the smile. Amin was grinning from ear to ear.

The mabaneth began by examining the back of Amin's head. "You say he was hit with a shovel?"

Mohamed nodded. "Yes, my eyewitness told me they hit him, dropped his body into a trench and buried him. I bet if we find that shovel it will still have the blood on it."

The mabaneth reached into the pocket of his cream colored coat and removed a pack of cigarettes. He thumped one out, placing it between his lips. "We'll get to that later. Right now I would question this man. Where is he?" The cigarette bounced up and down as he spoke. He opened a book of matches and struck fire, cupping the flame in his hands.

"I've asked everyone to stay in their quarters," Mohamed said, "Five men participated in this, but only one will talk."

They walked down the muddy path toward the men's housing, followed by the soldiers with their weapons. The sun burst through the clouds painting the side of the building a bright yellow. They stepped inside to find the men seated on their bunks. Heads turned. The whispered conversations of those huddled in small groups hushed as they passed by.

The two soldiers stationed themselves at the door subtly suggesting that no one leave. Followed by the mabaneth, Mohamed wove his way through the legs of the men seated on the floor. He wiped his nose with the back of his hand, the foul smell almost gagging him, worse now, with the room full, than it was before.

They passed row after row of bunks until they reached the far end of the room. Uthman was sitting on the edge of his bunk. He looked up as they approached. The turban on his head looked lopsided, keening to the side, and his beard, hanging from his sallow cheeks, covered the Koran in his lap.

He was surrounded by his four disciples who sat at his feet. Mohamed glanced at their faces. The man he had talked to earlier, his prime witness wasn't among them. He turned looking back, recalling how the man had been lying on a bed at the other end of the room. He couldn't see beyond the wall of bunks and bodies.

He brought his head back around. "These are the men I told you about. They were the last to see Amin alive."

The inspector folded back the lapel of his coat to reveal a badge. "I am Mabaneth Hossame El-Din," he said, the cigarette smoke curling into his eyes causing him to squint. "I am here to investigate the death of your fellow worker, Amin Taymur. You will please answer all my questions." He peered over his stomach at the man seated closest to him. "I'll begin with you. Please come with me." He dropped his cigarette and stepped back to crush it under his heel.

The man glanced at Uthman and then, pushing himself off the ground, followed the mabaneth through the tangle of arms and legs until they were outside.

Mohamed turned and made his way back down the center aisle to find his star witness. The sixty odd men stood and sat around the stacks of bunks, overcrowding the space, but as he approached, his heart began to pound. The bunk where he'd seen the man before—*was empty!*

He got down on his hands and knees looking underneath. *Gone!* It was the same bed. There were traces of vomit on the sheets. He got up and went to inspect the latrine, but came out a second later. Walking back down the center aisle, he leaned in to inspect the face of each man. When he reached the end, he swung around and foraged in the opposite direction, but the man wasn't to be found. It seemed the man had disappeared.

He didn't know the man's name, he didn't know the names of any of the workers, but he knew how to describe him, and the fact that he'd been sick, but each person he asked gave him the same shrug of the shoulders and the same shaking of the head. As far as his workers were concerned, the man didn't exist.

He shuffled his way back to the mabaneth shaking his head. "The other man I told you about seems to be missing."

The investigator nodded and looked at Uthman. "I understand there was one more with you. Where is he?"

Uthman raised his hands palms up, a thin smile playing on his lips. "I don't know what you mean."

Mohamed glared at Uthman. "The man who was absent when I made the announcement this morning, the one they said was sick? I spoke with him earlier." Mohamed swung his shoulders around, pointing toward the other end of the room. "He was resting on the cot down there. He told me he was with you."

Uthman and his four minions shook their heads in unison, feigning ignorance. Mohamed pursed his lips. Either his star witness had fled for his life, or they'd disposed of him. Either way, he was gone.

The investigator addressed Mohamed with a look of impatience. "So, do you have someone else for me to interview, or not?"

"Apparently not."

The man nodded. "Then, I guess we're finished here." He swung around squeezing by Mohamed and waddled down the aisle causing people to step back to avoid his girth. Mohamed followed him outside, the clean smell of the rain-washed air reminding him of how putrid the men's quarters were.

The two soldiers trailed behind, hanging onto their weapons as the four men walked toward the house.

"Well, I guess that about wraps it up," the mabaneth said.

"What do you mean?"

"I mean there's nothing more I can do. You say a man was murdered. That he was hit on the head with a shovel. He may have been, but for all I know he could've fallen and hit his head on a rock. You say those men killed him. They all say they didn't, and there are five of them and one of you. You say you have a witness but you can't produce him. If there's nothing more to go on, then this is not a crime I can solve."

"With all due respect, accident victims don't bury themselves."

Mabaneth Hossame stopped and turned to face Mohamed. "I'm not saying we're giving up, I just need more to go on. I *was* able to get your suspect's fingerprints. I dropped my cigarette lighter and then pretended to sneeze, and while I looked for my handkerchief he picked it up and handed it back to me. Chrome plated, see? Makes a nice print. Doesn't even work, but I keep it for just this purpose. We'll inspect the crime scene for more evidence. If I find his prints on a shovel and also blood," he shrugged, "then maybe we'll have something to build a case on, but without your eyewitness, I don't have enough to make an arrest today, let alone get a conviction." He reached into his pocket for his package of cigarettes, and tapping one out, placed the unfiltered tip into his mouth.

The two soldiers kept walking, slouching under the weight of their rifles as they headed for the front of the house.

The inspector leaned forward, his cupped hands glowing with fire as he leaned in to light his cigarette. He exhaled a stream of smoke, causing Mohamed to take a step back. The intensity of the sun beating down on the puddles was causing steam to rise. Mohamed felt the humidity in his shirt. "So you're just going to let them walk away?"

"Unless you can produce some evidence, I'm afraid that's the way it is." The inspector took another drag on his cigarette. Melon slices soaked through the polyester suit under his arms. He exhaled a blue cloud of smoke into the air.

"At least talk to the victim's wife. These men threatened him. She was afraid for his life."

"Afraid, why?"

Mohamed rubbed his arms, realizing too late that he shouldn't have said anything. If Amin was killed for converting, the mabaneth might conclude Uthman had done the world a favor... but there *was* another explanation. "They felt their jobs were being threatened. I hired the man to install an irrigation system. Some of the workers thought if I automated the farm, they would no longer be needed."

"You should have said this earlier. At least now we have motive. All right then, I'll talk to the wife. But if she can't give me specifics, like names and what was actually said, this is still likely to be written off as an unsolved murder."

They rounded the corner. The body was missing. The two soldiers were standing by a Land Rover smoking cigarettes.

"What happened to Amin?"

"Who? Oh, our victim. The men have put him into the truck. We must take the body to Asyut for an autopsy." Inspector Hossame flicked his cigarette to the ground and crushed it underfoot.

"But what about his burial?"

"You may pick the body up tomorrow. They'll be done with it by noon. Now I'd like you to show me the scene of the crime."

Mohamed nodded and started off in the direction of the road, but the mabaneth caught his arm. "Please, allow me to drive," he said, as he motioned for the two soldiers to follow in the truck.

A wet mound of dirt was piled beside the shallow grave, the trench now a soupy mix of mud and water. Mohamed sighed, expressing his growing sense of apprehension. Whatever evidence might have been left behind, had probably been washed away. A welder's tank stood off to the side looking like it had just been washed, and pipes, saws and fitting tools were randomly strewn on the ground.

The mabaneth went to his car and returned with a camera. He stood on the temporary bridge taking his photos from higher ground as though afraid of stepping down into the mud and getting his shoes dirty, though he did come around to the side of the bridge long enough to take close-ups of the footprints. He looked up at the soldiers. "You men gather all the shovels, and anything else that might have been used as a weapon. And wear gloves. Don't disturb the mud on the handles. There may be prints we can use later."

Mohamed watched as the mabaneth supervised the gathering of evidence. The two soldiers placed the tagged items in the back of the Land Rover next to the body of Amin, and climbed inside to wait. Hossame returned to the car, indicating he was through. Mohamed slid onto the seat beside him. The interior of the car smelled like a cigarette factory, the residue of the ash tray spilling onto the carpet.

The inspector fired up the engine and put the car in reverse. He swiveled his head around, backing up in an arc until they faced the opposite way. Then he eased forward bouncing over potholes and washboards all the way back to the house, with the Rover following close behind.

When they reached the front gate, the mabaneth pulled into the drive, shut the car off, and got out. He called to the men in the SUV, waving his hand. "Take the body to the morgue. Tell them I want the autopsy on my desk by tomorrow noon." He turned back to Mohamed who had climbed out of the car and now stood beside him. "I will interview the wife now."

They went to the side door, entering the kitchen through the service porch. Mohamed ushered the man down the hall to his old room. The door was slightly ajar. He nudged it gently letting it swing open, and took a tentative step inside to look around, but Sabah wasn't there.

"Excuse me," he said as he brushed by the investigator. "She must be with my wife."

Hossame followed him down the hall to the living room. Layla and Zainab were there, but it was obvious something was wrong. Zainab's hands were gripping the arms of her chair, and when Layla looked up, her eyes expressed anxiety.

"Where is Sabah?"

"Layla shook her head. "She's gone."

CHAPTER 16

If any man come to me and hate not his father, and mother, and wife, and children, and brethren, and sisters, yes, and his own life also, he cannot be my disciple. — Luke 14:26

THE BRUSH was wet, soaking into her clothes, the mud squishy under her feet as Sabah plowed through the field. Her sandals felt like they'd gained five pounds. She didn't know how much time had elapsed—*fifteen minutes, a half hour*— she only knew if she kept going, she'd eventually reach the road.

She had a vague sense of being headed in the right direction, but she couldn't be sure. She'd snuck out the window and raced across the driveway into the barn and exited out the other side. If memory served, the rows of cane ran parallel to the property, intersecting the main highway. All she had to do was stay on course.

She pulled her *hijab* around her shoulders to protect her arms. Her skin was prickling with perspiration. The soggy plants were wetting her on the outside, and her own sweat from within.

She didn't think about what she was doing; she just knew she had to get out of that house. She'd asked Layla for a little time alone and, with no one else around, made her escape. She reached out pushing back the stalks of cane, the palms of her hands hurting from the many small cuts she'd received. Beyond the wall of plants, the light was increasing. She broke through into a clearing just as a car zoomed by.

She ran out onto the road waving, but the vehicle faded into the distance leaving her standing alone. If she could get a ride to Asyut, she could catch a bus to Cairo. She only had what little money she and Amin had brought with them, which wasn't much, but surely it would be enough.

She turned around. A blip on the horizon was growing larger by the second, a fuzzy image emerging out of the haze. Another car? It was obvious she'd stumbled upon the main highway. She started waving and then stepped back as the car zoomed by, honking its horn and throwing up dust. Her *hijab* skirted up in the wind. She turned, and collapsed to the ground, tears streaming down her face. *Why won't they stop?*

She felt, more than heard, the rumble of a truck. Looking up, she started to raise her hand, but the truck thundered by. Her hand fell into her lap, her tears washing her dusty cheeks. Her husband was dead, and she was abandoned—*the price of betraying Allah.* She heard the squeal of metal and raised her head. The truck was pulling to the side. She forced herself from the ground and, picking up the hem of her *hijab*, took off running. She came up on the driver's side, out of breath.

The man opened his window, looking down. "Are you all right?"

"Please, I need a ride to Asyut."

"Then I'm afraid I can't help you. Asyut's in the opposite direction. You're going the wrong way."

Sabah glanced down the road, her face flushed as she grasped her mistake. She could feel the heat in her cheeks. She looked at the man, her eyes pleading. "You don't understand. I need to get to Cairo. I have to get home."

"Cairo? Why did not you say this? Please, climb in. I am going there myself."

Sabah patted the metal door with the flat of her hand receiving a sharp reminder of the cuts in her palm, but her lips broke into a smile. "*Shokran*, thank you, thank you so much, just a minute." She raised her finger as she ran around the front of the wheezing diesel and climbed up into the cab on the other side.

"So why are you here all alone?"

Sabah didn't respond and the man didn't press. He released the brake and the truck lurched forward. The rumbling of the wheels massaged Sabah's back helping reduce her tension. She wondered what would become of her husband's body, and how Layla would react to her unannounced departure. Maybe she should have stayed, but she couldn't. Right now, more than anything else, she needed the support of her family.

The driver seemed content to ride in silence, and for that, Sabah was grateful. She didn't feel like talking. She stared down at her feet. Her sandals were leaving clods of mud on the man's rubber mats. She wiped her cheeks on her sleeve and rested her head against the window, feeling the bumps in the road vibrating her skull. The side mirror was cracked. She looked at the double image—two of everything. Her eyes grew heavy. She'd been awake the entire night. She was thinking about Amin and his smile, one she would never see again. Perhaps it was all a dream—a bad *dreaammm*—she thought, as the vibration lulled her off to sleep.

She woke with a start. The truck was pulling off the highway, its brakes squealing as it slowed to a stop at the light. Out the window she recognized the familiar sights of the city.

"Ah, the sleeper awakes." The driver glanced over and winked at Sabah. "You must have been tired. You slept all the way. I'm heading downtown, but I can let you out where you please. Is there somewhere you are going?"

Sabah blinked a few times and yawned, straightening herself. Her eyes were scratchy, and they burned. She focused on the road to avoid looking at the man. "Do you know the Khan el-Khalili market?"

"Of course, this is where I'm going."

"Then that is where you can drop me. *Shokran*. You are most kind."

The truck rumbled through the downtown core using its size and weight to intimidate smaller vehicles, forcing them out of the way. Horns on every side blared nonstop, but it was nothing Sabah wasn't used to. It was part of the culture of Cairo; it felt like they were welcoming her home. They trundled past buildings on both sides, many in a state of gross disrepair, pockmarked, and peeling multiple layers of paint. But there were also modern buildings with glass facades and newly painted signs.

The brakes squealed every time they came to a stop. Finally the driver pulled to the side. "I'll let you out here. Otherwise you'll have to wait until they let me unload."

Sabah glanced over at the man, hoping he wouldn't notice the red in her eyes. "Thank you so much. May the blessings of Allah be upon you."

She climbed out and slammed the door, stepping back as the truck jerked forward.

The shadows were long and the day nearly spent. Vendors were pulling drapes down to cover their stalls. Pedestrian traffic was light. Sabah turned around, instantly distraught. On this very corner she had clung to Amin's arm, begging him not to go, but he'd insisted and...and now he was dead!

She brought her *hijab* up to cover her face and hurried through the market. Her father would be furious, and rightly so. They had left without a word, and now she was returning without her husband. How could she explain such behavior?

The street on which she lived was adjacent to the souk. She stepped onto the walkway. The high-rise buildings blocked the last remaining rays of sun, leaving the street in shadows. Heads turned as she passed. Her neighbors would know of her disappearance. She kept her face toward the wall to avoid being recognized.

She only had to travel a block before coming to the alley that bordered the brick high-rise she called home. She stopped, gazing down the long shadowy tunnel. That was where it all began, but there was no vision now, no ghost, only rotting fruit and scattered trash. She turned and entered the building, tramping up the stairs to the third floor, and then slowed as she walked down the corridor to her parent's apartment. The loose flooring beneath the threadbare carpet creaked, announcing she was home. She stopped and wiped the tears from her cheeks, swallowing hard, her heart pounding as she reached for the door.

Her mother stood in the center of the room holding a broom. She looked up and froze. Her father sat in a large overstuffed chair his eyes glued to a blaring TV. He glanced over only for a second and then returned to the program he was watching. "Move, woman, you're in the way!" Sabah's mother dropped her broom, letting it hit the floor with a *thwack*, as she rushed over to her daughter. "Sabah, you're home, you're home! I was so worried. What happened to you?" She looked beyond Sabah's shoulder at the door. "Where is Amin?"

Sabah told herself she wouldn't, she tried to hold it in, but tears gushed from her eyes washing around her cheeks.

"My child, why do you cry? Here, let me…"

"Are you two going to stand there blubbering?" Her father pulled himself from his chair and went to the set, clicking it off. "Can a man not have peace in his own house?" He turned to his daughter. "Where have you been?"

Sabah continued sobbing, her eyes puddles of water. She opened her mouth, a string of saliva caught between her teeth, but no words came out. Her lips quivered.

"Answer my question!"

Sabah's brother strolled in eating a slice of melon.

"Answer me," her father demanded.

"Amin is dead," Sabah blurted out.

"Dead? What do you mean?"

Sabah sniffed. She wiped her nose on her hand, and used her fingertips to rub her cheeks. "I don't know…I" *Sniff.* Her throat was constricted causing the air in her lungs to flutter. Her voice broke as she choked on her tears. "He…he said he received some kind of vision from…from the Christian God. He wanted to find out what it meant, and…" she swallowed, warm tears rolling down her cheeks again "…and now he's…dead!"

"Your husband is a Christian?"

Sabah nodded, hot tears washing down her cheeks. "Yes…he…"

"And you say he'd dead?"

Sabah nodded weakly. "Others found out and…" She blinked several times trying to stem the flow with the palms of her hands… "and they killed him."

Her father raised his hands with his palms up. "Al hamdullah. Thanks be to God."

"No Father. How can you say that? My husband is dead."

The tension in her father's face relaxed. "I'm more concerned about you, my daughter, that you were not also persuaded. Tell me it is so."

Sabah sucked in her breath, her body trembling, but she didn't answer. Her eyes darted away.

"Sister! Tell us you have not converted." Sabah's brother broke in, speaking for the first time. "You will not shame this family. If you have converted I will strangle you myself."

Sabah's father glared at his son, his eyes once again filled with rage. "Quiet boy! I will handle this." He turned back to his daughter. "Tell me now, Sabah, once and for all, have you, or have you not, converted to Christianity?"

Sabah shook her head, her eyes darting about the room, looking for an escape. "I don't know. I don't think so. I had a visitation, and…and there was something I said, but…but I don't know."

"Her father raised his hand as if to strike her but when she flinched, he held back. Instead, he pointed to her bedroom. "Go to your room. *Now!* And don't come out until you can lift your head proudly and say the *Shahadah*. 'There is no God but Allah and Mohamed is his messenger.' I will not have a daughter that believes otherwise."

CHAPTER 17

...then shall be brought to pass the saying that is written, death is swallowed up in victory. O death, where is thy sting? O grave, where is thy victory? — 1 Corinthians 15:54-55

MOHAMED HELD the door and took his mother's hand, helping her into the car. She'd insisted on attending Amin's funeral, even though she rarely went out in public and never attended church.

The sun beat down on the overhead canopy making the car's interior incredibly hot. Zainab grimaced, trying to get comfortable on the warm leather. Mohamed realized he should have started the car and cranked up the air conditioner before bringing the ladies out. Layla climbed in back, yielding the preferential front seat to her mother-in-law.

Mohamed walked around to the driver's side. He was wearing the black Armani. In spite of the ribbing he'd taken the other night, he felt it was appropriate for the occasion. He slipped in behind the wheel, starting the engine, and sat for a moment with his finger in his collar trying to relieve the pressure.

The Christian brothers had gone on ahead. They had asked to attend the funeral—the attack on Amin had been an attack on them all—and while Mohamed couldn't deny them, everyone agreed it was best if they left before the other workers began their morning trek to the mosque.

The crew had risen an hour before dawn and quietly rolled one of the trucks out of the barn and pushed it half a mile down the driveway to the road before starting the engine. The fewer people who heard them leave, the fewer questions would be asked. They would drive into Asyut and wait for the body of Amin to be released and then meet Mohamed and his wife and mother in Minya where a Christian pastor had agreed to conduct the funeral. None of the men said it aloud, but Mohamed sensed they were excited about attending a service in a *Christian* church.

He hadn't been able to contact Sabah. She should want to attend her husband's funeral. But getting the body into the ground before it began to putrefy was imperative. Sabah would know this. If she'd wanted to be there, she shouldn't have run off. He had no way of reaching her.

There was no one else to notify. Amin mentioned that he had no family. His body would be placed in a community tomb, just as the police would have done if the body wasn't claimed.

They pulled off the highway and headed into the thick traffic of Minya. A boy dodged in and out of the cars as he tried to get a kite launched into the air, ignoring the incessant honking. Merchants hawked their wares from baskets and wooden crates. The heat rose from the street in waves.

The church wasn't much on the outside, just a square cinderblock building painted white. A wood sign with writing in both Arabic and English spoke of church affiliation.

Mohamed led his wife and mother inside. Masud, and the other Christian brothers were already seated at the front, which only told Mohamed the coroner hadn't wasted a lot of time on the autopsy. He thought he'd have to wait for Amin's body to arrive. The men craned their necks around. No one spoke or smiled in keeping with the somber mood. Two large overhead fans churned, but the room still felt muggy. The men were fanning their faces with the paper hymnals they'd found on their chairs. Layla and Zainab waited while Mohamed made his way to the pastor's office.

The wood crate containing Amin's body was a harsh reminder of the high price of conversion, a place Zainab did not want to revisit.

Layla reached out and took her mother-in-law's hand, leading her down the aisle to the front. They slipped into the second row and sat down, the metal legs of their chairs screeching on the linoleum. The simple wood box containing the earthly remains of Amin rested on the raised dais in front of the pulpit. Layla leaned in close to her mother-in-law and whispered, "It's okay, Mother, men and women sit together in Christian services."

Zainab nodded. She sipped in a breath, shivering in spite of the heat.

Her son appeared followed by a man carrying a large black Bible. It had been more than a dozen years since she'd seen that face, but there was no mistaking it. She'd been fleeing from Sayyid, and he'd offered her a place to rest for the night.

He was dressed in contemporary clothes, a white short sleeve shirt with an open collar and black slacks with black leather shoes. Having never been in a Christian church, she wasn't sure what to expect, but it seemed odd that he wasn't wearing some kind of vestment or clerical robe. He stood at the pulpit and waited for Mohamed to take a seat beside Layla.

The minister looked at the small assembly, his eyes filled with sadness. "Since I don't really know most of you, allow me to introduce myself. I am Peter. I was born into a Christian family, which makes this service especially hard to officiate. Ostaz Mulberry," he nodded at Mohamed, "informs me that most of you are from Muslim families. I cannot begin to tell you how humbled I am by your presence. The Church in Egypt is persecuted. Daily we face physical threats and intimidation, but the pressure on those of us who have been brought up in the faith, pales in comparison to the difficulties each of you must face."

The pastor looked out over the small gathering. "It is the travesty of our times that we as brothers in Christ are forbidden from fellowshipping together. I want you to know it is my fervent prayer that this will one day change.

"What has happened to our brother is a painful reminder of the world we live in. Amin, a fellow believer in Christ, was robbed of his life. In the gospel of Matthew, Jesus said, 'Blessed are ye, when men shall revile you, and persecute you, and shall say all manner of evil against you falsely, for my sake. Rejoice, and be exceeding glad: for great is your reward in heaven.' And in the gospel of John, Jesus tells us, '…the time cometh that whosoever kills you will think he is doing God a service. And these things will they do unto you, because they have not known the Father, nor me.'

"The good news is our brother, Amin, knew Jesus. He may not be here among us, but he is with Jesus enjoying the reward promised to him in scripture. The Bible says, 'what does it profit a man if he gains the whole world, but loses his own soul.' Amin released his claim on the things of this earth, but he has gained an eternal reward.

"We can take encouragement from the Apostle Paul who at the end of his life said, 'I have fought a good fight, I have finished the race, I have kept the faith.' Paul realized there was something greater beyond this life, and it gave him courage to face death. He, like Amin, was executed by those who did not believe, but he knew something better was waiting for him in heaven. That was where he truly wanted to be.

"Paul's example, as well as our own, was Jesus. Christ gave His life as a ransom for many. He was a model of how we, through the power of forgiveness, can endure suffering and death. He said, 'Father, forgive them for they know not what they do.' Even so, we must now forgive those who did this to Amin.

"Jesus said, 'I am the resurrection, and the life: he that believeth in me, though he were dead, yet shall he live. And whosoever lives and believes in me shall never die.'

"With this assurance we know we will one day see Amin again. Christ our Lord died that we might live. Every sin committed by

Amin, or for that matter by you and I, is nailed to the cross of Jesus. Our part is to believe in the name of the only begotten Son of God and ask His forgiveness.

"I know this was true for Amin. I trust it is also true for you. Let us pray: Father, we are thankful for the life of Amin. Remind us Lord, that while we may think of him as dead, in your kingdom he is alive evermore. And, should you require it of us, help us to follow his example and be bold in our faith even to the point of death..."

The service was concluded with a hymn sung by the pastor. He chose *My Jesus I love thee*, and sang all four verses in Arabic, his baritone voice resonating throughout the room. His tiny congregation sat with tears in their eyes. The last refrain especially struck home...

> In mansions of glory and endless delight
> I'll ever adore Thee in heaven so bright
> I'll sing with the glittering crown on my brow
> If ever I loved Thee, my Jesus, 'tis now.

Only Layla joined in the chorus. Like Zainab, the men were unchurched. This was the first Christian service they'd ever attended. They'd never heard a hymn before, and while they held pamphlets that contained the words, they didn't know what they were and had used them instead as fans to cool themselves.

The assembly rose to their feet. Mohamed helped the others carry the unadorned casket outside. They placed the coffin in the bed of the truck for the drive to its final destination, but no one seemed anxious to climb aboard. The men stood around idle, reluctant to say goodbye. Masud caught Mohamed's eye.

"I want to be baptized," he said.

"Me too," one of the others chimed in.

"I do too," said a third.

"And me," said the fourth, raising his hand.

Mohamed looked at Nour, who nodded his assent.

"We don't know when God will call us home," Masud said. "Amin spoke to us about this. We all agreed that he would ask you, but…"

"What are you saying?"

"We have discussed it among ourselves. We don't want to put it off any longer. We want you to baptize us."

"Me?"

"Yes. We all agree. We want you to baptize us in the river, tonight…"

Chapter 18

For whosoever shall do the will of God, the same is my brother, and my sister, and mother. — Mark 3:35

SABAH SAT on her bed with her back to the wall, her knees up and her arms wrapped around her legs. She hadn't slept. The honking horns and sirens intruded into her thoughts all night, and just about dawn, when she thought she might be nodding off, the call of the *azan* came. Such things had never bothered her before, but now the room was driving her insane.

The only escape for her thoughts was the window. She'd been to it several times staring at the wall across the alley, thinking to throw herself out. She had nothing to live for—her husband was dead, and she a prisoner in her own home.

She dropped a hand to the bed, kneading the blanket with her fingers. On this very bed she and Amin had consummated their marriage. This was where they planned to start their family. She needed to be with him, even if it meant going to hell.

With a, *click*, the lock turned and the door swung open. Her mother entered carrying a dish of boiled beans mashed together with onions and tomatoes with an egg on top. She was a short woman, a characteristic accented by the fact that she was also slightly stooped. She wore a single piece *hijab* with the head scarf removed. She held the plate out to her daughter. "I wish you'd give up this foolishness and come join us at the table."

Sabah raised her head slightly, her eyes liquid and red. "Take it away, Mother, I don't want it!"

Her mother laid the dish on the floor and sat down beside her. "Sabah, you must stop behaving this way. Your father is a good man, but he cannot allow you to blaspheme. You are his only daughter. He's doing this for your own good, keeping you from hell, and if it means keeping you locked up in here until you come to your senses, that's how it must be."

"Father doesn't care about me. He's only worried about what his friends will think."

"Sabah!"

"It's true. You saw how he took the news about Amin. He doesn't care that he's dead, only that I don't embarrass him."

"I think you're being unfair. He's concerned for you. It's dangerous to renounce Allah."

Sabah looked at her mother, her eyes pooling again. Strings of saliva broke from her lips as she spoke. "I have not renounced Allah. You did not hear that come from me."

"But you said…"

"I said I didn't know. My husband saw a vision of someone he thought was Isa Christ and it changed him. I didn't know what to think, so I prayed to Jesus too, and I felt His presence. Don't you understand, Mother? It was so real."

Her mother reached out to take Sabah's hand, her soft brown eyes expressing compassion. "But why did you run away? If you had stayed we could have worked this out. I'm sure El Sheikh could have explained what Amin saw."

Sabah pulled her hand back, pressing her palms against her cheeks wiping them dry. "I tried, I did, but Amin wouldn't listen. He was too excited about what was happening. And now my husband is dead, and I come home to receive comfort from my family, and my own father locks me in my room."

"Sabah! You must not criticize your father!"

"Not if you want to live."

Sabah looked up to see her brother, Ahmed, and their overweight cousin, Ubaid, standing at the door. Ahmed, like his mother, was short, shorter even than Sabah, though he was a year older. "These people have poisoned your mind, Sabah. Father has sent me to get you. You will take us to where you were being held and we will deal with the matter."

"No, my brother, I cannot."

"Cannot? Or, will not?"

"Cannot. I had never been to this place before. Amin saw it in his head. And when I left, I hid myself in a field of cane and made my way to the highway. I flagged down the first truck I saw and he gave me a ride all the way home. I have no idea where I was when he picked me up."

Ahmed puckered his lips, his short mustache and beard bristling. He shook his head. "This does not matter. We will find it, even if we have to drive around until you see something familiar."

"But it will take hours."

"This may be your only chance to redeem yourself, Sabah. I suggest you take it. Father's waiting in the car. Grab your scarf and cover your head. We're going."

Reception was always poor in the desert, but who needed a radio? From the back seat Layla's voice could be heard, blessing the car with her songs. Most often she sang hymns of worship and praise, because her heart was filled with a love for God that needed to be expressed, but today her songs were subdued. Mohamed glanced at her. She smiled, but it was a sad smile, her eyes tinged with moisture as she continued to sing.

The song she chose was perfect. Mohamed couldn't help but compare the death of Amin to that of his brother. If it wasn't for him, they'd both be alive—a debt he owed but could not pay.

"He paid a debt He did not owe
I owed a debt I could not pay
I needed someone to wash my sins away

And now I sing a brand new song
Amazing grace all day long
Christ Jesus paid a debt that I could never pay…"

He was still under that burden, but Christ had lifted the weight. He looked over at his mother. She was joining in, softly humming. He couldn't sing or hum, and the reason, he was sure, stemmed from his childhood, a time just before his mother disappeared…

They'd only been on the farm a week and he couldn't believe what he was seeing: the barns, with chickens that provided eggs and poultry to eat, and goats with milk, orchards filled with date palms burgeoning with fruit, and acres of beans, cotton and sugar. The only thing missing was someone to share it with.

He walked the length of the hall, slowly, his finger tracing a line on the plaster. His mother's voice came from the bedroom. She was singing. Mohamed smiled. He hadn't heard her sing since they'd arrived. She hadn't even come out of her room. But now, if she was happy again, perhaps she would be open to his idea.

Before they were found by his uncle, his mother had taken him to Minya. It was where Layla and her family were supposed to be. He wanted to see her again. Maybe his uncle would help him find her. Maybe he'd let them spend time together on the farm. Exploring the property would be more fun if he had someone to share it with.

He was almost to his mother's room when his uncle stormed out of his office and powered by, huffing and wheezing, his two-hundred and fifty pound body pressing Mohamed against the wall. He used a key to unlock the door. Mohamed had been warned not to disturb his mother, but he didn't know her door was locked. He crept up, placing his ear to the wood.

"What have I told you about singing?"

"But...it makes me..."

Whack!

His mother yelped.

"Do not test me, Woman! Already, your life hangs by a thread. There will be no singing in this house! Do you now understand?"

Then there was silence. Mohamed took a step back. The door flew open. His uncle looked down on him with eyes raging.

"What are you looking at? If you have nothing to do, go study. Frivolous behavior will not be tolerated. Now go!" His uncle slammed the door and huffed off down the hall.

They were speeding toward Asyut with Ahmed at the wheel, his foot on the accelerator making up for lost time. Sabah's father sat up front beside her brother, leaving Sabah squished into the tiny back seat against the heavy bulk of her cousin, Ubaid, who was sweating like a pig.

It was her brother's car, a small oxidized Fiat that had seen better days. With the bumpers rattling and the engine whining, Sabah had to wonder if finding the farm was worth the destruction of their only family vehicle. She rested her head against the window, the glare making her close her eyes. The late afternoon sun was hovering over the Nile. They hadn't even reached the city yet.

They passed several farms, but they all looked the same, rows of green and brown, a patchwork of agriculture. An old man furrowed the ground with a tiller pulled by a water buffalo. They came up behind another car. Ahmed leaned on his horn and pulled to the left to go around. Sabah's hand went up to the window as her head spun around, an action noticed by her brother in the rear-view mirror.

Matthew, Layla and Haja Zainab were in that car.

Ahmed raced by oblivious to who he was passing. His eyes were focused on Sabah.

"What did you see, my sister?"

"Uh, nothing, I mean that car looked like one owned by a friend of mine."

"You have a friend who owns a Mercedes? Since when?"

"Amin introduced us. It's a girl he knew at college. Her father is rich, but it wasn't her." She sat back sulking into the seat.

... 🌙 ...

Uthman released his donkey into the corral with a pat on the animal's rump. He tossed the bridle and reins into his cart and backed the unit into the barn. Grabbing a pitchfork he trudged over to a bail of straw.

The workers were drifting in, tired and sweaty. Most went straight to the bunkhouse, ready to plop on their beds and rest until the evening meal, but Uthman's cohorts knew where to find him. They made their way to the barn, gathering around their leader.

"Do you not see? He treats us as criminals. If he suspects we did this, he should reward us, not have us questioned by the police."

Uthman nodded, his turban burgeoning like a dirty mushroom. "You need not worry. We are not under suspicion. The policeman left without arresting anyone. If he thought one of us committed a crime, we would right now be in jail."

"He probably knows. I think if we confessed, the mabaneth would say we only carried out the will of Allah. He would pat us on the back and let us go. No, it is our employer that worries me. He seems to regard this Christian as special."

"Yes, this concerns me also. We must stick together. No one should talk to him without letting me know, but take heart, the Christian cannot bother us any longer, and this foolish project will now come to an end."

CHAPTER 19

And there went out unto him all the land of Judaea, and they of Jerusalem, and were all baptized of him in the river of Jordan, confessing their sins. — Mark 1:5

THE MOON, large and white as an ostrich egg, shone brightly on the water illuminating the way for the five men and two women traipsing single file down the banks of the river. Their nightshirts hung down to their knees as they sloshed through the shallows, their bare feet leaving prints in the pasty mud.

The men had waited until after midnight before slipping out of their quarters one at time, to meet up with Mohamed, Layla and Zainab at the edge of a field of cane. All but Nour, who stayed behind, complaining about not feeling well. No one spoke a word. As soon as everyone was assembled, they slipped quietly down the road, heading for the river. The air was warm, the breeze, light. Frogs, with their deep throated warble, were singing up and down the shore.

Mohamed waited until he found a place where the river's bend backed the water into an oxbow, creating a large shallow pool.

Layla came up behind. "You want me to check the depth?"

"No, I can do it." Mohamed took a tentative step forward, then another, and kept moving. Images crossed his mind like frames of a motion picture. *He was standing in the shallows of the Nile with a line of men and women waiting to be washed, but they seemed nervous, like they were afraid.* He looked around, back in the present. He'd seen that vision, or whatever it was, more than a year ago, the very same night he'd seen Christ coming in the clouds on a white horse.

He stopped when the water reached his waist. "This is good," he said, turning with his arms out, trying to keep his balance. "Send the men in one at a time."

Layla took Masud's hand and ushered him out into the water.

One by one the men were asked if they believed Jesus to be the Son of God, and if they had asked His forgiveness and were ready to confess Him as Lord. And one by one, upon their profession of faith, Mohamed immersed them in the name of the Father, the Son, and the Holy Spirit.

The four men stood dripping at the river's edge, the water lapping their feet. The moon shone down on their shoulders and a warm breeze feathered their skin. Layla began quietly singing the chorus the pastor crooned at Amin's funeral.

> My Jesus, I love Thee, I know Thou art mine
> For Thee all the follies of sin I resign
> My gracious Redeemer, my Savior art Thou
> If ever I loved Thee, my Jesus, 'tis now

Masud joined in, trying but missing most of the words. They hadn't got through the first refrain before all the men were singing, or at least struggling to remember how the song went. All but Mohamed, who waited patiently until they were through. Tears rolled from their cheeks, reflecting the light of the moon.

> I love Thee because Thou hast first loved me
> And purchased my pardon on Calvary's tree
> I love Thee for wearing the thorns on Thy brow
> If ever I loved Thee, my Jesus, 'tis now

The last into the water was Zainab. Mohamed could hardly contain his emotion as he took his mother's hand. His throat felt pinched, making it difficult to speak. "Mother, do you believe?" and when he was through he hugged Zainab so hard she had to pull away to keep from being hurt.

The men on the shore clapped spontaneously. They began splashing about the water, gleeful as children. Mohamed tried in vain to shush them but their exuberance couldn't be contained. As he waded back to the shore he reminded them that sound carries in the stillness of night, and that the house was only half a mile away, but Layla called him a curmudgeon and scooped up a handful of water, throwing it at him. Giggling, she turned and ran which made him chase after her splashing through the shallows until he tackled her and brought her down, baptizing the only one who wasn't already wet.

They rolled over, laughing, water dripping from their chins. It felt good to be free, if only for that brief moment, to express the joy of the Lord. Mohamed got up and offered Layla his hand, helping her to her feet. She combed her wet hair from her face and wrapped her arms around his neck, the moonlight aglow in her dark eyes.

She smiled. "Do you remember the last time we stood in the water soaking wet on a night like this?"

"Un huh. We were just kids. You wanted to play hide and seek, but my father came looking for me and we had to duck into the reeds to avoid being caught."

Layla looked into his eyes, her face shining in the light of the moon. "You have a good memory. Your father came just when I thought you were about to kiss..."

But Mohamed was already moving in, and their lips met before she could finish.

Mohamed was up at dawn, standing by the open window. He could smell the sweet cane wet with dew, and hear the birds twittering in the palms. The sun shone through the mist like a fuzzy tennis ball. He fastened his belt and tucked the tail of his shirt in, then turned and leaned over to kiss his wife, but she didn't stir. The night hadn't ended until the small troop made their way back to the house and shared in the bread and wine of communion. He'd had less than three hours sleep. He wanted to crawl back into bed and wrap Layla in his arms, but he had to meet with his workers before they left for the fields.

He stood at the side of the road waiting for Uthman. The sun burning through the moist haze made the humidity cling to his skin. He reached up, rubbing his arm. The fronds of the palm trees behind him rustled in the breeze.

He heard the clomping of hoofs long before he saw Uthman's shadow break through the fog. Uthman pulled up short, looking peeved at being stopped again.

Mohamed sucked in a breath, trying to remain calm. He wanted to wring the man's neck, but that wasn't the way of Christ. He ground his teeth clenching his jaw tight, determined not to let his emotions show.

"Morning, Uthman."

"*Sabah el kheer,* Ostaz Matthew" Uthman repeated, though there was no smile in his voice.

"I want you to assemble the men." He turned toward the house. "Have everyone meet right where we did before. I need to address them again."

"But you…the men have work to do. We lost a whole day searching for your engineer in the rain. And yesterday was slow because you left me shorthanded, and many of the men were heavy of heart."

Mohamed spun around. "Just do as I ask, Uthman, please."

Uthman muttered under his breath but snapped the reins and turned his donkey cart, heading back up the road to catch the others as they drifted in from the mosque.

Mohamed sat at the dining room table, bowing his head to whisper a silent, "Thank you," then dipped a slice of baklava into his cup of black coffee.

Neither Layla or his mother had shown themselves, but they needed their rest. He could hear voices outside as the men tramped about. He looked at his watch. Breakfast would have to wait. He got up and went to the door. The sun was burning off the morning mist leaving a hot sticky day in its wake.

It appeared most, if not all, of the men were there. His eyes scanned the assembly searching for his witness, but the man was still missing. He let the screen door slam as he stepped onto the porch. A hush fell over the group but he waited until he had everyone's attention before starting.

"You men know we've had a hard week," he said, his eyes roaming the crowd, "but I trust we're ready to put it behind us and move on. My main concern is for everyone's safety. Until the mabaneth can put the man who killed my engineer behind bars, a murderer walks among us, and no one is safe. I want to ask each of you to keep your eyes and ears open. If you hear threats being made against anyone, I want to know about it. Violence on this farm will not be tolerated.

"Now I want to make something clear. This irrigation project is important, and it will move forward." Mohamed glanced at Uthman. The men surrounding him murmured among themselves but stopped at the pause in Mohamed's speech. They looked up, nervously shuffling their feet. "Any further interruption of this project will be dealt with in the severest possible manner. Have I made myself clear?"

No one moved. A breeze rustled the fronds of the palm trees on the other side of the road.

"Good! Are there any questions?" He held his breath, his heart pounding... "All right then, let's get back to work."

From the bench of his donkey cart, Uthman raised his whip. "Who do you suggest is going to do this? I need every hand cutting cane, and your engineer is…"

"Yes, I know, he's dead. I will have to find someone to replace him, but until I do, Masud will be in charge. All the men laying pipe will remain on the job. If you have anyone to blame for a slowdown of the work, it's the man who murdered Amin. Find that man and I'll see he is handed over to the authorities and immediately replaced. But in the meantime, I expect the harvest to be gathered on time. Masud, and those assigned to the irrigation project, I want you to stay behind a minute. The rest of you are dismissed."

The workers began to disperse. Uthman glared at Mohamed, his lips drawn tight, but he turned his donkey and whipped its hind-quarters, causing the animal to bolt. The cart wheels creaked as the donkey trotted off down the road in the direction of the fields, the haze still shrouding the cane in a gray mist.

Masud and four others stayed behind. Mohamed stepped down off the porch waiting to make sure they were alone, but Masud spoke first. "Haj Matthew, I cannot possibly do as you ask. I know nothing of water systems and pumps."

"You don't have to. I plan to hire another engineer, and hope-fully a Christian by birth. I'd like to find someone who can help disciple you in the evening, as well as manage the project by day. But until I do, it's important we keep everything moving forward. I need an excuse to keep you out of the main population."

"But what do we do until then?"

"I thought about that. Wait here, I'll be right back." Mohamed turned and bounded up the porch steps disappearing into the house, the screen door banging closed behind him. He returned a minute later with a sheath of papers in his hand. "These are the drawings made by Amin. They show diagrams of where the pipe is to be laid." He tightened his grip, holding on as the papers furled in the breeze. "You worked with him. You know how to keep the pipe angled to increase water flow, and you already know where the stringers cross the road. Just keep laying pipe in all the locations illustrated in the diagram. If you finish with that, and providing the harvest is in, we'll begin running the pipe into the fields. We really only need an engineer to tell us how to get the pumps connected and hopefully, I'll have found someone before we get that far."

Masud nodded, but the others remained subdued, processing the information. "What? You don't think we can do it."

Mohamed waited but no one spoke. "Are you afraid, because if you are, I understand. I have the same fear. Whoever killed Amin now knows they didn't achieve their goal. If they really want this project to stop, they'll have to kill me. But if any of you want to back out, please say so now. I'll make sure you get reassigned to work in the fields."

No one moved. Only last night these men were bravely celebrating Jesus. They were so boisterous he'd had to quiet them down, but now they seemed timid. "We'll just have to pray and trust God will protect us. I know it sounds strange, but I don't think God abandoned Amin and let him die for no reason. I believe God has a greater purpose in mind."

Mohamed looked at each man, trying to ascertain their thoughts, but they looked away, desirous of avoiding confrontation. The last man didn't. He held Mohamed's gaze. Mohamed saw his Adam's apple sliding in his throat as he swallowed.

"We are afraid, Haj Matthew," he said. "but if we are going to die let it be for Jesus, not for an irrigation system. If you will permit, I have talked with the others and we all feel the same. We want to stop hiding our faith. We want to witness of all we have seen. We will be happy to continue the work, but if our lives are to be put in danger, let it be for what we believe. And if we must die, let us die as Amin, proclaiming the gospel. May God grant us His favor and protection."

CHAPTER 20

Blessed are you when men shall revile you, and persecute you, and say all manner of evil against you falsely, for my sake. — Matthew 5:11

UTHMAN SAT on his cart enjoying the consternation on the faces of the irrigation crew. He smiled as Masud placed his hands on his hips, shaking his head. The trench they'd dug had been completely filled in. They would have to start over, only now they would be digging mud, and it was heavier. And the police had taken their shovels for evidence, so they couldn't even start.

Uthman climbed down and stood with his followers sideling up alongside. The donkey brayed and backed up wanting to leave but Uthman held the reins, stroking the animal's flank. His eyes narrowed. "You men are fools to continue with this. Do you not know Ostaz Mulberry only plans to use this watering system to get rid of many who work here? Do not be fooled. Do you think there will be more work for you to do when you finish this project? You are only hurting yourselves and your brothers."

Masud stooped over and scooped up a handful of moist dirt, squishing it through his fingers. When the body of Amin was retrieved, only the dirt that covered the corpse, along with the section directly under the bridge, had been filled in. Now the rest of the channel, everywhere the pipe had not yet been laid, was full, a segment that extended nearly all the way down to the river.

He straightened himself, glaring at Uthman. "Are you responsible for this? Did you not hear what Haj Matthew said about interfering with our work?"

Uthman brought a hand to his chest, his eyes widening in feint surprise. "Me, interfere? *No, no, no.* We have done nothing to inhibit your work. I only wish to let you know that what you are doing will take food out of the mouths of your brothers."

"If you didn't fill this hole in, who did?"

"And how would I know that?"

"Because you're the foreman. You should know what your men are doing at all times. You heard Haj Matthew. This work must not stop. I ask you again, do you know who did this?"

Uthman's eyes narrowed, the smile gone from his face. "You question me? I was born on this farm. My father's, father, labored in these fields building that which you now wish to destroy. Where were you when I worked behind my father with blisters and cuts on my hands gathering cotton bolls? Where were you yesterday? If you had been here, you might have caught whoever did this. But you and your rabble were taking the day off, while my men and I were hard at work. None of my men would have had time for anything else. I suggest you ask the police investigator and his soldiers. They were the last ones here. They probably filled in the trench as a public service. Someone might have fallen in and got hurt. But you have not answered my question. Why do you persist in taking food from your brother's mouths?"

One of the men standing behind Masud spoke up. "We are not your brothers. We are brothers of Amin. We too, have seen Jesus."

Nour leapt forward, his hands raised in front of him. "No, my brothers, don't!"

"*Bahhh.*" Uthman raised his whip. "You blaspheme Allah."

Another stepped around Nour, shaking his head. "We have not blasphemed Allah. We give Him glory through Christ our Lord."

"*Auugggghhhh!*" Uthman reached down, picked up a stone and threw it at the man, missing by a wide margin. One of his minions followed suit picking up a rock which he launched at Nour. The first stone was followed by a second, and suddenly it was raining rocks as Uthman's men joined in the stoning.

Masud's group raised their arms to defend themselves, fending off blows with hands, shoulders and elbows, but though they could have easily done so, no one reached for a stone to throw back. Masud took a hit to the shin, *awwwwah*, He reached down to grab his leg but as he did a second rock slammed into his head. There was a sound, like that of an egg cracking, as he fell first to his knees, and then toppled face forward into the mud.

A wagon filled with cane stopped at the bridge, the ox driver pulling back to observe the commotion. Several others, late in getting out to the fields, approached from the other side.

Uthman froze, looking around, realizing he was being watched. One of his lackeys, with a stone still in his hand, took a few steps back and ducked into the cane out of sight. The rest glanced at each other, dropped their rocks and fled after him. Uthman saw he was alone. He scrambled aboard his cart and seized the reins giving them a flick. "*Heyyyyya,*" he screamed. The donkey broke as it felt the sting of Uthman's whip. The cart whirled away with Uthman screaming "*heyyyyya, heyyyyya,*" the whip cracking in the air, his long beard trailing behind. He hit a bump so hard it dislodged his turban and sent it spiraling to the ground.

"This was not a good idea," Nour said, as the men dropped to their knees to help Masud. They rolled him over. One of them placed an ear against his chest to see if he was breathing.

Sabah looked up as her father entered the room. It was the morning of her third day of confinement. She wasn't in the mood to be nice.

He sat on the bed beside her, his breath smelling of sour milk. "Sabah, it hurts me that I must keep you in here. Will you not renounce this heresy? You're breaking your mother's heart." He began scratching his short white beard.

Sabah pushed back, distancing herself. She brought her knees up, wrapping them with her arms, picking at a toenail. "I have nothing to renounce, Father. I have done nothing wrong, unless it is wrong to receive a visitation from God."

He father stood, whirling about. "Allah does not visit men!"

"What about Muhammad? He received a..."

"Do you seek to provoke me?"

Sabah looked up. "No, but someone spoke to me, and I think it was God."

"Lies! Who is filling your head with such? Tell me!"

Sabah looked down again, ignoring the question.

"You think because you have hidden where this man lives, we cannot find him ourselves. You foolish wretch." Her father grabbed her by the wrist, dragging her to her feet to face him. "I want the name of the man you and Amin went to see."

"*Ouch!*" Sabah clenched her teeth. The face glaring at her was a portrait of rage. "Why, what would you do if you knew it?"

Her father squeezed her wrists, causing her to grimace. "Do not anger me. I want an answer, now!"

"I cannot. This man did me no harm, and I..." *Whack!* The backhanded slap jerked her head sideways. *Awwwwww.* The lights went black for a moment, but flickered back on. She wiped her mouth, bringing her hand back streaked with blood. She held it out for her father to see.

He turned and stormed out of the room, slamming the door behind him. She brought her hands to her face, feeling the heat in her cheeks. Tears burst from her eyes. The lock on the other side of the door clicked—a prisoner in her own home.

Mohamed sat in the El Fishawy café sipping tea and watching the faces of the shoppers as they coursed through the market. The café was one of the most trafficked places in Cairo. An established landmark, it had been part of the Khan el-Khalili market for two-hundred and fifty years, but the bazaar itself was older, a place of haggling and commerce which had been in existence more than six centuries. It was reputed to be one of the oldest places of trade in the world.

The customers seated at small tables around him bantered in conversation, eating cheese and basboussa. El Fishawy still catered to artists and poets, just as it had in ancient times, but most of its modern clientele wore casual and business attire. A pair of robed ladies with children in tow brushed by, busy shoppers on their way to purchase spices and weavings and pillows made of silk. Heaps of hand woven tapestries and knotted rugs occupied the empty spaces. The souk was a favorite of locals and tourists alike.

Perhaps it was a fool's errand, but Mohamed couldn't help feeling Sabah would come to regret her decision. According to Amin, the El Fishawy was near where they lived. He was hoping to find her.

Everything hinged on whether her encounter with Christ was real, or imagined.

If real, by now Isa would have put a longing in her heart to learn more. If fake, Mohamed was just wasting his time. He'd talked it over with Layla and his mother and both felt the plan was worth a try. They would be at home lifting him up in prayer. He looked at his watch again. He'd been there almost an hour, idly sipping his tea. He couldn't keep the table occupied much longer.

A woman stopped to examine the loaves of bread spread out on a vendor's cart. She was the same size and build as Sabah, and the color of her *hijab* reminded him of one he'd seen Sabah wear. Her scarf prevented him from seeing her face. She started to move away. He'd occupied the space too long already. There were customers waiting in line. He got up and threw a few Egyptian pounds on the table.

The crowds were thick. He had to shoulder his way through, causing him to lose sight of the girl from time to time. He almost passed her when she stopped at a perfumer's stall. He would have kept going if, at the last second, she hadn't stepped back, holding a bottle of gold liquid up to the light. He wanted to remain discreet, so he stood in the recesses behind a rack of men's belts, waiting for her to turn around.

On the way to Cairo he had stopped off in Minya to ask Peter if he knew a Christian engineer that might be looking for work. Peter didn't, but he promised to pass the word along to other churches hoping someone might know of someone—the girl was turning around—it wasn't Sabah.

He looked at his watch. It was getting late. If God had wanted Sabah to find him, He would have made a way. He pursed his lips, staring at the throng of people. Maybe he should take one quick pass through the mall before giving up. Then if he didn't see her, he'd head for home.

Sabah stood at the window looking down on the alley from her third floor apartment. If she were a bird, she'd fly, but she wasn't a bird and, except for jumping, there was no way down, at least, not without killing herself.

She tiptoed back to the door, trying the knob again, just to be sure. The skin around her left eye was yellow and blue, and her jaw ached, but not as much as her pride. Her father had a temper, but he wasn't a violent man. To think he could do such a thing was inconceivable.

She turned the knob quietly as possible, pulling back when the lock reached the end of its throw, but the door wouldn't budge. She released her grip and shuffled back to the window, the floor squeaking beneath her feet. The smell of fresh bread hot from the oven wafted up from the market. The curio stands, pastry vendors and falafel carts were only a block away. She rested her cheek against the shutter. The angle prevented her from seeing the market. Her window was on the alley facing another brick wall, but she could smell its fragrance. It made her want to jump. She was becoming claustrophobic.

She couldn't explain her own irrational behavior. Her husband was gone. Renouncing the God that got him killed should be easy. Her family would throw the door open wide and welcome her back, but instead she toyed with the idea of leaping to her death.

Why had she come? Fear? Yes, she feared the unknown. Some inexplicable force had taken control of her life, and it was unnerving. Perhaps her father was right. Maybe she was demon possessed, but it didn't feel like it. She'd seen demon possessed men and they always seemed angry—*like her father.* She leaned out the window, looking down on the tops of people's heads as they hurried by. *Wait! It's him!* It appeared Haj Matthew was crossing the gap between the buildings, but she couldn't be sure, not from that angle. She'd never seen the top of his head before. She leaned out the window waving her arms but it was too late, the ally was narrow and took him only three steps to cross. He was already out of sight. No, *no, no, no, noooooooooo.* She flung herself away from the window, staggered across the floor, and collapsed on the bed with her face buried in her pillow. *Please, God, help me, please...*

CHAPTER 21

Then came Peter to him, and said, "Lord, how often shall my brother sin against me and I forgive him? Till seven times?" Jesus said unto him, "not till seven times: but until seventy times seven." — Matthew 18:21-2

MOHAMED ROLLED the Mercedes to a stop under the canopy, leaving the engine running with the air conditioner on. Staring out from underneath the faded yellow fabric, the world appeared creamy, but that's not how he felt.

If it weren't for his foolishness, his brother would still be alive, and Amin too, for that matter. It seemed he was good at making bad decisions. He'd thought to redeem himself by saving Sabah, but it wasn't to be. Only Christ could provide redemption. He'd just wanted the chance to show God he could do something right.

He killed the engine, stepping into the sun, squinting to shield his eyes. It was less than fifty feet to the side door, but prickles of sweat were itching his neck by the time he entered the house.

The kitchen was empty, so were the living and dining rooms. He made his way down the hall hearing voices that grew louder as he approached his uncle's office. He paused just outside the door, listening for a moment, but the words were muffled and indistinct. Reaching for the knob he opened the door to find Layla and Zainab on their knees.

"Heavenly Father, please, do not let this situation get out of control. I ask that you deal with the hearts of those involved that it might lead to their salvation. And please help my son show forgiveness, that what was meant to be evil, might result in something good. In the name of Christ our Lord, Amen."

Layla got up, but remained over by the couch on the other side of the room. She brought her finger up to scratch her nose.

Zainab struggled to her feet, supporting herself on the arms of the chair. She turned to face her son. Her light green *hijab* made her look bulky, though she was actually quite thin. Her eyes, like those of his wife, were fretting.

"What's going on?" he said.

"We were praying."

"I could see that."

Zainab looked at Layla, then back at her son. "Please, sit down," she said patting the back of the chair. "I will explain everything." Following her own instructions, she took a seat and paused, waiting. "Please, Matthew, sit."

"I'm okay standing, Mother."

Zainab glanced at Layla, again. "As you wish." Her hand dropped to the wicker basket by her chair to retrieve the pillowcase she'd been mending. Layla found a seat on the couch. She tugged at the hem of her skirt, folded her hands in her lap, closed her eyes, and began to hum.

"Okay, *what?*" Mohamed snapped.

His mother looked up. "Not until you sit down and promise to remain calm."

"This is silly, Mother. I don't have time for games," but he conceded and went to take a seat beside Layla on the couch.

His mother folded the pillowcase, smoothed it in her lap, and returned it to the basket. She took an audible breath and looked directly at her son, her eyes dark and brooding. "There's been another incident," she said. "The men you have working for you were attacked, and Masud was hurt…"

Mohamed jumped up. "What! Who? *Uthman?* I'll have that man arrested before he can spit. Where's Masud? Is he okay?"

"Please, Matthew, sit down. The situation is…"

"Where's Masud?"

"Masud is in the hospital in Asyut. He was taken there unconscious, but he's awake now and doing fine."

Mohamed began pacing. "He's not getting away with it. Not this time." He spun around looking at Layla. "Have you called the police? I want Uthman behind bars."

"On what grounds? We don't know who did it."

"What?"

Layla rose from her seat. "Where do you think we are, Matthew? This is Egypt, not the U.S.. As long as we're here we have to accept that things like this are going to happen. It's what you wanted!"

"Wanted! Oh for the…I just want to minister. And I don't want my friends being attacked, but I guess that's too much to ask. Are you saying they didn't see what hit them? How's that possible?"

"I said *we* don't know who did this. The men have agreed among themselves not to tell us. They want to exemplify the love of Christ. Masud claims he wasn't assaulted until he said he was a Christian. He doesn't want his first act as a professing believer to be revenge. The men have decided not to file a complaint. They merely wish to return to their work as soon as possible. All except Nour. The poor man said he couldn't take any more. We gave him a ride to Asyut when we took Masud to the hospital." She reached out to take Mohamed's arm. "Please, sit down."

Mohamed shook her off and resumed pacing. "So, Amin's dead, Sabah's run off, Masud's in the hospital and Nour's gone? How many do we have to lose before we do something?" He whirled about, stopping in front of his mother. "This is ridiculous. These men are hurting people and we're supposed to turn a blind eye. Maybe Masud won't press charges, but I want Uthman and his kind off the property. That much I can do."

Zainab nodded. "If you must. I ask only that you go see Masud first. I promised I would ask you to speak to him before you do anything. Will you do this one thing, for me?"

Mohamed shook his head. "It's a waste of time, Mother. Uthman killed Amin, I know it surely as I breathe. And now he's hurt Masud. He belongs in jail where he can't hurt anyone." Mohamed turned on his heel, heading for the door. "I'll be back in a few hours," he said over his shoulder. "You might want to tell Uthman to start packing."

"Wait!" Layla said. "I'm coming with you."

The western sky was a deep shade of vermilion that bled into a star-studded indigo in the east. It was day's end for the workers who, with shoulders sagging, shuffled toward the bunkhouse, weighing the consequence of the rumors. News of the assault had spread through the cane like an uncontrolled fire, leaving them anxious about their jobs. They would not have been surprised to find Haj Matthew standing in the drive, waiting to dismiss every last man of them. The lights were on in the house as they snuck by, one by one, slipping into their quarters.

Uthman was there to greet them. He'd already closed the windows, making the room unbearably hot. As soon as everyone was accounted for, he instructed one of his henchmen to close the door trapping the men inside. Cutting off the air circulation made the smell, which was rank at the best of times, even more putrid.

The interior was illuminated by three bulbs with conical lamp-shades strung in a series fifteen feet apart. The light wasn't enough to read by, and hardly enough to see. Uthman stood in the shadows at one end of the room pacing back and forth in a freshly washed turban and white *galabia*. He held a copy of the Koran above his head as he continued his rant.

"We cannot allow these infidels to take over." He screamed. "Most of you were here when Haj Sayyid was alive, a man with a heart as big as the moon. You owe him your loyalty. Do you wish to stand by and let this woman and her son destroy everything he stood for?"

A number of men were seated on the floor in front of him, with others either filling the center aisle or positioned on their bunks straining to get a better view. Heads bobbed as a wave of murmurs rippled through the crowd.

"I say we drive them out and burn their house until it is no more!" Uthman's long beard swayed like a pendulum as he swung right and left. He waved the Koran. "Allah tells us what to do with those who disbelieve!"

A few of the men seated right in front of Uthman rose to their feet and began beating their fists in the air, chanting the *Shahadah*:

"There is no God but Allah, and Muhammad is his messenger!"
"There is no God but Allah, and Muhammad is his messenger!"
"There is no God but Allah, and Muhammad is his messenger!"

But their enthusiasm, as well as the volume of their shouts, waned as they realized they were alone. The arms of Uthman's followers, those who had participated in the stoning, fell to their sides.

"You presume too much, Uthman." The voice came from the other end of the room. Heads twisted around to see who was speaking. Whoever it was stood in the dim light at the back wearing a baseball cap and coveralls.

"Driving Haja Zainab out will not bring us good. Once we destroy the family, there will be no one left to employ us. We will all lose our jobs. Some of you have wives and families to feed. You need to think about that."

The room erupted in murmurs.

Uthman brought his hands up, holding the Koran in front of him. "Men, brothers, do not listen. This is deception. We must do what is right. The family wants to automate the farm and eliminate your jobs."

A man about halfway back stood. "That's what you tell us, Uthman," he shouted, "but how do we know. Haj Matthew will still need us to plant, and to fertilize, and to harvest the crop, will he not? Bringing in water is a very small part of what we do. I don't see this as a threat to anyone."

The murmurs rose again.

The man in the baseball cap cupped his hands around his mouth, raising his voice to be heard above the tumult. "You bring trouble upon us, Uthman. I think it's time for you to leave."

Another man closer to the front rose to his feet. "Yes, Uthman, I need this work. I have children to feed."

He was followed by another, and then another, until the whole throng was standing, backing Uthman against the wall.

Uthman groped behind him, his hands searching for the entrance to the latrine and finding it, slipped inside, slamming the door. His heart was pounding. The mob was beginning to chant.

His eyes scanned the room—*a mop—a bucket—a window.* He threw the mop aside and overturned the bucket streaming dirty water across the floor. The clattering bucket flew against the wall where he used it as a stool, but his beard got caught underfoot. Baaahhh! Untangling himself, he pulled himself up and with his feet kicking, scrambled through the window, his legs scraping against the sill as he fell to the ground on the other side. He quickly righted his turban and took off, fleeing down the driveway toward the road. He ran until his lungs rasped for air and his legs ached, but he kept going, never once looking back.

CHAPTER 22

Trust in the Lord with all your heart, and lean not on your own understanding. In all your ways acknowledge him, and he will direct your paths. — *Proverbs 3:5-6*

MOHAMED STOOD at the window watching the sun, like a giant pomegranate, slip behind the trestles of the Ibrahimia bridge. The room had a nice view, for what they paid, but that was chiefly because they were on the sixth floor. Below him, in the dark shadow of the street, cars snapped on their headlights while continuing to honk and beep.

He grimaced as he took a step back. The forty watt bulb in the lamp gave off an eerie glow. He went to turn down the bedcover. The mattress sagged in the middle, the springs creaked and the sheets furled like they'd already been slept in. He looked over at Layla and shrugged, glad they hadn't brought suitcases. The room was too small for storing luggage. Two walls were covered with burgundy wallpaper of a leafy weave design. The other two were painted mint green. The paint was old and flaky.

They'd arrived at the University Hospital in Asyut only to be turned away. The nurse informed them that visiting hours were over. Mohamed had argued, but she remained firm. The patient needed rest. She'd already chased three others out and wasn't making an exception for him. If he wanted to see Masud, he'd have to come back in the morning.

He had stormed out of the hospital, fuming about the wasted drive, and started for home—he didn't want Uthman staying one more night—but Layla reminded him of his promise. "You can't fire him until you speak with Masud," she said. "You gave your word." She suggested they get a hotel, and bolstered her argument by saying she'd already told his mother that, depending on Masud's condition, they might have to spend the night.

At least the room had a private bath, though it too, was small. You could stand and shave, or comb your hair, but there was only room for one person at a time, and even then you could barely turn around.

Mohamed swept his hand across the sheet. After driving all the way to Cairo to look for Sabah, and all the way back, and then into Asyut, he had to admit he was tired.

"Could you help me with this?" Layla stood at the end of the bed tugging at her zipper. The dress was a full length one piece with long sleeves, too hot for the weather but conservative enough to keep the locals from taking notice. It was a necessary precaution. Asyut was known for its fundamentalists, many of whom believed women were to keep themselves covered in accordance with strict Sharia law.

Mohamed squeezed himself around the bed and, pinching the material between a thumb and finger, slid the zipper down with ease. Layla spun around to face him.

"Thank you," she said. She raised herself on her toes, giving him a kiss.

"My pleasure." He turned and scooted around the bed again. "We didn't even get a television," he quipped, "but it's probably for the best. We need to get some sleep. I want to get up early so we can see Masud before he's released."

"I wouldn't be so sure about that."

"About what, catching Masud at the hospital?"

"No, about getting to sleep." Layla slipped out of her dress and laid it on the dresser.

"Uh huh, not so fast. You think you can seduce me and get me to change my mind. Not going to happen. I don't care what Masud says. Uthman is history." Mohamed slipped into the covers and lay on his back with his fingers interlaced behind his head and his elbows winging out.

Layla crawled up from the end of the bed. "Look, this whole thing has me scared, I mean we could be next, but I'm trying to trust God and let it go. Can we just not talk about it tonight?"

"I just wish..." but his words were cut off as Layla brought her lips down to meet his, her long hair wrapping his face in warmth. He reached out, taking her by the waist as he rolled over, but she broke free and slipped under the covers beside him.

"It's too bad we didn't think to bring luggage. I don't have any pajamas to wear," she said.

Mohamed wrapped his arms around her pulling her in. "Yeah, so I noticed."

Sabah sat in her small prison. That's what it was, wasn't it? Four square walls and a bed with a locked door. What other definition of prison was there?

She'd worked at staying asleep because once she was awake, there was nothing to do but pace the floor. This was her fourth day and according to her mother, who brought her a meager breakfast of asyh and tea, her father was showing no sign of relenting.

She went to her dresser and retrieved a handheld mirror. Her face was a mess. Her eye was a puffy purple glop surrounded by a yellowish tinge. Grotesque! She touched the swollen pulp with her fingers. Ouch! The bruise her father inflicted had only grown darker. She pushed her hair off her forehead. Amin used to tell her how pretty she was. What would he say if he saw her now? Her eyes began to fill, but she choked back the tears.

She reached for a brush but, with her arm raised, recognized the faint smell of body odor. Four days without a bath. She brought her nose closer to her underarm. Phew, disgusting. They should at least let her bathe. She set the brush down and went to the door, knocking the way she did when she needed to relieve herself.

They were usually pretty quick in responding, at least her mother was, but no one came to the door. Sometimes her father had the TV blaring too loud to hear. She placed her ear against the wood, listening. *Nothing.* "Mother! Mother, I need to use the bathroom!" Still nothing. She tried the knob, rattling the door, then raised her hand slapping it against the wood. "Mother!"

She gave up and went back to the bed, collapsing in a heap with her knees tucked up under her chin—fetal as a child. She wanted to cry, she wanted to scream, she wanted to throw herself out the window and die! "Why are you doing this God! You show yourself to me. You say I'll not be alone and…and You kill my husband, and…" Her lungs broke out in sobs. She kicked her feet out, rolling off the bed, pulling the blanket with her.

"Why do you assume I've left?"

She sat up, looking around. "Who's there?" She hugged the blanket to her breast, her heart softly pitter-pattering as she got to her feet, dragging the blanket with her as she went to the door again. "Mother? Are you there?" She put her ear to the door but heard only silence. What day was it? She counted off with her fingers. It was Thursday! Her brother always took her parents shopping on Thursdays!

She tried pulling the door open but it was firmly locked. Dropping the blanket she placed both hands on the knob, jerking it back and forth with all her strength, but it wouldn't budge. She slammed her shoulder against the wood and grabbed her arm in pain. It was no use.

Her eyes went to the window, then to the blanket at her feet. She stooped over, picking it up and began spreading it out on the floor. Kneeling at one of the corners, she began rolling it diagonally.

A second blanket was still on the bed, and a sheet. She did the same to each, and then tied them end to end, pulling the knots taut to ensure they wouldn't come apart. Treading over to the window she looked down into the alley. It wasn't that far. She would want to avoid the piles of refuse along the wall, but she should be able to get down, as long as she did it quickly.

She grabbed her bed and pulled it over to the window, securing the rope she'd made to its bottom leg. Climbing on the mattress she looked out again. All clear. She tossed the fabric cord out and watched it fall. It didn't quite make it to the ground, but it was close enough. Standing on the bed, she braced herself against the window's frame, slipping one foot out at a time until she was sitting on the sill. She rolled onto her stomach, clutched the rope, and pushed off feeling a sudden drop as the bed slammed against the wall. The jerk almost made her let go, but she managed to hang on.

Kicking off the building, she scooted down until she reached the end of the sheet, but her feet still dangled beneath her. She had misjudged. There was still a six foot drop. She heard the bed above her scraping against the wall. Her weight was pulling the leg up and turning the bed over. As the bed flipped, the knot slid off the bottom leg dropping her to the ground. She landed on her feet but fell backward onto her butt, bruising her hands.

She struggled to get up and stood for a moment picking pieces of dirt from her palms. She brushed herself off and collected her rope, looking both ways before limping down the ally in the direction of the road. She hadn't lied to her parents. She didn't know where the farm was. But she did have their phone number, which she'd memorized. All she had to do was find a phone.

Asyut University Hospital was supposed to serve all of Upper Egypt. It was a modern facility with seventeen-hundred and eighty beds, but that wasn't enough to meet the demands of twenty million people. It was a zoo. Mohamed and Layla made their way down one long corridor after another dodging wheelchairs and rolling beds until they reached Masud's room. Mohamed started to step in, but Layla grabbed his arm and pulled him back.

"What?"

She took his hands in her own, her wavy hair falling on her shoulders, her eyes dark and sultry. "I think we should pray first," she said.

Mohamed raised his eyes, glancing around. The corridors were filled with people in *galabia's* and *hijab's*. They were surrounded by Muslims who, as a rule, didn't stand in the halls and pray. But she was right. The man they were about to see was in the hospital because he'd refused to deny his faith. He nodded.

Layla bowed her head and closed her eyes. "Lord, we thank you for protecting Masud, and that he wasn't killed. And I pray You give my husband an open mind so the conversation they have will be profitable. Give us the strength to let You make the decision about what to do with Uthman. In Jesus name I pray, Amen."

Mohamed squeezed her hands, opened his eyes, and let go. He turned and started for the door, then stopped and reached out to take Layla's hand again so they could enter together.

Masud was not alone, his brothers in Christ were there, but they weren't huddled around his bed; they were standing around the beds of others. Two appeared to be engaged in a heated debate with another patient, while the third appeared to be praying for a man who looked unconscious.

"Well look at you," Mohamed said as they stepped inside. "You old faker. Some people will do anything to get a day off." He grinned, letting Masud know he was kidding. "How you feeling?"

The men in other parts of the room looked up and excused themselves, breaking off their conversations to make their way over to greet Layla and Mohamed. The space was crammed with beds. Private rooms were unheard of, at least without insurance, or a pile of money.

"I am fine, Haj Matthew," Masud said. "Very, good, and anxious to get back to the work you think I wish to avoid."

Layla took his hand. "Not so fast. We'll wait to hear what the doctor has to say." She leaned forward, looking into his eyes. "Your pupils look clear. How many fingers do you see?"

"Three, the doctors have been playing these games with me all morning."

"Just answer her questions. Doctors are trained to ask the same thing over and over until they get what they want. We came by last night but they wouldn't let us in."

"Yes, they also made us leave." One of the men behind Mohamed said.

Mohamed nodded, acknowledging the man, but spoke to Masud. "We would have been here sooner, but I had to argue with my wife about not firing Uthman. I should have done it before. He did this, didn't he?" He raised his hand indicating the bandage wrapped around Masud's head.

Masud ran his tongue around his teeth causing his lips to bulge, but he didn't answer.

"Okay, I give. Why are you protecting him? The man's a murderer. I don't want him on my property. I didn't fire him after he killed Amin because I didn't have proof and I didn't want the rest of the men to riot, but now...I have to ask you again, why are you defending him?"

Masud glanced around the room at his friends. "We are new believers," he said, "but we have kept this hidden from our brothers, though we know they also need what we have found. If we go back and make complaints about the way we've been treated, will that open a door of opportunity to witness? I think not. We asked ourselves, 'What would this God we now worship have us do?' And we look to the Holy Book and we find that Christ never sought revenge on those who hurt him. How can we do less? Please Haj Matthew, do not fire Uthman, or any of those involved in this act of violence. Allow us to return to work as though nothing happened. If anyone asks about this bandage," he brought his hand up to the side of his head fingering the gauze.

"I will say it is the result of an accident, which I truly believe it is. When word gets back to Uthman that we do not accuse him, will he not wonder at so great a forgiveness? Will it not testify of the love of Christ?"

Mohamed shook his head. "You, Masud, are an example even unto me. All of you are," he said looking around. He caught Layla's eye. She was growing misty.

A nurse wearing a black *khimar* stood in the door. "I'm holding a call for a Matthew Mulberry. They said I would find him here."

Mohamed whirled around, squinting. "That would be me," he said.

The woman spun on her heel and headed back down the hall expecting Mohamed to follow. His eyebrows arched with curiosity. He held a finger up indicating he'd be back in a minute and rushed after.

The nurse stepped up to a counter and pointed to the phone. Mohamed nodded and picked it up.

"Hello."

"Hello my son, how is Masud?"

"He's fine, Mother, just as you said. And yes, they're trying to convince me not to do anything."

"And?"

Mohamed sighed. "And I can't disagree with what they have to say. But I fear no good will come of it. Unrestrained evil only grows."

"So you don't trust God to handle this problem."

"Of course, but…"

"…Because I was having dinner last night and when I looked out the window I saw Uthman running down our driveway toward the road. And this morning one of our workers showed up at the door and explained that Uthman had resigned. So I guess just the threat of you going to the police was enough to cause him to panic. The young man said Uthman won't be back and volunteered to fill in until we can find a replacement, but that's not why I called.

Something else has come up. I just received a call from Sabah. She needs your help."

"Sabah? Is she all right?"

"For the moment. She wants you to come and get her."

"*Al Hamdullah,* Praise God!"

"Yes, *Al Hamdullah* indeed. She's waiting for you. She said there's a small park just down the street from the Khan el-Khalili market. She said you have to pass it on your way in. She'll be watching for you. I don't know what's going on, but she was very upset. You need to leave right away."

A thin smile creased Mohamed's face as he entered Masud's room. He found his friend sitting on the edge of his bed, sliding his *galabia* over his head. "We must go," Haj Matthew, he said. "One of those we spoke to reported our witness to the nurse. She has gone but I fear she will be back shortly, and not alone."

Mohamed sighed. "If it isn't one thing, it's another. I have news, but I guess we can talk on our way out. Okay let's go."

Masud stood, but teetered, reaching out to grab the bed.

Layla took his arm, supporting him. "Are you sure you're all right?"

He took a breath and straightened himself. "Yes, fine. Perhaps I should not have got up so fast. Come, we must go."

With Mohamed in the lead, the group moved as one man toward the door. "This way," he said. They veered to the left, heading the opposite way of the nurse's station.

The nurse, accompanied by two uniformed security personnel, turned the corner marching down the hall just as they ducked into the stairwell out of sight.

"I think I have good news," Mohamed said. The clomping of their feet echoed off the walls as they thundered down the stairs. "Uthman has resigned. He left the farm of his own accord. It appears he thought I was coming back with the police." He looked back over his shoulder. "Can you men see Masud gets back okay? And see that he rests." He was short of breath, his words sounding winded, but they had to keep moving. "I have to go to Cairo. When I get back, I'll work with you myself. If anyone else wants to stop this project, they'll have to go through me."

They reached the bottom of the stairs and found an exit sign off to the side, away from the main lobby. "Why are we going to Cairo?" Layla asked, as they wove through the streams of people in an attempt to reach the door.

"We are not going anywhere. You're going back to the farm to take care of Masud. I have to go pick up Sabah. She called Mother and said she wants to come back."

"Masud's fine, he just needs rest. I'm coming with you."

They pushed their way through the door, the hot air smothering them as they stepped outside. "Sabah's going to need a gentle touch, and *Habibty*, I love you, but you're not known for your tact."

They began scurrying through the parking lot. "No. I have to consider that her father may have put her up to this. He might be out for revenge. I don't want you getting hurt. Where did you guys park? I'm over there, he said pointing."

"All the more reason I need to be there. I can be a second set of eyes. Maybe I'll catch something you don't see."

"We're that way," one of the men behind Mohamed said. I'm afraid Haja Layla will have to go with you. There are four of us. The truck cab is full. We don't have room for anyone else."

Mohamed shook his head. "I can't seem to win. Okay Layla, but you're getting out before I pick Sabah up. I'm not going to risk letting anything happen to you."

"We'll talk about that later. Let's go."

CHAPTER 23

The Lord is my strength and song, and he has become my salvation...
— Exodus 15:2

SEEN FROM a distance, Cairo was but a pimple on the flat surface of the earth. The desert, except for a narrow belt that bordered the Nile, stretched for miles of endless monotony, a vast open space, virtually empty.

Mohamed took a breath and tried to relax. He'd been clocking one-thirty most of the way. His mother said Sabah's plea sounded urgent; the excessive speed was warranted. He pressed against the seat, hoping the supple leather would ease the tension in his back.

None of this was part of his original plan. His hope, in coming back to Egypt, was to live a simple life and maybe even one day return to the remote village where he'd been born. His happiest memories were there. A place where few people owned cars and traffic was the bleating of sheep crossing the road. It was where he and Layla had explored the Nile together, their backs growing brown under the hot Egyptian sun.

Layla had begun the trip with singing. He loved her voice. More than that he loved her songs. She frequently put scriptures to music. She said it helped her memorize verses. She'd sung Romans 8:28 *"And we know that all things work together for good to those who love God, to those who are the called according to His purpose."*

"Why don't you ever sing?" she asked.

"Come on Layla, we've been through this before. I just don't. And don't ask why, because I don't know…"

Mohamed was in his room with the door closed. It was his twelfth birthday and his mother wasn't there to share it with him. He lay on his bed feeling like an orphaned child.

They had celebrated at school. He rubbed the plastic housing of the disc player, pushing the button until it clicked on. The class had presented him with the gift, along with a CD of a female vocalist. Music poured from the tiny ear buds.

His classmates at the private school he attended were from prominent families. Some of the boys had pooled their allowance and bought him this nice present. The servants, too, had made him umm ali, a raisin cake soaked in milk and served hot, and his uncle had placed the annual soccer ball on his pillow, but his mother, so he was told, was off on one of her trips and her absence created a bigger hole than could be filled by cakes and gifts. The village would not have afforded him such luxury, but if he had to choose, he'd take his mother and poverty, over a life of privilege without her.

He dialed the volume up loud enough to hear the music without putting the buds in his ears.

> *"My heart, don't act so stupidly,*
> *Why do you play the fool?*
> *Sit still, the brother comes to you,*
> *And many eyes as well."*

The voice was soft and sweet, reminding him of his mother. The chorus started again and he found himself singing along.

The door burst open.

"What is that?"

Mohamed spun around, startled. His uncle's face was flushed, his eyes hard as stone.

"It…it is a CD player, Uncle."

"Give me that." Sayyid reached with his hand out, his meaty palm

turned up with his fingers wiggling, beckoning the device.

Mohamed looked at the player, rubbing the smooth plastic with his thumb. He wanted to grab it and run, but he handed it over.

"Where did you get this?" Sayyid said, examining the plastic housing.

"My brothers at the school gave it to me...for my birthday."

Sayyid ripped the wires from the ear buds and dropped the housing to the floor. Mohamed heard the plastic crack as his uncle began crushing it under his foot.

"Noooooo, it's mine, Uncle, it's a gift" Mohamed jumped off the bed hoping to retrieve his present before it was completely destroyed.

"You have no time to listen to such foolishness." His uncle kept grinding the player under his heel, pulverizing the plastic housing while ripping the ear buds apart. The CD popped up and rolled across the floor in a rainbow of light.

Mohamed looked at his uncle, his eyes pleading. "It...it reminded me of my mother. She used to sing and..."

"Your mother does not sing anymore, and neither will you!" Sayyid turned and stormed out of the room, slamming the door. Mohamed fell to his knees and clutching the broken player to his chest, crawled on his bed to cry.

Mohamed pursed his lips. A year later on his thirteenth birthday he would be told his mother was dead. He hadn't sung since.

The sun glistened on Layla's dark hair, enriching the glow of her olive skin. Her beauty captivated him, like that of a Pharaoh's daughter or Egyptian queen, but he would have loved her even if she were plain. They were childhood friends that grew to be lovers with memories of skimming stones on the river, giggling as they ducked into the reeds playing hide and seek, and running against the wind as they launched paper kites into a red autumn sky. They'd been inseparable. They'd shared too many hours together to ever be apart.

The city was growing on the horizon. Layla stirred, stretching her arms with a yawn. "Sorry, I nodded off. Did I miss anything?"

... 🌙 ...

Uthman sat in the open air market sipping tea, the cup trembling in his hand. He hoped the hot liquid would smooth his jangled nerves the way sitting in the shade made him feel cool, distilling his temper.

He could have gone to Asyut to look for work, but Upper Egypt was poor, and jobs few. And even if he found work on another farm, it would likely be as a laborer, and he wasn't ready for that.

He reached down, fingering the knot at his waist. At least he wasn't broke. His money was where it always was, in a pouch stitched inside his robe. *Al hamdulla*, thanks be to God. He might have to do without his precious donkey, but at least he wouldn't go hungry. He'd saved practically everything he'd ever earned. The hours he'd spent bouncing around the bed of a pickup, the only ride he'd been able to catch on his trek to Cairo, gave him time to count his reserve. He could live modestly—if not well—for years.

He coughed, *akkkhemmm*, and took another sip of his tea. The beverage sat like a thistle in his throat. How could men he'd known for so many years, turn on him so quickly? That witch woman, Zainab, that was the problem. Men, who had worked that farm all their lives, devout, faithful men, were being replaced by blasphemers. His grandfather had worked for Sayyid's father, and he and his father had both worked for Sayyid. It was the only life he'd ever known. And this was how they repaid a lifetime of service? If Haj Sayyid could see what they were doing he'd vomit—were there no windows in paradise?

Uthman looked up, distracted by three men shouldering their way through the crowd. They were grabbing people, spinning them around, examining their faces—not men, just the women—a diversion bringing mild amusement. He yawned, balling his hands into fists as he stretched out to relax.

One of the men spun around to study the faces of people in the café. Uthman brought his cup to his lips to take another sip. The man stepped back and, ignorant of the obstruction, tripped over Uthman's legs. Uthman jerked his feet in but his cup of tea slipped from his fingers, spilling down the front of his robe.

"Hey!" He jumped up. "Look at this. You have ruined my *galabia!*" He began kicking the fallen man, directing all the rage he felt at the smaller man's head. He plowed his sandal into the man's nose. "These are the only clothes I have," his foot assaulted the man again, "I have to find a job," another kick, "and I need my robe!"

A second man, taller, and at least fifty pounds heavier, grabbed Uthman in a bear hug. Uthman felt his lungs compress with the sound of air escaping a balloon. He brought his leg up, looking for leverage, but the man jerked around sweeping him back and forth. His feet dangled, unable to find purchase. He tried to inhale but choked. Snow began swirling in his head. His ribs felt like they were about to snap. He saw flashes of red and black. He tried to kick but his legs had no strength. Then his world went black.

Mohamed pulled to the corner and stopped at the light. Horns blared behind him. Most considered a stop sign a suggestion, not the law. He turned right to get off the main thoroughfare and stopped again. Another horn *beeeeeped.* He hit the gas, rolling slowly forward. A bevy of pigeons were circling the palms that grew out of the mostly brown grass.

It wasn't really a park, not in the sense of American parks with playgrounds and baseball diamonds; rather it was a small rectangle of land with a few benches and palm trees planted smack-dab in the middle of the city. Traffic surrounded it on every side.

He turned to Layla. "This has to be the place. I can't park the car, there's too much traffic. I'm going to pull over and let you drive around while I go in and wait. Just keep circling the area and don't stop. I'll be where you can see me. If this is a trap and, I'm not saying it is, but if something bad happens, you just keep driving. Go find the first police officer you can and bring him back. But don't worry. I'm sure everything will be fine. And don't expect to recognize Sabah. I imagine she'll be veiled. I'll wave if it's her. Just pull over and we'll get in."

"You figure all this out while I was asleep?"

"As a matter of fact, I did."

"Good. No point in asking what I think."

"Do I detect a note of sarcasm? It doesn't suit you, Layla."

There was no place to pull over without obstructing traffic. Mohamed squeezed to the right, stopped the car, and put it in park. "Okay, your turn." He swung the door open and hopped out as Layla scooted over. The irritated driver behind him was beeping his horn with growing impatience. "I'll see you in a few minutes," he said, closing the door.

Mohamed held his hand out, entreating drivers to stop as he slipped between their bumpers to cross the road. He entered the park searching, but didn't see Sabah. Sidewalks from each of the four corners met at the center forming an X. He took off in that direction. Several people sat on benches in the shade. Two women with their faces shrouded by scarves walked by with bags from the market, but neither looked his direction.

He stood in the grueling sun, unprotected by shade, but he had to be visible. The sweat under his shirt rolled down his chest. He scanned the street and saw the black Mercedes, inching along. Layla hadn't gotten very far. Exhaust fumes saturated the air. He looked up into the sun, squinting with his hand over his eyes.

He heard his name, "Haj Matthew, Haj Matthew, over here." Words spoken in a hoarse whisper.

He spun around, inspecting the shrubs. The bright sunlight had dilated his pupils making the image hard to see, but it appeared someone was waving at him from behind a tall clump of papyrus. He nodded and started walking.

"Sabah?"

The woman waited until he was at her side before unwrapping her scarf and pulling the shroud from her face.

"What happened?"

She didn't answer. She turned away, covering herself again.

Mohamed spun around and waved at Layla. "Come on, let's go," he said. He made no attempt to assist her. It was inappropriate to touch a woman in public. He simply took off, leading the way as they hurried to the car.

CHAPTER 24

Therefore they sought again to take him, but he escaped out of their hand. — John 10:39

LAYLA PULLED over and hopped out leaving the engine running and her door open, setting off another round of honking horns. Zigzagging through the cars she crossed the road and raced up onto the grass, "I'll help her," she said, taking Sabah by the hand. "You get the car."

Mohamed nodded and took off in a sprint, his face dripping sweat. Frustrated drivers tried to squeeze around his stopped vehicle. One tipped his head out the window and called him several rude names. He climbed in behind the wheel and yanked the door closed. Checking his rearview mirror, he saw the guy behind him shake his fist and give him another blast on the horn.

Layla kept her arm interlocked with Sabah's as she guided her to the car. Mohamed stepped out again, opening the door so Sabah could climb in as Layla ran around to the passenger side slipping into the backseat so she could talk with Sabah while Mohamed drove. Mohamed ducked behind the wheel, threw the car into drive, and pulled away—a successful extraction—but they didn't get far. Traffic inched forward like ants on their way to a picnic.

It was like that in Cairo. Gas was cheap, and the streets were narrow, the combination creating a nonstop glut of traffic. The fumes made him nauseous. *Honk, honk, beep, beep, beep.*

He checked his rearview mirror. Sabah had her head turned away from Layla, staring out the window. He caught Layla's eye. She shrugged and settled back in her seat. Mohamed understood. If Sabah wanted to remain quiet, so be it. She was still grieving the loss of her husband.

He studied the cars behind him. It was impossible to tell if they were being followed in this traffic, but he wasn't ready to dismiss the idea that Sabah might be bait in a trap. Her father might have forced her to contact them. It would account for both the bruise on her face, and her sullen behavior. But Mohamed wasn't worried. If he could spot the FBI following him on the crowded freeways of Los Angeles, he should have no problem spotting someone tailing him across miles of open desert.

Uthman leaned against a table holding his beard to his chest. A crowd had formed, circling the fracas like tourists ogling street performers. Someone had flipped open their cell phone and summoned the police.

He was trying to explain his version of what happened to an officer who was having a hard time hearing him over the screams of the other man who, with his arms swinging wildly, continued to assail him with invectives.

Uthman was at an obvious disadvantage, not just because his sore lungs prevented him from screaming as loud as his opponent, but also because the man was joined by his two friends who were equally vociferous. One was the man who'd grabbed him and nearly choked him to death; the other was older with a white beard.

The police officer wore a khaki military uniform with a blue beret. He placed his hand on his baton as he shouted over the melee. "One at a time," he screamed. "You," he pointed at the shorter man, "you go first."

The man wiped his nose leaving a smear of blood on his upper lip. "My father and my cousin and I," he said, nodding at the men with him, "were looking for my sister. I turned around and this man," he raised a finger pointing accusingly at Uthman, *sniff*, "he stuck his leg out and tripped me, and I fell and he jumped on me and began kicking me for no reason."

"Liar!" *kuff, kuff*, Uthman grabbed his chest. "I was drinking tea." *Kuff*. "You came in here pushing and shoving, and you ran into me!"

"Silence!" The police officer spun about, causing Uthman to flinch. He took a deep breath and turned back to Ahmed. "Now, you said you were looking for your sister? How long has she been gone? Do you have a picture? Give me one half hour and we'll put together a search."

The man raised his hands, palms outward. "No, no, this is a family matter. My sister, Sabah, ran away, it is true, but she's an adult, a married woman. She was staying with her husband on a farm outside Asyut but he got himself killed and she had to escape, but now we fear she's gone back…"

Uthman sighed, placing a hand against his chest to ward off the pain. He smiled, his lips thin and taut. *Who can know the will of God?* He stepped out from behind the police officer. "I must apologize," he said, bowing his head in deference. "I did not know of this tragedy. Please, forgive me and allow me to buy you and your father a cup of tea. Perhaps I can provide information that will make you want to thank these clumsy feet of mine."

Mohamed raced through the desert, anxious about getting home. He checked his side mirror. His was the only car on the road. He leaned back, looking out the sunroof just to be sure they weren't being followed by plane. It was a silly thought. Sabah's parents probably couldn't afford such a measure, but it made him feel better to check—lots of blue open space, but nothing else.

Layla and Sabah were in the back talking, though they kept their voices hushed. Mohamed couldn't hear what they were saying, but

Layla would tell him later. He glanced at his rearview mirror for the umpteenth time. Sabah wiped her eyes with a tissue, gently dabbing the side with the bruise. She hadn't stopped crying. He looked at Layla who had scooted over to sit beside Sabah. She'd been right to insist on coming.

As the road moved closer to the Nile, the farmlands came into view. The rows of crops swept by like a picket fence. Many of the properties were as fruitful as the one Zainab now owned, a rich harvest of sugar beets, corn and beans.

Farming along the Nile was prosperous for wealthy landowners like Sayyid...Mohamed clenched his teeth. His mother now owned the land, and she was putting it to good use.

His mother had loved his father, not his uncle. She would never have married Sayyid without a knife to her throat. His father had been an unwitting tool in Sayyid's hands, a means to an end. King David loved Bathsheba and sent her husband into battle to be killed so he could have her for himself. In much the same way, his uncle got rid of his father by sending him out on a personal jihad. The lust of the eye, and the pride of life—two of Satan's favorite tools.

The farm was just ahead. The mosque that stood on the neighboring property was coming into view. He pulled off the road, turning onto the lane that led to the house, pleased to see his workers out in the field cutting cane.

He pulled the car up the drive and rolled around back to park under the canopy, gravel crunching under his tires. A dusty film drifted up as he pulled to a stop. He looked in the mirror at Layla. "Okay ladies, we're here." His eyes drifted to Sabah, but she kept her head turned away.

"Sabah wants to be left alone." Layla said. "She's not ready to talk about it yet."

Mohamed nodded.

"She's upset about missing her husband's funeral, but she's glad we had a Christian service. He would have wanted it that way. She also wants to know if we have an extra Bible. I told her she can borrow mine. We can share yours, if that's okay with you."

"Of course."

"I'll show her to her room and help her get settled." Layla looked at Sabah and squeezed her hand. "If you need anything, just ask."

Mohamed placed his arm across the back of the seat, straining to see over his shoulder. "I...I haven't had a chance to say it, Sabah, but I'm glad you decided to return. And don't worry; no one knows you're here. You'll be safe."

CHAPTER 25

There is neither Jew nor Greek, there is neither bond nor free, there is neither male nor female: for you are all one in Christ Jesus.

— *Galatians 3:28*

TOURISTS WOULD HAVE called the yellow fans of light spreading across the valley a spectacular sunset, but not the men working in the fields. When you spend all day toiling under its scorching rays, you're just glad to see the sun going down.

Sabah closed the book she was reading and moved to the window. Workers were drifting in, silhouetted by the amber sky. They moved slowly, fatigued, ready for an evening of rest. Wrapping the Bible in her arms, she turned and began her trek to the living room. She was wearing her new yellow *hijab*. Her hair was down and intentionally combed forward to mask the bruising of her face.

Zainab and Layla looked up as she entered. They were seated on the couch, Zainab mending a worn sock and Layla, keeping her company, sipping a cup of tea. The room was warm, an evening breeze ruffling the curtain of an open window. Sabah looked at the Bible in her hand. She'd behaved poorly. This day would not end without an explanation.

... ...

Mohamed trundled up the front steps. He'd been gone all after-noon gathering as many men as he could to deliver another one of his speeches. Perhaps they were weary of his constant inter-ruption of their work, but the risk of seeing their displeasure was overridden by the importance of what he needed to say. He had complimented the men on their willingness to continue with the harvest even after the announcement of Uthman's resignation. More importantly, he asked who had assumed the roll of assigning the men to their tasks.

From the back, a young man stepped forward. "I guess that would be me," he said, tipping his hat. In contrast to the tradi-tional white *galabia,* he wore a faded blue T-shirt with denim coveralls and a baseball cap. And while practically everyone else was barefoot, he had on a pair of muddy tennis shoes.

"I suggested they get someone to carry on for Uthman, but they chose to appoint me."

Mohamed's eyebrow rose slightly, but he tried not to show surprise. "What's your name?" he asked.

"I am called Hamadi al-Zahraa Ibrahim."

Mohamed nodded. "Hamadi, if you don't mind, I'd like to speak with you for a moment."

The men began drifting back to their labors, some to the cutting of the stalks, others to the gathering, and yet others to the loading of the carts. Mohamed drew Hamadi aside. "We've lost several days. You think there's any chance we'll get the crop in on time?" he said.

... ...

Mohamed had stayed the entire afternoon walking the fields with Hamadi, discussing the importance of soil maintenance, harvest planning, crop rotation and livestock distribution. In addition to sugar cane, the farm produced maize, cotton and beans, many of which were grown on different parcels of land at the same time, and others of which were rotated to replenish the soil and reduce the proliferation of pests.

Mohamed found Hamadi to be well versed in the fundamentals of farm management. More importantly, the young foreman spoke well about the benefits of irrigation. By the end of the tour, Mohamed was convinced they had the right man for the job.

Workers were drifting in from the fields. Mohamed pulled the screen door open and stepped inside. He could hear the creaking wagons rolling past. One man had ingeniously utilized Uthman's donkey. While the cart was little more than a seat with wheels, the man had it loaded with bundles of cane for the donkey to haul in. Mohamed didn't deliberately eavesdrop on their conversations, but he did hear Uthman's name being mentioned more than once.

The room was warm. Sabah stopped mid-sentence as he entered. Her eyes went to Layla, as though looking for reassurance. Layla gave a light shrug and Sabah continued.

Mohamed sensed she'd be more comfortable if he weren't there, but now his curiosity was piqued and he couldn't leave. He went to a chair and sat down as she continued her story. She never once looked at him, keeping her attention directed at Zainab and Layla. The story she told was all too common, a story of a patriarchal family where her value as a human being was frequently in question, and her self worth often in doubt.

Her marriage to Amin was a bright star on a very dark night. Her father had wanted a second son. He saw her birth as more of a burden than a blessing. Long were the hours she spent scrubbing floors while her brother was out with his friends. It was her *brother* whose birthday was worthy of celebration, her *brother* who sat at the table and enjoyed conversation while she was ignored, and it was her *brother*, not her, who they insisted receive a good education.

Perhaps if her parents had been blessed with other children it might have been different, but her mother's premature hysterectomy left her brother to be viewed as a gift from God, and she a curse.

It was pure chance that brought her and Amin together. Her brother was attending university, and her father, who had fallen ill, sent Sabah to find him to deliver a message. She had never been to Al Azhar. With so many doors to so many rooms, she didn't know where to begin, and quickly became lost wandering the halls. Several times she passed Amin. He was standing under an arch reading the poet, Malak Hifni Nasif, a twentieth century Egyptian Muslim who sought an improvement in the status of women. He couldn't help but note Sabah's look of distress and in keeping with what he'd just read, offered to help.

She was moved by his kindness, but shied away when he asked her name. He escorted her to the Islamic studies group where her father said they would find Ahmed. Amin stepped aside as Sabah relayed her message, but as soon as she was gone, he approached the brother to ask whether or not she was betrothed.

Ahmed eyed Amin curiously but instantly decided to help. He later told Sabah he'd done it because he wanted to see her married so she would be less a burden on the family. He was looking ahead. If their father died, he would be the family's sole provider. Having one less mouth to feed, not to mention the dowry, would be an asset. He let Amin know about Sabah's weekly trips to the market and suggested that if he just happened to be there in the early afternoon, he was sure to see her again.

Amin chanced seeing Sabah almost every week thereafter until it became clear, even to her, that these meetings were more by design than happenstance. Before long he was offering to carry her bags home, which she refused to allow, but which more than anything else, won her heart.

Though by no means well off, Amin still had the remainder of the money from the sale of his parent's shop and the promise of a summer job with the ministry of natural resources. He approached Ahmed with a proposal.

At first, Sabah's father was furious and argued that his wife needed Sabah to help around the house, but when Ahmed explained how he had found the suitor himself, and had arranged a sizable dowry, his father acquiesced, if for no other reason than it made him proud to see his son acting so prudently.

But when his father came up with the idea that, after the wedding, Amin would move into the apartment and live with the family, Ahmed found himself regretting his decision. Now, instead of reducing the number of mouths to feed, he found he'd increased the number by one.

Those first few months had been the happiest of Sabah's life. Amin would rush home from classes just so they could be together, taking long walks through the outdoor market and enjoying falafels at a roadside cart. He even got a college friend to loan him a bicycle and rode her out to the Qasr El Nile bridge where they sat one evening watching the massive golden orb of the sun sinking into the river's blue waters.

But Amin was still a student, and religious studies were part of his curriculum. He began to read the Bible, hoping, he said, to show the illogic of the Christian faith. Sabah had never felt such love, so even when she saw Amin starting to change, and watched him receive a revelation that, at the time, seemed crazy; she reconciled herself to standing by him whatever the cost.

As for herself, she wasn't looking to convert. It wasn't until she realized she was feeling something she'd longed for her whole life that she decided to investigate what her husband was saying. The change within her was subtle. She couldn't explain how the transformation occurred, she knew only that she'd found something she didn't want to lose.

"I'm sorry I ran off. I...I was so confused. My husband was gone and all I could think about was that he died because we came here. I went home hoping to find peace but all I found was the same anger I'd known all my life. You see my face," she said, dragging back her hair, "this is how my father shows his love. He kept me locked in my room the whole time I was there."

Zainab stood and went to the couch. She sat beside Sabah and placed an arm around her shoulder. "Can I pray for you, Sabah?"

Sabah's answer was muffled. She was biting her lip to keep from crying but her eyes were glassy all the same. She nodded.

"Lord, please take care of your child, Sabah. She's going through a hard time right now, Lord. I ask that you protect her and fill her with the joy that can only be found in You…"

Zainab's head jerked back. Someone was pounding on the door. Not a friendly, "Hi, I've just stopped by for a visit," kind of knock; it sounded like someone was attacking the wood with a hammer.

Mohamed's eyebrows furrowed in. He looked at Layla, then at his mother. Sabah pushed the hair out of her eyes and stood, wiping her cheeks, and then ducked into the hall. Mohamed rose from his chair and went to the door.

Two men stood on the porch, veiled by darkness. Mohamed didn't recognize them, but he perceived they meant trouble.

"You have my sister," the shorter man said. "I insist you bring her here now."

Mohamed looked back over his shoulder. Sabah was standing in the shadows shaking her head, her eyes like those of a mouse facing a snake.

He turned to address the men again. "What makes you think your sister is here?"

The older man turned toward a car parked in the laneway and pointed. "That man." Through the dusky light Mohamed could make out two men sitting in the backseat. One looked huge, like he could barely squeeze into the cramped space, and the other, the one closest to the window appeared to be wearing an oversized turban. *Uthman?*

"Now please, if you will bring my daughter out. We are her family. We know what is best for her."

"That's not possible. I don't want to seem impolite, but I must ask you to leave."

"Not without Sabah." The younger man stepped forward, but Mohamed raised his hand to block him. "Do not try my patience. This is my house, and you will not enter without my blessing."

Several workers, late in coming back from the fields with their scythes and hoes, stopped to watch.

Ahmed saw they were outnumbered and backed away. His eyes were a dark fire. "*Rabena yehrakak*—may God burn you, you son of Isa. I will be back. And if it is true you shelter those who blaspheme, may Allah have mercy on your soul."

Chapter 26

In the fear of the Lord is strong confidence, and his children shall have a place of refuge. — Proverbs 14:26

MOHAMED WAITED until the car was turned around before closing the door. He spun around to face Layla, combing his fingers through his hair.

Sabah stepped out of the shadows. "Please, I do not want to go with them. I…"

"They're not going to take you, Sabah. We'll hide you if we have to, but you can stay here as long as you want," Layla said.

Marching into the dining room Mohamed drew back the curtain, watching until the vehicle's tail lights disappeared behind the wall of cane. "It's not just Sabah we have to worry about," he said.

"How did they find us?"

Mohamed stood in the arched entry. "I think Uthman was with them, in the backseat. I recognized that silly turban. What I want to know is, what's his connection to Sabah's family?" He looked to Sabah, but she shook her head.

"Ladies, I need you to do something for me. I need you to pray." He stepped into the vestibule reaching for the door.

"Where are you going?" Layla asked.

"Same place I always go when I need to hear from the Lord."

Mohamed hurried down the dirt lane, heading in the opposite direction of the car. The moon was full and bright, illuminating the palm trees, their fronds jutting into a night crowned with stars. The uncut cane shone with a buff light. He walked briskly, his shadow running before him on the ground.

It was coming apart, all he'd hoped to accomplish—*everything!* He hadn't been home six months and his ministry was already compromised, his hope of creating a place of refuge for those called out of Islam, dashed.

Voices carried through the stillness of the night, the sound of men working. He held his watch up to check the time. He'd made it clear the delayed harvest wasn't anyone's fault. Working sunup to sundown was enough. The men should be resting.

He reached the end of the row and, as he suspected, found men still at work, but not bringing in the harvest, they were laying pipe. At least twenty men were engaged in the project with shovels and hoes, digging a trench. It looked like the pipeline stretched about fifty feet into the field waiting to be buried. Masud was holding a sheath of paper up to the moon trying to read by the pale glow.

"Masud, what's going on? I thought we agreed you were going to stay in bed and rest."

Masud lowered the paper, smiling, his teeth bright in the moon's light. "I am okay, Haj Matthew. And as you can see, we are constructing the pipeline, as you requested."

"So it seems. And it appears you've found a few extra hands."

Masud looked around. "Yes, we have. Your workers are very good men. They have been taking shifts, each man giving a few extra hours after filling his daily quota on the farm. They came saying they wanted us to know they had no part in what happened to me, or to Amin. They say Muslims and Christians should live together in peace. See, God is using their guilt to get your pipeline laid. Is this not wonderful?"

Mohamed looked around. Hamadi was standing in a trench holding a spade with his baseball cap glued to his head.

"Everyone?"

"There are a few who refuse to participate. They spit on the ground when they pass, but they cause us no difficulty."

Mohamed took Masud by the elbow and stepped away, pulling him along until they were alone. "Unfortunately I have bad news. The wife of Amin has returned."

"I do not understand. Why is this bad?"

"Because her family has already come to get her. I sent them away, but they'll be back. I'm sure of it. And that's only part of the problem. I believe Uthman is involved. I'm afraid we're in for a bit of trouble."

"This is not a problem, Haj Matthew. We are ready for whatever comes." Masud waved his arm in the direction of the ongoing work. "Do you not see how God provides for those who remain faithful? I, for one, will not recant, even if they drag me off and throw me in jail. Think about what a testimony that would be for these other men."

"I'm afraid it's not that simple. I believe they'd rather see us dead than in jail. And even if they choose to punish us legally, they won't arrest just you, they will arrest my wife and my mother for sheltering you, and turn Sabah over to her father. And if Uthman has his way, he'll get his men to burn our barn, and our crops. My mother's too old to handle such abuse. If she is sent to prison, I doubt she'll survive."

The smile disappeared from Masud's face. He rolled the sheath of paper. "What would you have us do, Haj Matthew?"

"I'm not sure there's anything we can do. Wait a minute, yes, there is." He lowered his voice leaning close to Masud's ear. "As much as I hate to, I need you to stop what you're doing and return to your quarters. I need you and the other brothers to cover me in prayer. You can tell the workers I'm insisting they call it a night. Just go back to your room and pray. I feel a great evil is about to be unleashed on us. We're not fighting against flesh and blood. We have to battle in the spiritual realm. I'm going down to the river to inquire of the Lord."

Mohamed kicked off his shoes and pulled his socks from his feet leaving them on the shore as he pushed his *felucca* into the water. The river was alive with the sound of frogs, crickets, and mosquitoes. Taking hold of the boat he lifted the bow, and slid it back, walking out knee deep into the shallows. The small boat turned on the tide, causing him to almost lose his grip as it pulled away from the shore. He hauled the boat in again and pushed himself up on the rail, rolling over the side.

He lay on his back, looking up at the stars, a myriad of constellations proclaiming the glory of God. *Where were you Job, when I laid the foundations of the earth, answer that?* He crawled to his feet and stood debating whether to raise the sail, or just let the boat drift. The current would take him further downriver than he wanted to go. With the sail he could tack across the wind. He unfurled the canvas. The pulley at the top of the mast screeched. The triangular lateen immediately caught wind, nearly ripping the boom from his hand, but he caught its rope and let it out, turning the rudder to cut across the current. The boat rocked on the water. He felt the rustle of the wind in his hair and the spray tickling his face.

He drove the small *felucca* into the current until he was about a hundred yards off shore, then pulled the boat around, holding the rudder as he dropped the sail and reached for the bag of rocks that served as an anchor. He could see the lights from the house just off his shoulder. His wife and mother, and hopefully Sabah, would be praying. *Kaplunk.* The sack of rocks went over the side heading for the bottom.

Breathing in the musty smell of the river calmed his soul. He still didn't like water, but he somehow always felt safe in a boat. It was a place of refuge. Liquid lapping against the hull broke the moon's refection into a thousand white petals. The night was clear and full of stars. When Christ had appeared to him the first time, He had come on the clouds. As Mohamed stared into the rolling deep he had seen a most wonderful thing, the clouds had gathered together and become a man on a white horse. He had just finished reading the book of The Revelation and knew immediately who the rider was.

Many times since, he'd taken the boat out onto the river seeking the face of God, and while he'd never seen the image again, it always made him feel he was standing in God's presence. The boat rocked back and forth. No clouds meant there would be no vision, but he was undeterred. He leaned back to gaze at the starry host.

God, I know You're there, no not there, but right here beside me, and God I really need Your help. Already, one of those You brought to my door has been killed, and another has been wounded. And while I'm thrilled to find the men working together, and this is a miracle that could only come by You, still, Lord, every time I turn around we face another threat. I don't have the answer Lord. I thought this was where You wanted them. Did You bring them here to die? And what about Sabah? Has she come to bring the rest of us more grief? You gave my mother the farm, I know You did, and we're only trying to use it to protect Your children, but first Amin, and then Masud, and now this? What do you want from me? What am I supposed to do?

Mohamed leaned over the side looking into the river for an answer. He heard the water sloshing, the clinking of the pulley against wood, and the creaking of the mast in the wind, but not the voice of God.

As a child, he'd seen men filled with hate destroy the home of Layla's parents. Sabah's brother would be back, bent on destruction. Was there no end to the madness? How long would it be before men realized God didn't call them to murder, or drive people from their homes? *Please Lord, let me see your face. Appear on your white stallion and tell me what to do*—the white stallion!—of course. *Thank You Lord. Thank You.*

He pulled himself up and began taking in the anchor, drawing the rope from the water hand-over-hand until the wet sack of rocks lay in the hull. Raising the sail, he dropped the rudder and turned the boat around, heading for shore.

Mohamed dove in silence, his mind deep in thought. He knew where he was going, but God hadn't revealed what they were supposed to do once they were there, or how long they were to stay. Layla sat beside him, her eyes open staring straight ahead, though the yellow beams of his headlights didn't reveal much. He'd told her of this place, but she'd never seen it. Sabah sat next to the window. Mohamed didn't know if she was awake or asleep.

He glanced in the rearview mirror but couldn't see the four new Christians sitting in the bed of the truck with sacks of food and other provisions in their laps. Maybe Nour was smart to leave when he did.

They were crossing the desert by night, using a road that hadn't been driven in years. It wasn't much to begin with, just a dirt track carved into the desert, and since the passing of his uncle it had sat fallow and wasting away. Sandstorms had buried entire stretches, hiding the road from view, and torrential rains had washed out other parts completely. The truck rolled over bumps, jostling the men in the back. Mohamed hit his brakes. A *fennec* raced in front of his tires.

Driving the thirty kilometers took an eternity—he'd had to stop several times to get out and find the road after it disappeared—but now the barn with its facade of hand painted tile, sat in the beam of his headlights. His uncle had called it, "Seventy Palms," because of the natural spring and the large number of palm trees that surrounded it but it was a really a shrine built for Sayyid's prized Arabian stallion. It was where his uncle held his mother prisoner. The memory of finding her bound to a chain barely long enough to reach the toilet, curdled his stomach. He swallowed, trying to push the image from his mind. Leaning forward, he switched off the key, shutting down the engine and killing the lights. The barn stood directly in front of him, its tiles shining in the glow of the moon.

"This is it ladies. We're here."

He let the door swing open, and climbed out of the truck, grabbing a flashlight from under the seat. The men scrambled over the sidewall and hit the ground. They would stay in the barn. There weren't any beds, but they'd brought blankets and providing the hay wasn't moldy, would find comfortable sleep. The girls would stay in the small residence where Zainab had been held prisoner.

Layla questioned the decision to leave her behind, but he insisted. It was inappropriate to leave Sabah alone with four men. Besides, Layla could help the new converts become established in their faith. He didn't tell her it was also for her own protection.

"There it is," he said. "It isn't much, but my mother called it home for twelve years. As I recall, I broke the lock off the door." He handed the flashlight to Layla. "You ladies go on in and make yourselves comfortable. There's no electricity, but I saw kerosene lamps and a stove the last time I was here, and there were cans of fuel in the cupboard. The important thing is, no one knows this place exists. You saw how hard it was for me to find, and I've been here before.

"Men, let's get everything out of the truck. The barn will still be locked but I have an answer for that." He walked to the door of the residence, and searching by the light of the moon, found a tire iron on the ground, just where he'd left it after rescuing his mother. "You can use this to pry the hasp from the barn door." He handed the tool to Masud. "I'm sorry I can't stay and help but I have to get back before Sabah's brother shows up. This time I'll let them in, and when they don't find Sabah, they'll dump on Uthman for making the story up."

CHAPTER 27

Be sober, be vigilant, because your adversary the devil walks around like a roaring lion, seeking whom he may devour. — 1 Peter 5:8

UTHMAN WAS GLAD to be sitting up front. The little red Fiat didn't have much of a back seat. He'd ridden all the way from Cairo to the farm with his long legs folded under his chin. And if that wasn't bad enough, the dimwitted oaf sitting beside him took up three quarters of the space, making him feel like a bug under a thumb. Being squished by the man who'd already nearly squeezed him to death, was an affront, but he'd deal with that later.

Now he was being shown the respect he deserved. Ahmed had made idle threats but couldn't back them up. It was *Uthman* who suggested they contact the Muslim Brotherhood, *Uthman* who knew the Brotherhood's representative in Asyut, *Uthman*, who by dropping the name of Sayyid El Taher, was able to get them an audience.

Ahmed stomped on the brakes, throwing Uthman against the dash. He lay on his horn, *beeeeeeeeeeeeeep*, and pulled around a taxi that had stopped in the middle of the road to collect a fare. He thrust his hand out the window, waving it in indignation. The Fiat continued weaving in and out of traffic like a needle stitching crochet.

The little car sputtered, the gray fumes of its exhaust contributing to the smog as it *puff, puff, puffed* along. Its paint was oxidized, its chrome pitted, and its seat covers coming apart, but it still ran, and it was the only car Ahmed's family owned.

"I think this is it," Uthman said.

Ahmed pulled to a stop in front of a tenement that matched the description given to Uthman over the phone. The century old building was crumbling, the plaster falling from the brick in huge mottled chunks. Someone had spray-pained graffiti on the walls. A wooden lean-to, probably the home of a vagrant, was perched on the flat roof. The building looked brownish-gray in the morning light. The man giving directions had said it was pink, but it was on the right side of the street, centered in the middle of the block, and looked like a square cube three stories high with a peaked arched entrance, so the description fit.

The car doors slammed, sounding like warbling sheets of tin. They got out and stood at the curb. Uthman arched his shoulders and stretched, easing his cramp. The car was too small even without Ubaid. His long beard dangled from his chin.

He had never seen so many children. They polluted the sidewalk, scurrying about screeching and chasing one another. Several danced around with their palms held out begging for coins, but he ignored them. Useless noisemakers, that's what they were. He didn't like kids.

They climbed the stairs to the top floor and marched down the hall. Two men stood outside leaning against the wall smoking cigarettes. They turned to block their approach.

"You have business here?" the taller of the two inquired, breathing smoke into Uthman's face. They stood eye to eye, but though Uthman matched his height, he still took a step back.

"We have an appointment to see Sharifa ah-din."

"I asked your business."

"I…I mean we, we want to discuss what's going on at the home of Sayyid El Taher."

Uthman's stomach jittered, his arms hot with perspiration, but the man turned and disappeared into the apartment closing the door behind him.

"Do not let my brother intimidate you," the shorter man said. "You are expected, but we must make sure Sharifa is ready to receive you."

The door behind him opened and the guard stood back allowing Uthman and Ahmed to enter. The room was formerly an apartment that had been transformed into an office. They stepped inside what used to be the living room, though the furniture had been removed. The walls were covered with shelves filled with commentaries on Islamic law. They were ushered past the library into one of the bedrooms where a man sat behind a desk reading a newspaper. He stood as they entered.

The man introduced himself as Sharifa ah-din, executive administrator for the Brotherhood in Upper Egypt. Uthman recognized him from his visits to the farm. Working in concert with Sayyid, he had overseen the deployment of martyrs for the cause. His face was that of a soldier, lean and hardened, with thick dark eyebrows and an abrasive day old beard, but he wore the robes of a cleric, with a circular flat-topped hat. Uthman knew he was a lower level functionary reporting to the General Masul.

But Sharifa's lower rank didn't diminish his authority. The Muslim Brotherhood was one of the strongest organizations in the Arab world. It had been founded in 1928 by an Egyptian schoolteacher, Hassan al-Banna, with the primary mission of restoring Islam by upholding Sharia law and, through Jihad, eradicating western ideologies which were believed to have contaminated the Muslim world. Sharifa was the Brotherhood's local linchpin, a man to go to when things needed to get done.

Sharifa stepped out from around his desk. The Brotherhood's creed was fastened to the wall behind him—a banner of blue linen embroidered with gold thread. The words read, "Allah is our objective; the Quran is our constitution, the Prophet is our leader;

Jihad is our way; and death for the sake of Allah, the highest of our aspirations."

"Please, sit," the man said, his hand gesturing to several large floor pillows.

Uthman and Ahmed did as they were asked, attempting to make themselves comfortable. Sharifa folded his legs and sat facing his guests.

"I hear you once worked with the great Sayyid El Taher. To what do I owe the honor."

Uthman bowed his head deferentially, his oversized turban momentarily hiding his face. "Please, the honor is all mine."

The cleric smiled and nodded. "Tell me, what is it I can do for you?"

"You mentioned Sayyid El Taher."

"A great man, yes, one about whom it can truly be said that Allah's gain is our loss."

"Then I'm sure you know of his efforts to restore Islamic rule. I was merely one of his servants, but he demanded of us strict adherence to the teachings of the Prophet. All who came into his employment were required to maintain stringent observance of Sharia law. But sadly, since his passing, things have changed. I come to you with a concern that greatly troubles me. His wife, the woman Zainab, now controls all he once possessed. She has a son…"

"Ah, Mohamed El Taher, a martyr for Allah. I am familiar with his story, and his tragic end. We had such great plans for him."

Uthman shook his head, his turban hovering over him like a cloud. "No, that is not of whom I speak. I also knew Mohamed. As a boy, he would often run through my crops, much to my dismay, but it is of his brother I speak, the one they call Matthew. He was raised in America, indoctrinated in all the ways of the West, and now lives with his mother."

Sharifa's eyes narrowed. His lips pinched together in a thin white line. "Yes, I have heard these rumors."

"Have you also heard he is bringing men to work the farm who were once Muslim but now embrace Christianity? He dares to hire these men and shelter them, even giving them a place of honor."

Sharifa's jaw tightened, his cheeks moving ever so slightly with the grinding of his teeth.

"It is true," Uthman continued. "I have seen this for myself. There are five that I know of. There were six but one recently met an unfortunate end, an accident made by these hands," he turned his palms up with a shrug. "And for this I have been unjustly fired. And my friend," he said, motioning to Ahmed, "has a sister who is being held there and forced to worship Isa."

Sharifa nodded slowly, his fingers forming a steeple as he brought them to his lips. "'They surely disbelieve who say Allah is one of three, when there is no God but the one God. If they desist not from so saying, a painful doom will fall on them.' The words of the Prophet Surah 5 verse 73." He paused, taking a breath. "Is it not enough that they call the Brotherhood an outlaw organization? Surely they think we are weak. They are fools. The strength of Allah is the Jihad, and the strength of Jihad is in men willing to die."

CHAPTER 28

When the righteous are in authority, the people rejoice: but when the wicked rule, the people mourn. — Proverbs 29:2

DUST LOOMED up in a cloud that blew across the driveway and settled on the fields cane. It looked to Mohamed like there had to be at least half a dozen cars. He held the curtain back to get a better view.

Gravel crunched under their tires as they slid to stop, the cars splayed out like the fingers of a glove. Two continued on, roaring down the road past the house disappearing into the distance. Uthman was in the passenger seat of the lead vehicle—Mohamed caught a glimpse of his billowy turban as they sped by—probably going after the crew laying pipe.

Car doors slammed, and the dust settled. Mohamed stepped back from the window, but kept watching from the side. The group huddled together, one man pointed toward the barn and bunkhouse. Five from the group split off and ran in that direction. The last contingent turned and marched toward the house. As far as Mohamed could see, only two of the men held rifles, but he was sure most, if not all, had knives girded under their sashes.

He turned and went to the living room, listening to the sound of their shoes clomping across the porch. The screen creaked. His heart raced. He waited for the knock, but it didn't come. The door flew open letting in a breath of musty air, warm and humid. Mohamed found himself facing an unshaven cleric.

The intruder glared at him but said nothing as he stepped into the room. He walked past Mohamed to the coffee table and paused to pick up a Bible, thumbing quickly through the pages before tossing it down.

He spun around. "It is reported you are teaching the way of Isa to who are born Muslim. This is against Sharia law."

Mohamed walked over, picked up the Bible, and held it out to the man. "It's okay. You can read it if you like. The Koran says: 'And we caused Jesus, son of Mary, to follow in their footsteps, confirming that which was revealed before Him, and we bestowed on Him the Gospel wherein is guidance and a light, confirming that which was revealed before in the Torah—a guidance and an admonition unto those who ward off evil.' I believe that's Surah 5, verse 46. The words of the Prophet. According to him the *Injil* contains guidance and light. Go ahead, read it." He held the book out a little further.

"Do not blaspheme, son of Isa."

Mohamed's arm dropped to his side. "If you're saying I'm a Christian, that's no secret. I was raised in the United States by a Christian family. My faith has followed me here, just as your faith would follow you if you went to America. But as for instructing others, this is my home, not a school. Look around you. There's no one here to teach."

The man smiled thinly and glanced at the two men behind him. Without a word they raised their rifles pointing them at Mohamed. "We shall see. Ahmed," he raised his chin, looking at the man standing behind him, "says you are holding his sister."

Mohamed shook his head, his bottom lip protruding. "If that's why you're here, I'm sorry you've wasted your time."

"As I say, we shall see." He looked back over his shoulder at one of his men, tipping his head to the side. The man lowered his rifle and started for the hall."

"I wouldn't do that if I were you."

The cleric raised his hand causing his man to stop. He eyed Mohamed suspiciously. "No? And, why not?"

Mohamed shrugged. "You may not like what you find."

The cleric's face relaxed. "Ah, perhaps it is you who will not like what we find." His expression grew serious again. "Do you not know, son of Isa, that the price of blasphemy is death. You may want to pray we don't find anyone back there, or I will have the pleasure of killing you myself."

That was all the mabaneth needed. He stepped around the corner followed by four soldiers armed with automatic weapons.

"Well, if it isn't my old friend, Sharifa ah-din. *Salam*, Sharifa. Pardon my intrusion, but I just heard you threaten a man's life."

Sharifa stepped back in surprise. He glanced at Mohamed, his eyes squinting, his face growing hard, and then back at the officer. "This is none of your business, Hossame, I suggest you take your men and leave."

"I'd like to do that, but you've put me in an awkward position. The Brotherhood's an illegal organization and I just heard you make threats to a man who, as far as I can tell, hasn't broken any laws."

"So now you defend Christians, Hossame? Your mother weeps in Paradise."

"I just uphold the law. I'll take those rifles if you don't mind."

Behind him the four soldiers raised their automatic weapons. It was a stand off, four MP5's against two Enfield bold action rifles. Sharifa's men stooped over, laying their weapons on the floor.

Mohamed eyed Hossame. Only a few days ago the same mabaneth didn't have time to run a thorough investigation. But today, Mohamed took a call from the mabaneth who told him about a tip he'd received regarding trouble at the El Taher estate. Then he'd volunteered to stop by and had been there within the hour. Somehow the mabaneth knew Sharifa would show up. It was obvious the two men had history.

"We're not going to let this get out of hand, Sharifa."

The mabaneth's eyes shifted to Ahmed. "You are free to search the house. If you find your sister, take her with you."

Ahmed took off. His feet could be heard tromping up and down the hall, searching every room. Doors were being opened and slammed shut. "You see, Sharifa, there is a lawful way of doing things, and an unlawful one. I suggest the next time you have complaint, you come to me."

Ahmed reappeared empty handed. "She's gone," he said.

Uthman and his cadre pulled to a stop at the construction site. The men climbed out of their cars and rallied around as he led them onto the bridge for a better view.

The channel now extended a fair distance into the field following a path through a section of cane that had already been cut. Several workers were digging at the far end. A long line of pipe was already laid in, waiting to be buried. *Bahhh.* He hawked up phlegm and spat. The workers were fifty yards up the trench with their backs turned away.

Uthman leaned toward the man standing beside him. "Grab those men and bring them here. Tell them Ostaz Matthew wants to see them, but don't mention my name. There's no need to make this more difficult than necessary. I'll be standing over there out of sight," he said pointing toward the cars. "If they see me, they may not be willing to come."

The men hopped down from the bridge and tromped off in the direction of the workers. An ox cart turned the corner. The wagon was empty, probably coming back from the barn. Two men, one on each side, held the harness of the ox, guiding it down the path.

Uthman turned his back, walking as far away from the road as possible hoping they wouldn't be inclined to stop. He heard the ox hoofs pounding the wood bridge, the wheels creaking as they passed by.

He waited until he saw the cart was well beyond the bridge, then spun around and made a beeline for the car, moving as fast as his spidery legs would allow. He was opening the door as he heard the sound of hoof-beats. He slipped inside, ducking down waiting until he could no longer hear the cart in the distance. He tipped his head up to see, and quickly sat upright. *That's my donkey!* His fist pounded the seat. *May God burn you!*

Sharifa's men were returning with the workers. He watched through the dusty windshield, examining each face as they stepped out from behind the trestle.

What? He flung the door open and squirmed out from behind the wheel. The tail of his long *galabia* got caught in the locking mechanism as he slammed the door, stopping him short. He spun around pounding the roof of the car. Yanking the handle back, he freed himself, and marched off toward the group.

"What is going on here?" he screamed, his hands fanning the air. "I want the irrigation crew, not these men. These men work for me!"

"You pointed at these men. You said to bring them."

About a dozen men were coming in from the field. Uthman looked around as several more joined them, hopping out from behind the tall cane. *What is this? It's that that little weasel, Hamadi.* There had to be twenty or more by the time the men reached the bridge. Hamadi wearing his baseball cap, stood in front.

"Why are you here, Uthman?" he said. "I thought we made it clear you should leave."

"I'm here to right a wrong." Uthman looked behind him. "First these Christians devise a scheme to replace your jobs, and now they have you working for them."

"No, we do this for ourselves. This watering system will make our jobs easier, not replace them."

"So where are the men that should be doing the work?"

"Every time you show up, there's trouble, Uthman. You're not welcome here. I suggest you go."

Hossame withdrew a cigarette, lit it, and placed the package back in his pocket. "So, here's the situation," he said. Smoke rolled into his eyes causing him to squint. He waved out the match and knocked an ash to the floor. "I can arrest you for making threats against this man, or you can leave peacefully. Your choice."

Sharifa glanced to the right, looking out the window. The two cars he'd sent to rout the Christians had returned and were pulling up in front of the house.

Mohamed could see the gears turning in Sharifa's head. He needed a way of ending this without losing face. "I think you've been misled," he said. "That man with the turban, the one getting out of the car, he used to work for me but I fired him and now he's trying to use you to get back at me. He knows if things go wrong, he'll walk away leaving you to take the blame."

Sharifa nodded. His mouth curled in a frown. "Perhaps we were misinformed," he said.

Hossame sandwiched his cigarette between his lips. Blue vapors swirled about his head. He nodded. "It's good to see we're on the same side." The cigarette bounced up and down as he spoke.

Sharifa ah-din nodded and turned to leave. His men bent down slowly, retrieving their guns, and fell in behind, followed by Sabah's brother.

Mohamed went to the door.

"They're gone," Uthman screamed. His hands were waving in the air, his beard swaying back and forth. His *galabia* flowed behind him caught on a breeze.

"So it would seem. Your friend here searched the house," Sharifa turned to Ahmed. "There is no woman inside."

"He has hidden them. Have you searched the barns? Come. We must force him to tell us where they are." Uthman started for the steps, but paused when no one followed. "Hurry, what are you waiting for?"

"That would be an act of aggression. Everyone knows the Brotherhood disavows violence. We are a peaceful organization. I came here to help you seek justice, not to hurt innocent people. That is not the way of the Brotherhood."

"*Bahhh.* This is a house of blasphemy. They must be punished."

Sharifa had begun walking toward his car, but he paused and turned around. "The man said you were recently fired, something you yourself admit. This gives you a reason to accuse him whether he is guilty or not. I will not raise my hand against the innocent."

The cleric climbed into his car, as did the others. Sabah's brother ducked into the little red Fiat and started the engine. He began backing out of the drive followed by one vehicle after another until Uthman was left standing alone. Uthman looked back over his shoulder at the house. "Wait," he yelled. He took off after them, running with his beard trailing behind him in the breeze.

Mohamed turned and nodded at the mabaheth. "Thank you," he said.

"Sharifa ah-din is a little fish in a big pond, but he does have influence. I'm glad he opted for the easy way out. Arresting him would have only caused me grief."

"Why did you? Help me, I mean. You defended a Christian over a Muslim. Not everyone would do that. In fact, not many."

"There's your mistake. You assume everyone's either a Muslim or a Christian. I am neither. I've seen too much bloodshed in the name of religion to believe in God. As far as I'm concerned, you can both blow yourselves up. I'm just here to do a job."

CHAPTER 29

Then they came to Elim, where there were twelve wells of water and seventy palm trees; so they camped there by the waters. — Exodus 15:27

THE TABLE was set with clean white linen, a vase of fresh cut roses, and a silver pitcher filled with cream. The sun, streaming through the window, was resting on Zainab's shoulders like a warm blanket. The breath of the morning was fresh, carrying with it the sweet smell of the cane harvest.

Mohamed sat across from his mother wolfing down a poached egg. "The crew at Seventy Palms will be anxious to get back." he said.

Zainab sipped her *shai*, the sun from the window highlighting her silver hair. She held her cup in both hands, warming her fingers. "I'm not sure that's a good idea. You yourself said Uthman will probably try something else. Why don't you see if you can hold them off, at least for a while?"

Mohamed's face puckered. "I miss Layla, but you're probably right. I doubt she'd mind staying another week. She's pretty nervous about all this. We'll see how it goes. Anyway, I have to get going. I promised to pick her up and take her to Asyut for supplies. It'll be nice to have some time together, give us a chance to talk." He popped the melon slice into his mouth realizing that such luxuries weren't available to those in hiding. It was a hard thing he was asking, but it had to be done.

... 🌙 ...

The sun rippled off the desert floor in waves of corrugated heat, a mirage of water flowing across the burning sand. The truck dipped into a hole. Mohamed grimaced as his backside landed hard on the flattened cushion. The chassis of the truck creaked.

The barn came into view, its tiles glinting in the sun. He eased up beside the corral and killed the engine, the motor *tick, tick, ticking* as it cooled. Hot air from the outside began to seep into the cab.

The natural spring that made this an oasis was off to his left, surrounded by palms. He couldn't say there were seventy, he'd never bothered to count, but there were enough. The vast majority were down by the water, but several grew closer to the barn.

It was midmorning, too hot to be outside, but he thought it odd no one rushed out to greet him. He let the door fall open and stepped out looking at the small residence attached to the side of the barn—his mother's prison for twelve years, where she'd been a slave on the end of a chain, used by Sayyid for personal gratification.

The women should be inside, but it seemed quiet. *What if...* He pushed the thought from his mind. They were safe here. The oasis was on private property. He and his mother were the only ones who knew it even existed.

The sun glinting off the tiles made him squint. Such foolish-ness—such vanity. His uncle had spent a fortune building a barn of hand painted tiles to house a horse, only to shoot the animal and end up using the palace as a prison. He tapped on the door.

The screech of taps shut off the flow of water. A few seconds later, Layla appeared. She stepped outside, blinked a few times and immediately went to her purse for her sunglasses. She slipped them on before closing the door behind her.

"Morning, *Habibty,* glad you could finally make it. I thought you'd be here sooner." She stood on her toes, giving him a quick peck on the cheek, and popped down, leaving him behind as she took off in the direction of the truck. "We're short of everything. I have a list so there's no point in fussing around. We need to get going." She kept walking, talking over her shoulder as her long dark ponytail bounced in the sun. It took him several long strides to catch up.

"Where are the others? I should let them know I'm here."

"Believe me, they know. You can hear a car coming for miles. It's spooky knowing your mother spent so many years in that shed. She must have been terrified every time she heard a car approach. I mean, because she would have known it was Sayyid. I can't imagine what that must have been like."

"All the same, I should probably say hi. Maybe they need us to pick up something for them."

"I have a list, remember?" Layla held up a slip of paper. "They're in the barn doing a Bible study and I promised not to let you interrupt." She climbed into the cab on the passenger side. *"Ouch,"* she said, fanning her fingers. "The seat's hot."

Mohamed shrugged. He pulled himself up to sit behind the wheel, but kept his foot on the running board with the door open to evacuate the hot air. He cranked the engine over. The truck didn't start with the ease of his Mercedes. It moaned, and took three tries, but the engine finally caught. At least the air conditioner was still cool. It immediately began discharging frosty air. He drew his foot in, slammed the door, and pulled away, making a large circle to head back the way he'd come.

"You missed it," Layla said, turning her head toward the barn. "We had an incident this morning. Sabah went out to the spring, insisting on getting water for the men. We have running water in our quarters, but there's nothing in the barn, so she grabbed a bowl and went outside, thinking to be nice and help out, but Masud was already there taking a bath.

"Sabah screamed and I thought she'd seen a snake. I came running outside but she was too flustered to say anything, and when the men came rushing out of the barn, they thought we'd been discovered and were in a panic, until Sabah started pointing and they saw Masud climbing out of the water and realized what happened. Everyone broke out in hysterics. Poor Sabah, she was so embarrassed. I felt guilty laughing about it, but it was hilarious." Layla had her hand to her chest as though still trying to contain her amusement. "But don't say anything, okay? That's why she didn't want you going inside. She's afraid someone will say something and she doesn't want it brought up again. I just had to let you know so you wouldn't think it's all dull and boring out here."

"Is Masud teaching?"

"I think so."

Mohamed smiled. "I think it would be more embarrassing for him, than for Sabah. Every time she looks at him, he's bound to wonder what she's thinking."

Mohamed wove through the suburbs of Asyut, the traffic thick as honey, rolling slowly. Layla's song was fresh in his mind, her voice still humming in his ear. All the way through the desert she had sung songs of praise, reducing the stress he felt over the uncertainty of their situation. He had to wonder if God, in some mysterious way, hadn't given her an overabundance of songs to make up for what he lacked.

No, that didn't work. God desired everyman's praise. They might, in the biblical sense, be one flesh, but the fact that she always sang didn't somehow make up for the fact that he couldn't.

It wasn't that he didn't want to sing. Sometimes he could feel the songs bursting from his heart, but the words always got caught in his throat. It probably had something to do with what that Russian guy, Pavlov, called a "conditioned response." If dogs could be made to salivate when they heard the ringing of a bell just because they'd previously heard a bell when they ate, then he could understand how, if he associated singing with violence, it might be difficult for him to sing. He'd prayed about it, but until God decided to fix the glitch in his brain, he would have to depend on Layla for his songs.

He'd dropped her at the market. The combined grocery and mercantile would have the bulk of what she was looking for. It was where the servants usually did their shopping. The owner made a point of stocking the items the farm needed most.

Layla had her list but when she tried to get Mohamed to join her, he begged off saying he wanted to visit an electronics store and see what it might cost to get a solar panel to charge the battery of the laptop, and maybe a satellite dish. If Masud was going to teach, he would need access to on-line resources.

"That's not nice," Layla said. "You know I'm not comfortable wandering around Asyut alone, not with all that's happened."

Mohamed smiled. "You'll be fine. I just need an hour. I'll probably be back even before then. I want to be on the road before sundown so I don't have to navigate the desert after dark."

"You'd better. I'm holding you to it. One hour, no exceptions. It won't take me that long to pick up these few things." She turned and hopped down from the cab, walking away with her short heels clicking on the pavement. She looked back over her shoulder, waving as she blew him a parting kiss. Her hair, flicked by a sudden breeze, looked glossy in the morning sun. He smiled. *Such a rebel.* Blowing kisses just wasn't done in public.

The store was small, with boxes of miscellaneous electronic parts cluttering the aisles. Squeezing through was a challenge, and only worth doing because the sign in the window said they specialized in internet connections.

The man behind the counter at the back of the store was lighting one cigarette off the butt of another. He exhaled a cloud of blue smoke through his missing front teeth and snuffed out the old butt in a sardine can. His hair was oily and matted, his cheeks unshaven, and his eyes weighted down with sacs that seemed to ooze water.

"Welcome, welcome. What is it you are looking for? Whatever it is, I'm sure we have it. We carry a huge inventory."

"I'm looking for a satellite dish and solar panel. I want to be able to connect to the internet from a remote location. You have anything like that?"

The man rubbed his grizzled chin, thought for a moment, and then nodded. "Just one minute." He disappeared into a room behind him and returned with a dish about a foot in diameter, but it was just a dish, no cables, or mounting bracket, or the box in which it came, or instructions. The man placed it on the counter.

Mohamed picked it up turning it over. It had a set of military numbers stenciled on the back.

"Army? No, I don't think this is what I'm looking for."

"I beg to disagree. This is Israeli equipment. You know how those Israelis are, high tech everything. It was removed from a disabled tank by a close friend of mine. If anyone knows how to transmit information, it's the Israelis."

"That's fine, but I'm looking for a dish to transmit internet signals. That one was probably used for radio."

"A signal is a signal. I'm sure you can make it work."

Mohamed shook his head. "Do you have anything else? The sign in the window said you do internet connections."

"DSL only." The man gave him a toothless smile. "All you need is a telephone line."

"If I had a telephone line, I wouldn't need a satellite dish. How about a solar panel? I need something I can use to charge the computer's battery?

The man shook his head. "How about a computer? I have many very good used computers in practically new condition. Very good prices. The lowest anywhere."

"I have a computer, thanks. I want to get hooked up to the internet."

The man took a drag off his cigarette and placed in on the pile in the can. He shook his head, breathing smoke out his nose. "Maybe you come back tomorrow. I'll ask around and see what I can find for you."

Mohamed nodded, but he knew he wouldn't be back.

Layla brushed by a woman in a full-body *burka* with a cell phone to her ear. If the head-covering hadn't masked the woman's face, she might have recognized her as one of Zainab's kitchen staff. The woman seemed to be watching her through her veil.

She continued outside with her arms full, trying to manage the load. She had enough beans to feed an army; she also had several two foot long salamis, salted fish, and plenty of dried fruits, nuts and cereals. She even bought a metal pail for carrying water. Mohamed had urged her to buy food for at least a week, but that was short term thinking. Once things settled down, she would take him aside and propose the idea of moving back to the States.

She set her bags down at the curb and rubbed her palms, glancing at her watch. It hadn't been quite an hour, but it was a bright warm day and the sun felt good. She didn't mind waiting.

Mohamed pulled up and stopped in front of the market. Several bags were sitting at the curb, but he didn't see Layla. He glanced around. The horn of the car behind him was blaring. He couldn't sit holding up traffic. He glanced over his shoulder one last time as he pulled away.

He did two rounds before deciding to go inside and let Layla know he was there. The sign said parking was for tenants only. If he hurried, he'd make it back before anyone noticed his car didn't have the right sticker.

The bags were still at the curb. A beggar sat a few feet away with his back against the wall, holding out his hand. He was blind, a permanent fixture of the store, as regular as the sun when it shines. Mohamed reached into his pocket and removed a five pound note, dropping it into the man's hand as he passed by.

Walking up and down the aisles, he began checking out the produce and dry goods expecting to see Layla, but she wasn't there. He paced the store one more time, taking longer strides, his concern growing. She wasn't in the store.

He went back outside, looking down the street. The crowds were thick, a mix of *hijabs* and business suits meandering in and out of traffic. She could be anywhere. He looked at his watch. It was fifteen minutes beyond the time they'd agreed to meet. His eyes fell on the bags at the curb, only this time he saw something he hadn't noticed before. His heart began thudding in his chest. Sitting beside one of the bags, spilled over like it had been recklessly tossed aside—was Layla's purse.

CHAPTER 30

Hear, you deaf; and look, you blind, that you may see.

— Isaiah 42:18

BEADS OF SWEAT broke out on Mohamed's forehead. He stooped over picking up Layla's handbag, inspecting it more closely. Blood was rushing to his head, his eyes throbbing. It was definitely hers. For a moment the street became blurry, the cars, people, and buildings losing resolution. He shook his head and felt a sharp pain. *No!* He wasn't going to accept that. She was there, somewhere, had to be. He blinked and swallowed hard, his mouth like sandpaper. He whipped his head around searching the street. He could feel a pulsing at his temples. His eyes slowly regained focus.

The sidewalk was as crowded with pedestrians as the street was with cars—the incessant honking, conversations, and bustle of shoes on cement—a constant flow of human noise. His sweat began to pour. He didn't see Layla anywhere.

He spun around and rushed back into the store, running up and down each aisle, convincing himself she had to have gone back inside. He must have somehow missed her. He approached the front counter, still holding her purse.

"*Hal beemkanek mosa'adati.* Can you help me? I'm looking for someone, a Christian woman in a blue dress, not a *hijab*. This is her purse." Mohamed thrust the handbag into the man's face.

The man stepped back and nodded, but seemed tentative. "Yes, the woman was here, but she bought much food and left."

"Did you see where she went?"

The man raised a hand, pointing with his finger. "She went outside; that is all I know."

Mohamed spun around suddenly realizing the store's entrance was at an angle, preventing the proprietor from seeing beyond the door.

He rushed outside again shouldering his way through the crowds. *Alma'derah!* excuse me, excuse me. He stopped, taking a moment to scan the street—*nothing*—then began rummaging through Layla's bags. There was no question they were hers. Salami, breads, beans, it was everything on her list.

"You are seeking someone?"

Mohamed raised his head looking around, but the people passing by didn't stop. *The blind man?* "Did you say something?"

"I asked for whom you were seeking."

"My wife. I was to meet her. She left her things at the curb, but she's not here."

"This is because someone took her."

"What? *What* did you say?"

"I am blind," the man said, "but Allah gives me ears to see. I hear things others do not. This makes up for the loss of my eyes." People continued to pass the man by without rewarding his outstretched hand.

Mohamed stood and reached into his pocket for another five pound note. He walked over placing it into the man's dirty palm. "If you have something to say, say it."

The man grinned broadly, taking the money and folding it before tucking it into a leather pouch. "I heard your wife come out of this store. I know she is either a tourist, or Christian, but not Muslim. Do you know how I know? Because her feet clicked the pavement with the sound of a shoe with a small heel. See, I can identify many things without eyes." He smiled. His teeth were as brown as his eyes were white. "She stood only for a moment when a car stopped. This I know because I heard the brakes screech, and I also heard the door open and someone climb out. The woman at the curb, she seemed not to notice, but then I heard a struggle and the woman started to say something but her voice was muffled like someone covered her mouth. The next thing I heard was the sound of doors slamming and the car left like it was in a hurry.

"Are you sure? Are you absolutely certain they took the woman?"

"Quite certain, yes."

"How?"

"Because, as the car pulled away, I heard the woman scream."

For a second Mohamed froze. He swallowed, feeling his temples throb, and then drew back. "Who? *Who* did this?" The beggar started to shrug but Mohamed was already rushing back to the curb. He scooped up the bags, took off running and didn't stop until he reached the truck. Flinging the door open, he threw everything onto the seat, climbed in, and ground the engine to a start.

Mohamed used his windshield wipers to clean the glass. He had the air conditioner off and the windows rolled down. After driving through the desert, his windows on both sides were layered in yellow dust and he needed to see. He plowed his way through downtown traffic, using his own horn as much as those around him. His head was swiveling back and forth looking for any car that might have a woman in back.

This couldn't be happening—not that Uthman wouldn't do such a thing, Uthman was capable of anything—but this was the second time Layla had been taken hostage. The Americans had a saying, "lightning doesn't strike twice in the same place." Layla had already been kidnapped once, while living in the States. His fist pounded the wheel. How could God let it happen again? Did anyone ever get kidnapped twice?

It was his fault—his vendetta against Uthman, his actions, his pride, had put the one he loved in jeopardy. *Just the way it happened before!* She'd warned him, but he'd been too self-absorbed to listen. God wants us here, he'd argued. Did God really want them putting their lives at risk?

How did Uthman know where Layla was? As quick as he thought it, he knew the answer. The store he'd taken her to was where the farmhands shopped for supplies. Layla had dropped into Uthman's lap like a gift. Mohamed grit his teeth chipping away at the enamel. And all because he'd refused to stay with her. He'd gone to a stupid electronics store, leaving his wife unprotected.

Dust scattered up behind the truck as he turned into the drive bouncing over potholes and washboards in his race for the house. He pulled to the front, slammed on the brakes and skid to a stop, and with the engine still running, jumped out taking the porch steps two at a time. He flung the door open.

Zainab was sitting on the sofa wearing light blue *hijab*. She usually wore her hair pinned up, but this time, probably because she was alone, her silver tresses fell loose on her shoulder. She looked up, her eyes expressing surprise at her son's intrusion.

"Have you heard anything from Layla?"

"Why would I hear from Layla; isn't she with you?"

"Yes, I mean…I did a really stupid thing. I dropped Layla at the mercantile and left her alone because I had to take care of something else, but when I came back she was gone. Her purse and bags were at the curb but she wasn't around. The beggar who sits there heard a car pull up. He said there was a struggle and someone grabbed her and took her away. He said he heard her scream."

Zainab stood, the newspaper in her lap sliding to the floor.

"They got Layla, Mother. Someone kidnapped your daughter-in-law. It had to be Uthman. He probably saw the truck and started following me, or he was already there, I don't know, but…it had to be him, and that Ahmed character, the brother of Sabah."

"Why would they do such a thing?"

"I don't know, revenge maybe, or maybe they want to trade her for Sabah. Please, just pray." He spun around heading down the hall.

"Where are you going?"

"To call the police."

The car squeaked and rattled as it raced down the road, tossing Layla to and fro. She worked at counting the turns, left, right, stop, trying to draw a mental map of where they were going. She'd been thrown inside and had her head forced down between her knees with her hands flat on the carpet. The man beside her, holding her in place, smelled of sheep manure and his body took up most of the space. The car turned onto a long stretch of road, leaving her with nothing to listen to but the relentless drone of the tires.

By now, Mohamed would have been to the mercantile and discovered she was missing. He would be searching for her—*God, please help him find me.* She'd always prayed for him, not herself, not that she didn't need prayer but she wasn't the one taking risks. Now he'd see why she'd fought coming to Egypt in the first place.

Exhaust fumes seeped throught the floorboard making her nauseous. She noticed the ring on her finger, just a simple band of gold, nothing fancy, but the most valuable thing she owned.

She had wanted to be married in the States, surrounded by family and friends. She'd envisioned walking down the aisle in a white gown through a gauntlet of flowers with Mendelssohn's Wedding March booming from the organ. But Mohamed wanted to be married in Egypt. He didn't have anyone to invite. His childhood friends were Muslims, and they all thought he was dead. The only guest he wanted was his mother, but she'd never been on a plane and flatly refused to fly.

They'd settled on Greece. Layla and her parents boarded a plane and flew into Athens, while Mohamed and his mother caught a ship out of Alexandria and sailed across the Mediterranean.

A tip from a tour guide led them to a small basilica on the Via Egnatia, the second century Roman road that crossed the provinces of Illyricum, Macedonia, and Thrace. The church, with its ancient bell tower, was erected over the crypt of Adalfo Crynerus, to whom the church was dedicated. It was pre-Byzantium, with stone walls that supported a high vaulted ceiling. Candlelight illuminated a mosaic floor of hand painted ties depicting the Last Supper surrounded by a collage of Christian symbols.

They couldn't have asked for a more romantic site, especially in view of their desire to serve Christ. The story of the thousands who, over the centuries, had lived and died defending their faith inside those hallowed walls was an encouragement and a blessing.

Layla was radiant in her white wedding gown, which she insisted on wearing even though her friends weren't there to witness her vows. She chose to read a passage from the first chapter of Ruth: "Entreat me not to leave you, or turn back from following you, for wherever you go, I will go; and where you lodge, I will lodge, your people shall be my people, and your God my God."

And Mohamed, in his rented black tux, selected an adaptation from Proverbs 31: "Who can find a virtuous wife? The heart of her husband safely trusts in her. She will do him good all the days of her life. Favor is deceitful, and beauty is vain, but a woman who fears the Lord shall be praised."

And when they kissed the candles flickered all at once, revealing the presence of God.

A tear leaked from Layla's eye. If she was about to die at least she'd have the joy of knowing Mohamed as her husband, however short the time. *No!* She and Mohamed had just begun their life together. She swallowed. Her abductors were not going to take that away. *God help me, please...*

CHAPTER 31

For out of the heart proceed evil thoughts, adulteries, fornications, murders. — Mark 7:21

MOHAMED HUSTLED down the hall to the office and picked up the phone, turning to see his mother standing at the door. He caught her eye just as the phone was answered.

"Yes, can I speak with Hossame El-Din, please…He's not? When do you expect him?…Okay, just let him know Matthew Mulberry called, and tell him it's urgent…Alright, *Shokran, Ma'asalama.*"

His eyes continued to hold his mother's. "I tried to notify the police but I had to leave a message." He felt the lump in his throat as he put the phone down. "I'm headed back to Seventy Palms. If the kidnappers call, try to find out what they want. We can't give them Sabah. There has to be another way. I have Layla's purse, so I have her cell but there's no reception at the oasis. I'll try to call as soon as I can."

"And I will continue to pray."

Mohamed raced down the highway, his gut fizzing like seltzer. If he knew where Sabah lived, he'd already be pounding on her parents' door.

He checked to make sure no one else was on the road before pulling onto the dirt track and heading out across the desert. Dust plumed up from the skirts of his truck, but the wind was brisk and carried it away quickly leaving no trace of his passing.

He squinted, trying to relieve the strain on his eyes. The truck had run out of wiper fluid, and the sun's glare through the dust on the window made it hard to see. *Ooufff*, the truck bounced over another rut, his head nearly hitting the roof. One of the bags of groceries spilled, dumping its contents to the floor. He reached down to find an onion rolling around his feet.

What filled Uthman with so much hate? He found the onion and brought it up, examining it for bruises before tossing it onto the seat. Was it Islam? No, he of all people knew better than that. He knew many good Muslims. And there were bad Christians. No, it had more to do with Satan's agenda, than any particular doctrine.

It was Satan who in the guise of a serpent seduced Adam and Eve, which ultimately brought death on the entire planet. Christ called Satan a murderer from the beginning. He said Satan had come to kill and destroy. So yes, Satan had an agenda. He hit another bump, *ugghhh!* If he didn't slow down, he might not arrive at all. Satan just wanted people dead. He wanted unbelievers dead so they would never have a hope of knowing Christ, and he wanted believers dead so they couldn't tell others how Christ had come to give them life.

Uthman wanted Amin dead—*"You are of your father the devil, and the lusts of your father you will do. He was a murderer from the beginning"*—and he would have killed Mohamed, and his entre family, had the mabaneth not intervened. Now there was a conundrum, an atheist with more concern for the preservation of life than a man who claimed to serve God. But that was the point. The God Uthman served was the God of death, not the God of life.

The barn emerged out of the hazy heat, its tiles glistening in the sun. He pulled up alongside the fence and once again jumped out leaving the engine running. He didn't plan to stay long. He went around to the passenger side and opened the door, scooping handfuls of spilled beans and greens back into the bags until his arms were full. It was all he could do to balance the load as he headed for the barn. It appeared the place was deserted, but there was no reason for people to be outside. Except for the palm trees that shaded the oasis, the only thing the property had to offer was the natural spring.

The shed and barn would be excruciatingly hot. But the barn, being bigger, would be less stuffy than the shed, especially since both wagon doors were now open.

The men were clustered around Masud who held Layla's Bible in his lap. They jumped up, taking the bags from his arms. "See that these get into the shed," he said. "Sabah, I need to talk to you. It's important."

But the men surrounded him jabbering all at once.

"*Wahashtena,* we missed you."

"We are reading the Bible. Come join us."

"Are we going home?"

"Where is Layla?"

"Did you remember the pita?"

"Quiet everyone, please, I beg your patience. No, you cannot return yet, and as much as I'd like to stay and talk, I'm right now in the middle of another crisis. I'm sorry, but we'll have to catch up later. Sabah, I need to speak with you in private for a moment." He handed the last remaining bag to Masud and ducked outside, raising his hand to hold everyone back. The men shook their heads muttering, but stayed where they were. Sabah followed him out into the sun. "How are you doing?" he said, trying his best to be patient and not let his concern for his wife overshadow the needs of others.

Sabah bowed her head, choosing to stare at the ground rather than directly at him. "I'm fine," she said, "but I miss Amin." She raised her eyes, looking around. "But where is Layla?"

"That's what we need to talk about. First, I want you to promise you won't tell the others what I'm about to say. I don't want anyone becoming anxious or worried or insisting that they have to jump in and help. Everyone needs to remain calm and stay here where it's safe. Can you promise me you won't say anything?"

Her eyes drooped, heavy with sadness, but she nodded.

"Okay. Layla isn't here because I think your brother and my former foreman have kidnapped her. I think they want to trade her in exchange for you."

Sabah stiffened, her eyes widening. "Then I must go at once and turn myself over to them and get Layla released."

"You'll do no such thing. I'm not taking you with me and that's final. And if you try to cross the desert on your own, the heat will kill you, so just get that idea out of your head. But I do need your help. I need to know if you can think of any place they might try to keep her. Some place your brother might try to hold someone hostage."

"I know what they did with me. They locked me in the bedroom."

"That was my first thought too, and it might be where she is, but you escaped, plus they'd know that would be the first place I'd look so I doubt they'd keep her there. Is there anywhere else you can think of?"

Sabah shook her head, her face blank, but then her eyebrows furrowed and she squinted as though wrestling with a troubling thought. "Yes, I know where she is," she said. "My cousin, he works in a cement factory in Asyut, that is how he makes his living, but he also raises sheep for extra money. He has a place just outside Asyut where he takes the sheep to be sheared. There's a shack there. It's small but it's windowless." Her voice grew quiet and she turned her eyes away. "It has a lock on the door. This is where they would take her."

Mohamed's heart began to race. The back of his neck felt prickly. Twice before, once for his mother, and once for Layla, God had led him to the right place. Whether it was God speaking now, he couldn't say, but in his spirit, Sabah's words rang true. "You're sure?"

Sabah nodded, but kept her eyes averted. "Yes, my cousin took me there once. I was very young. He said he wanted to show me his sheep, but…when we got there he desired to molest me…but my brother came looking for me." She caught Mohamed's eye. "That's where they would take her. I'm sure of it. Please, promise me you won't hurt my brother…"

Mohamed felt like he was going around in circles: from the farm to Seventy Palms to Asyut, to the farm to Seventy Palms to Asyut, but that didn't matter. Asyut was closer than Cairo, which was where he'd be heading next if this didn't pan out.

He knew the exact place Sabah described. It was a small wood shack built at the top of a knoll just off the main highway. He'd seen it dozens of times and never given it a second thought. There were even pens for holding sheep.

He reached over and felt the tire iron, the metal rough and cold to his touch. He was glad he'd had the good sense to toss it into the truck before leaving. It was for his protection. He wasn't worried about them having a gun, but they might have knives.

He turned onto the dirt driveway, giving the throttle only enough gas to keep the truck coasting for about a hundred yards, and then cut the engine and rolled quietly to a stop without using the brakes. The shed was still another thirty meters ahead, with a vehicle parked to the side, which meant someone was there.

He slipped out of the truck, his heart pounding as he closed the door making sure the latch didn't make a sound. Picking up his feet he moved quietly, thankful there weren't any sheep whose bleating might warn those inside.

His hands felt sweaty. He wiped them on his pants and realized he'd forgotten to grab the tire iron. He turned, looking back at the truck—he'd come too far. *Please God, give me strength.* He crept up to the shed, afraid of making a noise those inside might hear. Sabah was right, there were no windows. The only opening was the shabby wood door made of boards that were too short. There were wide gaps at the top and bottom. He felt the adrenalin rushing through his veins as he stood to the side making sure his feet weren't seen as he leaned in to listen. He heard something that sounded like a voice, but the words were muffled. It was Layla! He threw the door open and bolted inside.

What he saw ripped his heart from his chest. His wife lay in the dirt with her hands tied behind her and a gag in her mouth. Her eyes were closed, but she opened them wide, causing Uthman who was on top of her, holding her by the hair, to spin his head around and smile the most wicked smile Mohamed had ever seen. His lips emitted a groan, his eyes rolling to the top of his head.

Mohamed lunged at Uthman grabbing him by the neck, dragging him off. He pulled back, feeling the hair of Uthman's beard caught under his fingers as he squeezed Uthman's skinny throat, his own eyes becoming blurry as he directed all his strength to his hands.

Uthman struggled kicking and flaying with his arms trying to reach back to hit Mohamed, his eyes bulging from their sockets, his lungs already raw from the choking they'd received from Ubaid. He grasped Mohamed's fingers, trying to pull them off but they were clamped around his throat like a vice. His breath extinguished, he began to weaken. Mohamed felt the surrender and squeezed tighter. In a moment, Uthman would be gone.

He heard Layla and opened his eyes. She was shaking her head and trying to scream through the rag in her mouth *"Mmmnnooooooooo..."*

He released his grip on Uthman and stepped back, staring at his hands as Uthman sank to the ground, coughing and gasping in spurts. On impulse, Mohamed reached down and yanked the ridiculous oversized turban from his head and kicked it out the door.

Score! He hadn't made a kick like that since college. He started to raise his hands in a victory dance, but Layla grunted, interrupting his reverie.

He lunged for his wife tugging her skirt down to cover her violation while bringing a hand up to remove the gag from her mouth. He struggled to hold her as he reached around to untie her wrists.

"Ohhhhhhhhhhh, God, Ohhhhhh" was all she managed to say.

But it wasn't over. A shadow filled the door. Instinctively Mohamed turned. The silhouette of a giant stepped inside followed by Ahmed. The larger man reached behind him and produced a knife. He lunged at Mohamed.

Mohamed let go of Layla and turned to block the man's thrust, taking a slice in the arm. He managed to grab the wrist of the larger man before he could bring his arm back for another strike. Mohamed felt himself being lifted to his feet. He kept both hands on the man's wrist and lost his wind as the man's other fist plowed into his side.

He gasped, unable to breathe, but he refused to let go. The man brought the dagger overhead pulling Mohamed with him. *Please, God, help!* The arm came down in a powerful thrust but Mohamed turned the wrist, twisting the blade so that it went to the man's own side. The man's eyes popped open. He gurgled, *auggggggg.*

Mohamed released the man and jumped back.

Ubaid looked down and pulled the knife from his side. He tried to raise it over his head again but *groaned*, and instead, buckled at the knees. He dropped the knife, grabbing his side as he fell.

Mohamed turned to face a possible challenge from Ahmed but Ahmed backed up and fled out the door. Mohamed spun back around. Uthman scooted back looking rather silly without his turban. He coughed as he tried to raise his arm protectively.

Mohamed heard a car. He saw a red streak sweep by the door as the vehicle sped away. He staggered over and picked up the knife, flinging it outside, and inhaled to catch his breath, realizing for the first time how the room was ripe with the smell of sheep manure. His arms felt weak, his forearm dripping blood as he scooped Layla up, holding her with one hand under her shoulders and the other under her knees. *Déjà vu.* He'd done this before—another place, another time—*Oh Lord, is this to be our lot?*

Ubaid held his side and tried to push himself up, but only succeeded in flopping onto his back. He lay in the dirt staring up at Mohamed, his breathing labored.

Mohamed stepped toward the door but before exiting, turned to look at Uthman. "You can shear a sheep many times, but you can only skin him once," he said. Then he stumbled out the door. Ahmed had disappeared, but he would be back as soon as it looked safe. They would have to get their friend to the hospital on their own. He was taking Layla home.

CHAPTER 32

Let lying lips be put to silence, which speak grievous things proudly and contemptuously against the righteous. — Psalm 31:18

THE TEMPERATURE in the room was a mild seventy degrees, but Layla sat on the edge of the bed wrapped in a blanket, trembling like she was cold. Mohamed sat beside her, trying to lighten her heart, but his words couldn't penetrate the darkness. She wasn't ready to listen. She sat staring into the void, oblivious to everyone and everything around her, her mind a daze.

She'd been there all evening. After arriving home, he'd taken her by the hand and led her inside. She hadn't fought him, nor had she welcomed his assistance, she'd simply stumbled behind him like a zombie unaware of its own mortality. He seated her on the bed and tried to explain to his mother what had happened. Layla did not provide input, or offer explanation. She had entered another world and locked the door, shutting everyone else out.

His mother cautioned him, saying he needed to give Layla space and the time to work through her emotions herself, promising him she would respond when she was ready. Being violated was as much a mental degradation as it was physical.

It was after midnight when he finally lay back with his arm bent over his forehead, staring into the darkness. Never had he felt so useless, so inadequate, so completely incapable of understanding. Amin was dead, Sabah and the Christian brothers in hiding, Layla a victim of…rape! Everything was crashing down around him, evil carrying the day. *Why God, wwhhhyyyyyyy? Please don't let this be about my brother.* He reached up to massage Layla's back. Her hair felt warm and soft to his touch. If it wasn't for him she'd be sunning herself by her parent's pool in California.

He hadn't meant to fall asleep but the long day, and mild evening temperatures, and the weariness in his bones, made his eyes heavy. They slid closed and before he knew it, fluttered open to a room dusted with predawn light.

He sat up. Layla hadn't moved.

"You're still awake?"

She didn't respond.

Mohamed struggled to his feet and yawned. "Are you hungry?"

No response.

He heard voices, and went to the window to look outside. Several men were walking through the morning fog with their prayer rugs under their arms. Would the God they worshipped expect them to forgive, the way the God of the Bible did? All the way home he'd struggled to control his hatred of Uthman. "Love your enemies, turn the other cheek, be kind to those who despitefully use you," concepts difficult to grasp, let alone put into practice.

One by one, the workers disappeared into the mist like ghostly aberrations. He shook his head. Sometimes being a Christian was hard. He made his way around the bed, returning to check on Layla. Her eyes came up to meet his, but then turned away.

"I wish I would have let you kill him," she mumbled.

"Don't say that." He grimaced, feeling his stomach churn. He'd wanted the same thing. Uthman was a destroyer. *No!* Uthman was just a tool in Satan's hand, a man full of selfishness and pride, no different than he himself. A year ago, he was plotting to kill hundreds. Had Layla not introduced him to Isa and the God of the Bible, he would have carried out his mission believing he was doing God a favor. Uthman just didn't know any better.

"They'll be preparing breakfast. Can I get you a cup of tea?"

"I'm sorry I said that. I didn't mean it." Layla shook her head.

"I know. Is there anything I can do for you? Can I get you anything?"

"No. I just want to be left alone."

He nodded. "Okay, I'm going out for a few minutes, but I won't be long. I'll ask Mother to check in on you in case you need anything." He leaned over to kiss his wife's cheek but she turned her head away. *What?* He straightened himself, arching his back to stretch the kinks. At least she was talking.

Mohamed sauntered down the hall to the kitchen. Two ladies wrapped in *hijabs* were assembling the morning meal. His eyes were drawn to a corner cabinet. He walked over and opened it, and there, down at the bottom, was a soccer ball, just where he'd left it. He pulled it out, balanced it on his finger and gave it a spin, watching it whirl as he kicked off his shoes and walked outside. Here, with the wind in his hair, the ball at his feet, and earth, water, and sky melded into one, he could forget his problems, if only for a moment.

He kicked the ball, keeping it in control, watching it spin down the path. The ball dipped into a runnel and bounced out on the other side causing him to veer off course to recapture it. The grass along the banks of the river tickled his feet.

He'd spent nearly all his summers practicing soccer down by the Nile. He had dreamed of one day becoming a star, of hearing people in the stands chanting his name and being surrounded by fans clamoring for his autograph. And for a brief period, he'd seen the dream fulfilled. But those days were gone. He'd traded his soccer ball for a fishing pole. The praises of men were no longer important. He wanted the accolades of God. He leaned over and picked up the ball as he continued to walk along the shore.

When I was a child, I did childish things but when I became a man I put such things aside... Soccer was only a game, but—he dropped the ball and kicked it down the path—it was also good exercise.

He didn't realize how far he'd gone until he stumbled upon the construction site. Picking up the ball he placed it under his arm. The new trench now extended about ten meters into the field, with dirt piled along its ridge where lengths of pipe were being assembled. It appeared they were doing an excellent job.

He glanced up to see three men approaching, though they were a fair distance off. They stopped to inspect a stand of cane. He wasn't in the mood for conversation. Stepping off the path, he disappeared into the field, the stalks towering over his head. What they'd accomplished was marvelous, digging trenches and laying pipe, but he still needed to hire an engineer. Installing tanks to hold the water, utilizing the right combination of pumps and valves, and maintaining the correct water pressure for distribution through the network of pipes, required technical expertise.

The point was, he was creating jobs, not eliminating them. He had another project already in mind. They needed apartments for the men and their families. Married workers stayed on the farm all week, going home to visit their families only on their days off. Their children were growing up without fathers, and that wasn't right. He wanted to bring their families here. One way or another, he planned to show these men the love of Christ.

He cut across several rows making his way back to the path. The morning dew dampened his shirt as he moved through the plants. It was a relief to step back into the open. He brushed himself off and looked up. Sami was hobbling toward him, his bald head and bowed legs giving him the look of a walking bowling pin.

His mother's *khadem* slowed and staggered his last few feet, bowing over with his hands on his knees, out of breath.

"What is it Sami? Is Layla all right?"

"Yes, yes, she is fine, I think," he said, though panting hard. "It is a phone call for you, from *el shorta*. The policeman said you must call him at once."

"The police?" Mohamed placed his hands on his hips, arching his back as he began walking with Sami toward the house. "Why would the police want me?" In his mind he saw the mabaneth showing him evidence that would put Uthman in jail. He'd toyed with the idea of accusing Uthman of rape, but he knew it would be futile. Rape was a charge that seldom resulted in a conviction. Men had the right to subdue their women. And even if a charge of rape could be laid, once they realized it was a Muslim man taking advantage of a Christian woman, the charges would disappear, either that, or be twisted around to where it appeared Layla was guilty of seducing Uthman. He couldn't put Layla through that.

They entered the house. The smell of boiled eggs filled the kitchen reminding Mohamed that he hadn't eaten. He placed his ball back in the cabinet and made his way down the hall determined to check in on Layla before making the call. He opened the door slowly, so as not to disturb her in case she'd fallen asleep, but she hadn't. She was sitting hunched over in the same place he had left her, a statue without ears to hear or eyes to see. His mother sat beside her with her Bible open in her lap. She was softly reading scripture. He turned and went to the sitting room. Sami had the number scrawled on a piece of paper by the phone. He picked it up and dialed.

"Hossame, here."

Mohamed balked, caught off guard. It was the mabaneth's direct line. "Yes, this is Matthew Mulberry. You asked that I call?"

"I did. Excuse me for a second."

Mohamed heard a clunk as the phone was set down, the shuffling of feet and the sound of a door closing. A second later the mabaneth was back on the line.

"Sorry, but I have to be careful."

"About what?"

"About being overheard. Look, there's no easy way to say this. I'm coming out to your place. I'm supposed to place you under arrest and bring you in."

"Me? On what charge?"

"The charge is murder."

"Murder?" The struggle for the knife went through his mind.

A fight, *yes*, self defense, *yes*, but when he left, the man was still alive.

"Your foreman, Ostaz Uthman, is saying you assaulted him and the other man I met at your place, Ostaz Ahmed. The victim is a man named Ubaid. Ostaz Uthman says you attacked the three of them with a knife. He claims you were in a frenzy, screaming about how you were going to kill them all. He says you knifed Ubaid but then Uthman says he overpowered you and wrenched the knife from your hand, and you fled."

Mohamed was pacing the floor with his elbow winging out, the phone jammed to his ear. "That's ridiculous! Just the opposite happened." He spun around and went to his own door, closing it so his Mother and Layla wouldn't hear. He lowered his voice. "They kidnapped my wife, is what happened. Check your messages. I called you about it, only you weren't there so I went after them myself. I caught Uthman in the act of defiling Layla. He was raping her. The other man came at me with a knife and I fought him off, but I was defending myself, not attacking, and I did get the best of him and I stabbed him with his own knife, but I only wounded him. When I left, he was still alive."

"I suspected as much, but it's not for me to judge. They brought the body here and it's been sent to the morgue for an autopsy. The man was stabbed twice, once through the heart, and once in the side."

"See, right there. I only stabbed him once, in the side. Ask my wife. She'll verify my story."

"I'm not sure why, but I believe you. But as you know, a woman's testimony in court is of little value. Especially if she's the wife of the accused. You may, of course get a doctor to verify the rape, if it is as you say, but the prosecutor will likely paint your wife as an adulterous woman who seduced Uthman, and say their affair was consensual. He'll use it to establish motive. We see this all too often, so again, who is the court going to believe."

It took less than a second for Mohamed to realize the thinness of his case. They would have the knife with his prints on it. And he'd just confessed that he stabbed the man.

"Normally I wouldn't call to let you know I was coming. I do so out of courtesy. At this point, as long as you're still there, I have no choice but to make an arrest. But I'm tied up this morning and won't be able to make it until about three o'clock. I hope you understand my meaning."

Mohamed put the phone down. He understood. The evidence was in Uthman's favor, but the police officer didn't buy his story. Hossame was giving him a chance to escape.

CHAPTER 33

Deliver me, O Lord, from my enemies. I run to you to hide me.
— *Psalm 143:9*

MOHAMED'S JAW tightened, his lips forming a pout. He had two choices: be arrested and go to jail, or become a fugitive for a crime he didn't commit. He collapsed against the desk, a wave of emotion washing through him, but he pressed his eyes closed, fighting to hold it back. He pushed off the desk, breathing deeply to clear his head. Spinning around, he opened the drawer and retrieved his and Layla's passports. He slipped them into his hip pocket and straightened himself, taking another deep breath. He had to put on a good front—for Layla's sake.

Thirty seconds. That's how long it would take him to walk down the hall to their room. That's how long he had to come up with a plan. He had to convince them that everything was under control. He blinked several times making sure his eyes were dry.

The floor tile was cool under his bare feet. He turned down the hall toward the kitchen to collect his shoes, buying a little more time to think it through. The truck needed to be loaded. Was Layla strong enough to travel? She needed his support now more than ever. They would go together or not at all. She would want it that way, even if she couldn't say it. He started thinking about things they might need.

Sami was standing at the sink, his bald head shining in the window's light. He shuffled forward, his knees curved like wishbones. "Is everything all right, Haj Matthew?"

"I'm not going to lie to you, Sami. Things are not all right. Layla and I have to leave. I want you to get one or two of the servants together and load the truck in the front yard with as many things as a person might need for travel, things like toothbrushes, soap, towels, bedding, food—*lots of food,* anything to make us as comfortable as possible for a few weeks."

Sami nodded but looked confused. He stood for a moment, smacking his gums, then turned and shuffled off to go get help.

Mohamed slipped into his shoes. He wished there was some other way, but Hossame was right; he couldn't expect a fair trial.

He entered the bedroom. Layla was still slumped on the edge of the bed looking helpless, her eyes distant. His mother looked up. He walked over and sat beside her, speaking loud enough for Layla to hear.

"Mother, I think we have to leave."

Zainab closed her Bible. "Leave? Why?"

"Things have changed. I want you to know everything I told you about what happened yesterday is true. Layla would say the same thing if she could." He leaned forward trying to connect with Layla, but her eyes were staring at the wall. "I had to drag Uthman off of Layla, and another man attacked me with a knife. This cut on my arm," he rolled his forearm up so she could see the bandage, "I received this defending myself. I nearly choked Uthman to death. I admit it, and I wrestled with the other man and ended up stabbing him with his own knife, but when I left, both men were alive. Sabah's brother was there too, but he ran off."

Zainab's rust colored *hijab* rustled as she nodded. "I believe you, Son. So why…?"

"I just spoke with Hossame El-Din, the mabaneth. Apparently, the man I stabbed died, which is crazy. I only pierced his fat, but

Uthman is saying I killed him. And Mabaneth Hossame said the man was stabbed twice, once in the side, and once through the heart. I only stabbed him once, in the side. As awful as it sounds, I believe Uthman killed him just to frame me."

Zainab reached out to take her son's hands. Her eyes were dark and strong, though perhaps lacking sleep. Tiny wrinkles he hadn't noticed before appeared around the corners of her mouth. "This man certainly seems to have a lot of anger."

"Yes, he does. He took the body to the police. Apparently Sabah's brother confirms Uthman's story and they have the knife with my fingerprints on it. The mabaneth will be here in a few hours, but I could tell he doesn't believe Uthman. He's aware of the problems we've been having, how I accused Uthman of murdering Amin. I think he knows Uthman's just trying to get back at me. But Layla's the only one who saw that man attack me, and they won't accept her testimony because she's my wife, so I don't have a case. If I'm still here when the mabaneth comes, based on the testimony of his two *so-called* eyewitnesses, he'll be forced to take me in and, as you know, I'm not likely to get a fair trial. That's why we have to leave. Hopefully, once the mabaneth starts his investigation, he'll be able to clear my name."

Mohamed let go of his mother and stood. Layla glanced up. Her skin was pallid, her eyes moist and red. He reached out to take her hand. Her fingers felt cool to his touch. With a gentle tug, he lifted her from the bed. Her long hair was draped over her shoulder in tangled strands. He put his finger under her chin, bringing her head around so he could see her eyes. "Layla, *Habibty*, I love you. Nothing is going to change that. You understand?"

Her head nodded lightly, but her eyes darted away.

"I think you heard what I said to Mother. We can't stay here."

Zainab stood. "Do you have to go, Son? Maybe we can get a lawyer and work something out."

Mohamed looked at his mother. Her silver hair was pinned up in a French roll, her eyes brimmed with moisture.

"I'd like to stay, Mother, believe me. But the mabaneth said he was on the way. He said if he finds me here he'll have to arrest me. He was doing me a favor by letting me know."

"Yes, but…"

"No buts, Mother. Uthman's a liar but he's not dumb. He'll leak to the press how I've been proselytizing Muslims, making that the real crime and before long I'll be public enemy number one. Even Hossame said I wouldn't get a fair trial. My only hope is to disappear and give the mabaneth time to sort through the evidence. If there's a way to establish my innocence, he'll find it."

She nodded, but her eyes conveyed sorrow.

Layla trailed behind Mohamed with her feet shuffling across the tiles. He held her fingers lightly but he didn't have to pull, she came freely.

The fog had dissipated leaving the sky in a yellow haze. A breeze ruffled their clothes as they stepped down off the porch, the air filled with the musky smell of the river. Mohamed noticed that Layla was still wearing yesterday's clothes, and realized the same was true of himself, but there was no time to change.

Sami stood by the truck. Two other servants were securing the load under a tarp and tying it down. Mohamed helped Layla into the cab and closed the door. He hopped around to the back and dropped the tailgate. The bed of the truck was loaded with boxes.

"I think you will find everything you need, Haj Matthew."

Mohamed turned to see Sami.

"Sorry I didn't mention it before, but we're going to need a few changes of clothes."

"Ah, but Haj Matthew, this is already done. Yesterday was laundry day. I had all your things folded and ready to be put away. These are now in boxes." He raised his hand toward the back of the truck, his smile revealing a mouthful of brown gums. "And your soccer ball is in there too, I think." His eyes bugged from their sockets.

Sami always seemed to know his thoughts. Mohamed wanted to hug him, but was afraid the little man might break.

"Thank you Sami, you've always been a good friend," he said.

Mohamed drove through the desert, taking the bumps slowly, with Layla gripping the seat and holding on. The sky was overcast and the humidity thick enough to make it rain. The air smelled sultry. Off to his right, fifty miles in the distance, dark clouds sparked with electricity.

He prayed for the kind of faith his mother had. She'd hugged him and told him not to fret, that God was in control. He knew she believed it. Intellectually, he knew God would see them through, but in his heart, he still worried. *And we know that all things work together for good to those who love God, to those who are the called according to His purpose.* All things? He couldn't see the end from the beginning the way God did.

Layla hadn't said a word the entire trip but there were small signs of improvement—her eyes meeting his, her mobility, and those few words she had spoke—all indicated she hadn't gone into a shell from which there was no return.

The palm trees, listless in the absence of wind, drooped under a hazy sun. He parked over by the corral and got out. The barn door was open. Inside, they would be studying the Word. He helped his wife out of the truck and taking her by the hand, led her to the barn.

Mohamed and Layla stepped into the shade waiting to be acknowledged but no one gave them notice. Beams of light filtered through the open windows revealing the dust floating in the air; the floor was littered with straw. The men weren't studying the Bible as he'd thought; they were on their knees. A rapid staccato of words filled the room, everyone praying all at once. It was cacophony of noise. It was music. He'd never heard a sweeter sound.

"*Uhhummm,*" he said, clearing his throat.

Masud's head popped up, followed by the others. The men scrambled to their feet rushing over. "Ah Haj Matthew. We were so worried." Masud turned to look at the woman behind him. "Sabah said you didn't want us to know, but she said we needed to pray so she told us everything, and we have been praying all night, and until now, and here you are, with Layla. *Al hamdullah,* praise be to God." His eyes went to Layla, but she turned her head away. "Is everything all right?"

"We're fine." Mohamed said. "Sabah, could you take Layla to the shed and get her settled, she needs to rest. I'll be there in a minute. As for everyone else, I would rather you didn't ask anymore questions. The important thing is that your prayers were answered. We are alive and safe, but the story of what happened must remain a mystery for now. Suffice it to say I was able to get Layla free, but it cost a man his life, and though I acted in self-defense, I'm being accused of murder. So, as much as I'm glad to see everyone, now's not the time to stop praying."

CHAPTER 34

You shall tread upon the lion and the cobra, the young lion and the serpent you shall trample underfoot. — Psalm 91:13

FROM THE OUTSIDE looking in, the barn seemed dark. A diffused light fell through the open doors in front, and there were two small windows, one on the side and the other at the back, but the central area, where the students sat huddled together, was dim. The low light was a blessing. It helped everyone stay cool, and provided a measure of solemnity.

Layla and Sabah sat on two upended boxes close enough to rub shoulders and hold hands—two saints with burdens drawing strength from the Lord and each other. Layla found more of her voice with each passing day, and while she had yet to laugh, or even smile, she no longer sat alone, staring into space. She exchanged ideas with those around her, using her knowledge of scripture to clarify passages they read. Their appreciation of her commentary gave her purpose, instilling within her a reason to live.

Two were missing from the group: Masud, who after waiting several days and watching their food supply dwindle, was finally commissioned to take the truck into Asyut for supplies; and Mohamed, who was leaning against the barn with one foot propped up on his soccer ball and his eyes fixed on the horizon, awaiting Masud's return.

Mohamed worried about his mother. They'd been away more than a week. The lack of information about himself and Layla was bound to make her anxious, but there were no phones, and the risk of sending someone to see her was too great.

He prayed she wouldn't try to find them, but he wasn't overly concerned. Zainab didn't know how to drive, and she couldn't ask someone to bring her because she didn't know where Seventy Palms was. He glanced over at the small, one room shack attached to the barn. She'd been in the trunk of Sayyid's car when he'd brought her here, and had been unconscious when Mohamed brought her out.

Mohamed looked at his watch. It seemed like the hands on the dial were inordinately slow. He pushed himself off the wall and brought the ball up with his toe, flipping it to his elbow, then to his head, and down again. Even as rusty as he was, keeping one ball in rotation was easy. He needed two balls to make the routine a challenge.

He had wanted to go with Masud. He'd wanted to call and let his mother know that he and Layla were fine, but he couldn't chance being recognized. He had given Masud their number. Once he was in Asyut he would find a phone and call Zainab to let her know everything was alright. But under no circumstances was he to attempt to see her. If the police weren't watching the house, Uthman, or his spies, would be.

He bounced the ball off his knee sending it against the wall of the barn, picking up the rebound with his other knee, alternating between the two until he realized the *whap, whap, whap* might be disturbing those inside. He leaned in to listen. They were still asking questions of Layla and debating her answers.

His heart yearned to participate. He longed to be part of the group because, in some strange way, they had become his family. Wasn't a family composed of people who cared for and depended on each other? It was something he'd never had.

But he had reasons for withdrawing. He wanted to keep Layla talking and she seemed less inclined to speak when he was around.

And he felt he should keep his distance because he didn't want his growing doubts rubbing off on anyone else. He dropped his ball, letting it roll away, and stooped over to pick up a rock. The sandstone started to crumble in his hand. Cocking his arm, he threw it at a post, smashing it to smithereens. A residue of sand splayed out like a star where the stone made impact. The others in the group, after seeing Layla's safe return, were so full of faith, they couldn't accept any harm might have come to Masud. But he, their spiritual mentor, had worms of apprehension growing in his gut.

Masud had been told to avoid the store where Uthman grabbed Layla. He was to transact his business south of the city, but the task should have taken three or four hours—*at most*—and he'd been gone two days.

Mohamed leaned against the wall, cupping his hand over his eyes as he scanned the horizon searching for any sign of the truck's approach. The sun sizzled overhead. Masud wouldn't reveal where they were staying, but they'd torture him, and when he wouldn't give into their demands, he was sure to be killed—*another death laid to his account*. He kicked off his shoes, swallowed the bile in his throat, and with his eyes starting to burn, picked up his ball and raced into the desert.

He began looping the ball in and out of his feet, dancing around as he kept it moving forward, trying to get his mind on something else. The ball was spinning as he kicked it, sending it ricocheting off a sand knoll. He raced across the burning sand, pounding the ball further and further into the desert. He was about a hundred meters out when he was brought up short by a sound he knew all too well—*sssssssppppffff*. He stopped the ball and froze, looking around slowly to see where the sound was coming from, *sssssssppppffff*.

Behind him the viper was looped in coils ready to strike. Any sudden movement would attract the snake's attention. *sssssssppppffff*. He slowly lowered his foot to where it was in front of the ball, kicking it backward. The snake, sensing movement, struck, *poof*. The ball began loosing air as the fangs sank into leather.

Mohamed, seeing the viper uncoiled and unable to strike again, bolted, sprinting back to the barn, huffing and puffing and dripping with sweat. He leaned against a post placing his hands on his hips and had two totally unrelated thoughts: one, *that was my only ball*, and two, *Satan's a snake!* He straightened himself and wiped his forehead as he began walking in small circles, trying to catch his breath.

A flicker of movement caught his attention. He stopped and turned scanning the desert to make sure it wasn't a mirage. *There!* Was that a cloud spinning up off the wheels of the truck, or just the wind picking up dust against the yellow sky? He watched, cupping his hands over his eyes as the cloud grew larger. Minutes passed, and then he saw it clearly—*headlights!*

He turned around peering into the dark interior of the barn, his eyes adjusting to the shadows. "I see a car coming!"

The men jumped up and hustled over, followed by Sabah who wrapped her *hijab* around her body holding it in as she hurried to catch up. Layla remained alone. Mohamed reached out, wiggling his fingers, inviting her to take his hand, but she stayed put with her elbows on her knees and hands clasped together. The men surrounded Mohamed at the door, waving, though Mohamed doubted the driver could see them from that distance. He felt an arm slip through his and turned to see Layla.

The cloud grew larger and the sound of the chassis, taking bumps with a metallic screech and groan, became clearer. Mohamed held Layla's arm, patting her hand and feeling relief, but as the truck drew closer he could see there were two people in the cab. He stiffened. Either Masud had picked up a passenger, which wasn't a smart thing to do, or they were about to find the truck filled with militants bearing arms. He held his breath as the truck slid to a stop, the sand swirling around the cab was too dense to see inside.

The doors swung open, and as the dust began to settle, Masud and Zainab climbed out. Zainab used a sheath of newspapers to fan her face. Her eyes went to the shed. She froze for a moment, then looked away. Bringing her here was not part of the plan, Mohamed sighed, but she was a welcome sight. He began to breathe easier as he walked over, bringing Layla with him on his arm. He let go long enough to give Zainab a hug, kissing her on both cheeks. "It's good to see you Mother, he said."

"As it is you, my son." Zainab took her stack of newspapers and placed them under her arm as she turned to Layla. "And how are you, my child?" Her eyes were full of compassion, and for once, Layla didn't look away. She leaned in and embraced her mother-in–law.

Mohamed placed his arms across their shoulders, urging them forward. "Come, let's get out of the sun. Mother, I'm really glad you're here, but I had asked Masud not to go out to the house. He took an awful chance picking you up." He looked back at Masud. "I hope you weren't followed."

Zainab stopped, causing Layla and Mohamed to halt beside her. She folded her arms around her newspapers and looked at her son. "You think having gray hair makes me senile?"

Mohamed took a step back. "No…of course not. Why…"

"Because age doesn't necessarily make one a fool. Masud followed your instructions to the letter. He called to tell me you and Layla were safe. I asked him to wait where he was. I had a cab pick me up and take me to him. But even then I watched to see if we were being followed." She began walking again bringing the procession with her as they plodded toward the barn.

It was slightly cooler in the shade. Mohamed looked at the boxes. I'm sorry mother, we don't have any chairs. Maybe we should go into the…" but Zainab was already shaking her head.

"No, this will do fine." She grabbed a box and pulled the hem of her *hijab* up so she could take a seat. "Besides, I want everyone to hear." The small group clustered around as she began tossing the newspapers to the ground, making sure they were face up so the headlines could be read.

American Implicated in Shepherd's Slaying
Murder Victim's Relatives Cry Out for Justice
Border Locked Down as Manhunt Continues
Guilty Man Flees, Police in Pursuit.

"It's not good, Mohamed. The police came just as you said. They searched the house. I don't know what they were looking for but I assure you they found nothing. Mabaneth Hossame took me aside and let me know that Uthman was making a major case of this. He's the one feeding stories to the newspapers. They're making it like you've already been tried and convicted.

"The mabaneth would not presume to tell me what to do, but he inferred you must lay low as long as possible. They have a photo of you. I'm not sure where they got it, but it's a good likeness, and it's being broadcast all over Egypt. There are posters in stores, stapled to telephone poles, even glued to walls. Everyone's looking, but no one knows where you are. I think it's safe to say this place is still a secret."

"Yes, but we can't stay here forever. If people continue to go back and forth, whether it's to get food or make visits, someone's bound to notice. People don't just drive into the empty desert for no reason. And truck tracks aren't that hard to follow. I hate to admit it, but I'm starting to agree with Layla. I think it would be best if we left the country," he raised his chin toward the headline that read, 'Border Locked Down,' "but according to that, the minute we try to cross the border, we'll be stopped."

His mother smiled, her mouth turning up at the corners, though her eyes remained sad. "I'm glad we think alike, my son. I regret only that your departure will leave a hole in my heart, but my grief will be lessened in knowing you are alive. This is why I had Masud drive me to the southern tip of Egypt. I have arranged for escorts for you and Layla. You will cross the desert into Sudan the way your father did. Once there, you can find your way to the U.S. Embassy, show them your passports and claim asylum."

"Why can't we just go to the embassy in Egypt? They would not turn American citizens over to the Egyptian police."

Mohamed turned his head, surprised to find Layla was listening. "They might," he responded. "It's not their mandate to protect Americans accused of murder. But once we're in another country, where we're not being sought, they might be open to letting us return to the States, as long as we can prove our American citizenship."

Zainab looked at her daughter-in-law. "The journey will be difficult, but God will be with you. I have hired Bedouins, honest and good men, to guide you. I have not told them why you must get into Sudan secretly. Nor did they ask. They care nothing for the government outside of their own community. They have agreed on a price, and I have agreed to pay. That is all that matters. But they were breaking camp when I arrived. Three of their members agreed to stay behind but they won't wait for long, so come, we must go quickly."

"But what about Sabah and Masud, and the others? What will become of our irrigation project, and the ministry, and the farm?"

"You need not worry about us," Masud interrupted. He reached up stroking his beard, pulling the white stripe through his hand. "I will take care of Sabah. You just go. And God be with you."

Sabah took Layla's hands, nodding as tears flooded her eyes.

Layla turned, the two women held each other. "You are my sister, Sabah, do not forget that. Maybe once we're settled in America, I can send for you to come and visit."

Zainab's eyes scolded Mohamed. "Do you not think me capable of keeping these men employed? Your project will be completed even if I have to send someone to school to become an engineer and learn how it's done. Now, your escorts made me promise not to delay, so let's go."

Mohamed nodded, then looked at Layla. "I don't think we have a choice," he said.

CHAPTER 35

Out of Egypt I called My Son. — Hosea 11:1 & Matthew 2:15

FOUR PEOPLE were crowded onto the bench seat of the rusty pickup as it clattered across a thirty kilometer stretch of desert. They were crammed shoulder to shoulder with Masud at the wheel, Zainab seated beside him, Layla next, and Mohamed jammed against the door. The truck was made to seat two people comfortably, three in a pinch, but never four. They teetered back and forth, absorbing the shock of every rock and rill, suffering the crowding because they knew Mohamed was destined to lay under a tarp for the remainder of the seven hour drive. Letting him enjoy the air conditioner, if not the benefit of sitting upright, for the first thirty kilometers, was the least they could do.

The sun waxed yellow on the horizon as they pulled up short of the highway. Mohamed checked his watch. It was three o'clock. If they drove nonstop, they could make it by ten. He slipped his hand down beside his leg and found the handle, snapping it back. The door popped open almost spilling him onto the ground, but he swung his feet out in time to keep from falling. He straightened and reached in to help Layla and his mother. Masud was already undoing the tarp. Mohamed stepped around and stood beside him looking at his ride for the next seven hours, a sandy blanket on a ribbed metal bed.

Zainab took her son's hand and then Layla's, pulling them away from the truck. "Masud, would you join us? We need to pray." Masud reached in and completed the circle.

"Lord, You alone know all things. Twelve years You ministered to me while I was in chains, never once forsaking me. In my hour of need, You stood beside me. You were there to comfort me, to hold and strengthen me. And when I prayed for my son's salvation, You answered. Now I ask, Lord, that you do not take back what You have given, but grant him safety for the journey ahead. In the name of Jesus most Holy, I ask. Amen."

Mohamed gave his mother a hug, folding her small body into his arms. He caught Layla's eye as he let go. Her expression was flat. He leaned in to whisper in her ear. "No matter what happens, I will always love you," he said. He released his hold, looking at Masud. "Let's go Masud, take us home."

Without prompting, he crawled into the back of the pickup, feeling grains of sand pressing into his palms. He spread the blanket out to lie down as Masud began stretching the tarp back over the truck's bed. Mohamed stared up at the faded brown material. He heard the doors slam. The engine revved and the truck lurched forward, scratching his arm on the metal as he slid back. It was going to be a rough ride.

Masud took it slow. He was doing his best to avoid jarring Mohamed as he dipped into holes and eased over mounds of sand. When he was about a hundred feet from the road, he pulled up behind a sandstone hummock and hopped out, running to the edge of the pavement to check and make sure there were no other cars in sight before jumping back into the truck and venturing onto the asphalt.

He tried painting a visual image of the journey. The first city they'd encounter was Asyut. He could already see its gray walls growing in the distance. Getting beyond those city limits was the real test. They would stay on the highway and drive across without going through town. The newspapers said the police were setting up roadblocks and doing random vehicle searches. If they were doing it anywhere, it would be there.

Asyut was the center of Islamic fundamentalism. The Muslim Brotherhood had a healthy presence there. And they had a vested interest in seeing Haj Matthew brought to justice, especially in light of the embarrassment they'd suffered at the estate. Masud checked his gas gauge. He'd filled the tank before heading out to pick up Mohamed. He should have enough to make it all the way to Aswan.

The city swept by without incident. Behind him Asyut was fading from view. *Al hamdullah.* Thank you, God. The wilderness spread before him with a line of sandstone hills off to his left that seemed to follow him wherever he went. Zainab, seated on his right, and Layla next to the window, were quiet. Each appeared to be lost in thought, but neither seemed ready to voice what they were thinking. His only companion was the constant hum of the tires.

The scenery changed as they drew closer to the Nile with the barren desert on one side, and fields of green on the other. They passed a donkey pulling a cart loaded with sorghums. The man leading the animal plodded along barefoot in a *galabia* with a sickle slung over his shoulder.

The road narrowed as they passed through cliffs outside Qena. The sun, just off the horizon, shot its rays out horizontally, momentarily blinding Masud. He pulled down his visor and tried to make out what appeared to be a spark of light. He squinted. *Da-aeh-da!* What? No! A Jeep with a flashing light bar was parked at the side of the road, and a soldier, standing in the middle of the street, was waving him over. His heart began to pound.

The slowing of the truck woke Zainab and Layla. "What's going on," Zainab said.

"Pray," Masud answered. He rolled down his window to greet

the uniformed man standing outside. A second officer made his way around to the back of the truck.

"*Masaa el kheer,* evening officer. What have we done?"

The soldier was six foot tall and had to be at least two hundred pounds. He wore a khaki military uniform with a blue beret, and had a thin mustache hovering over thick purple lips.

"Masud?" The man set his hand on the edge of the window, his thick fingers smudging the glass as he looked back at his fellow soldier. "Hey, look, Karim, this is my friend Masud from Beni Suef." He swung his head around addressing Masud again. "What are you doing all the way down here?"

Masud's eyes widened. "Abas?" He hadn't seen the man in half a dozen years, and wouldn't have recognized him, had he not been recognized first. "Look at you, you've grown. Whatever happened to that little skinny kid I used to know?" Masud glanced in his rearview mirror and saw the man standing at the tailgate squinting into the intense rays of the sun as he lifted the tarp. *Oh God, please hide Haj Matthew from his eyes.* Masud's heart continued to pound. His hands held the steering wheel keeping them from shaking.

The man at the back of the truck came around to the side. "It's empty," he said. He took a step out into the street to flag down another car.

Masud's hands felt slick, his heart throbbing. *Empty?*

Abas slapped the side of the truck with a meaty hand, creating a dull thud on the metal. "Sorry Masud, I have to get back to work. We should get together. Are you living here now?"

"Ah, no, unfortunately. I'm just taking this woman and her daughter into Luxor to see a doctor. Friend of the family. Her husband passed on and she doesn't drive."

"You always were a good man. Hey, it was good seeing you. I'm going to have to write mother about this; she won't believe it. Such a small world. *Ghoore, ghoore,* get out of here," he said, waving his hand forward. The big soldier turned away, walking toward the car that had just been pulled over.

Masud rolled up his window, his palm slippery with sweat. He raised his hand to give a final salute.

His friend turned and smiled congenially, waving as the truck trundled by.

"You see that?" Masud exclaimed. "*Sobhan Allah*, Praise God!"

But Zainab only nodded. "We were never in danger. Not with God on the throne."

Masud looked in his rearview mirror. The flashing lights faded into the distance. "Think we should pull over and make sure Matthew's still back there?"

There was a thump against the back wall, followed by a second. The sound was muffled, but loud enough to be heard.

Masud looked at Zainab and shrugged. "I didn't know he could hear us back there."

The lights of Luxor flickered against dark shades of purple as the city embraced the night. Mosques, bathed in green fluorescence, dominated the skyline, their tall minarets spiraling into the heavens like missiles about to be launched. Strings of incandescent bulbs reflected off the water from a cruise boat out on the Nile.

Masud checked his gas gauge. Their fuel was low, but he didn't stop. There was too much risk of being pulled over in the city. One brush with the police was enough. He kept his speed at the lawful limit trusting God to stretch the gas. He didn't think they'd see another roadblock. They were only a few hours away from connecting with the Bedouins and he was determined, now more than ever, to deliver Haj Matthew to his destination.

The monotonous scenery was reduced to what could be seen in the two narrow beams of his headlights. At one point, when the road swung close to the river, he'd had to swerve to avoid a crocodile slinking across the highway. Another animal, one he couldn't identify, stared at him with eyes that shined like flashbulbs. He thought he ran over a snake, but it might have been a stick. He reached to snap the air conditioner off, and rolled down his window letting in the warm evening air. The stream circulating through the cab helped him stay awake. The ladies beside him had nodded off again. Zainab's head was tilted back, restricting her windpipe causing her to snort. Layla lay against her mother-in-law's shoulder.

He knew he would have to wake Zainab soon. They were well south of Aswan. They must be getting close. He had been there the previous day but it had been light outside, not dark. He wasn't sure he'd recognize the encampment...*Ahhhh,* he squirreled the wheel to the left to avoid hitting a man riding a camel along the shoulder of the road.

Whew, close. They should put taillights on that beast. His heart was throbbing again. He saw the glow of a fire off in the distance, and a tent bathed in the light of its flames. He pulled the truck to the side. "Haja Zainab, wake up, I think we're here."

Mohamed scrambled from the truck. The soldier hadn't bothered to tie the tarp down again. It had flapped like a flag in the wind, creating a racquet that kept Mohamed awake and cognizant of the ache he felt in his back. It was good to be standing. He pushed the heel of his hand into his lumbar. A car passed, its headlights sweeping the road. He turned his face away.

Masud hopped out of the cab. "Haj Matthew, I am so glad to see you're all right."

Mohamed nodded. "What happened back there? I mean at the roadblock?"

"I don't know. The one officer was an old friend of mine, but I think he would have considered it his duty to arrest me if they had found you."

"That's amazing. Thank you Lord. That man lifted the tarp and stared right at me and then set it down again, and I heard him say the back was empty. I mean it was a miracle. God blinded him. I mean physically. I saw the sun shining directly in his eyes making him squint. I'd scooted all the way back and covered myself with

246

the blanket. He must have looked in and saw only blackness, but I was there. Thank you Lord!"

Zainab brought Layla around and placed her hand into Mohamed's. "I prayed the whole time," she said. "In my spirit I had this deep inner peace. Don't ask me how, but I knew you would not be found. Hold on to your wife. I need to go speak with one of your guides."

The man on the camel turned off the road and clomped by, heading for the fire. They were an ancient people living in a modern world, untainted by its lust and greed. Zainab turned after the man, disappearing into a tent that glowed from the inside like a hollowed out pumpkin with a candle.

Another car passed, slowing to veer around the truck parked at the side of the road. Mohamed took Layla's hand, and with Masud alongside, gently moved away. A shallow indentation had been scooped out of the sand to contain the fire. They stood in its glow, but mostly for the light, not because they were cold. The flaps of the tent were thrown back and Zainab came out with a man dressed in a long multi-colored robe. The cloth draped over his head was held in place with corded bands, and his leathery face was deeply tanned, standing out in contrast to his white neatly trimmed beard. His eyes were smiling, reflecting the fire's light.

"*Masaa el kheer,* I bid you good evening. Welcome," he said, bowing courteously. *Ismi Seif,* my name is Seif. Your mother, most kind and generous, has asked us to escort you into Sudan. Please, come. We have been awaiting your arrival." He waved his palm to the side with a light bow, and turned to lead the small group around to the other side of the tent where five camels stood, four with empty saddles, and one with bundles of supplies.

Two men sat on the ground with their legs crossed. Masud recognized one as the man they'd passed on the road. Ropes leading to the camel's harnesses were looped in their hands. They stood as the elder approached. One of the men singled out a camel and tapped its leg with a rod. The camel knelt obediently.

"Please," the elder said, waving his hand at the beast.

"You want us to get on, just like that. We're leaving right now, tonight?"

The man looked confused. "Yes, of course. We have been waiting."

"But at night. Shouldn't we wait until it's light so we can see where we're going?"

"No, no, no. It is too hot to travel by day. We use the stars to guide us. You shall see."

Layla dropped Mohamed's hand. She walked up and swung her leg over the saddle. The man with the stick tapped the animal and it immediately rose, causing Layla to rock back and forth as the animal clambered to its feet. She sat perched above looking down on Mohamed and Zainab "Remind you of anything?" she said.

Mohamed had a flashback of Layla as a little girl. He turned and kissed his mother, tasting the salty tears on her cheeks. "I don't know what to say, Mother. This is all happening so fast."

"Just promise to call me as soon as it's safe. Now," she said, breaking free, "Get on that animal, and go. My prayers will be with you all the way."

Mohamed embraced Masud. "I'll never forget you, my friend. I thought God had sent me to teach you, but as I look back, I see God has used you to teach me."

"You utter words of nonsense, my brother. Go with God, and we will pray for your soon return."

Mohamed wiped his cheeks, embarrassed by the moisture in his eyes. He went to his animal, climbing on.

The saddle was made of wood in the shape of two wishbones pinched over the camel's hump. The thick woven blanket underneath kept the wood from chafing the camel's back, and a large skin of thick fur covered the top, providing padding. *"Whoa,"* he quipped. He grabbed the pommel, hanging on tight as the camel stood. He looked at Layla. "Don't laugh. The last time we did this, you got on the camel but I stayed on the ground."

She giggled, bringing an unexpected warmth to his chest. It was the first time he'd seen her smile. He raised his eyes looking into a blanket of stars so thick it appeared there was more light than dark. *"Thank You Lord,"* he whispered.

Their guides were mounting their own camels. In an instant, the first guide moved forward. The second guide flicked his stick prodding Layla's camel to follow, and then Mohamed's. He fell in last, leading the fifth camel loaded with supplies. Mohamed looked back over the caravan, watching his mother and Masud growing smaller and smaller until they disappeared.

It didn't take long to settle into the rhythm of the journey. There was a knack to flowing with the roll of the beast's hips, a certain undulation that once you were in sync, enabled a more comfortable ride. Still, after an hour he was feeling numb in his seat, and sore in his back.

In the distance a long belt of clouds seemed to rise off the desert floor. The man leading the group brought the camels to a halt and made his animal kneel to dismount. The man bringing up the rear did the same, and came around to lower Mohamed's and Layla's camels as well.

Mohamed drew his leg over the saddle and stood, breathing a sigh of relief. "Are we taking a break?"

The man tipped his head toward the brown horizon. "Dust storm," he said.

While one man took the camels and made them kneel in a line, the other set about unfurling a large canvas. They didn't solicit Mohamed's help, nor did he offer. These men were skilled in the ways of the desert. They knew what they were doing. He felt the wind picking up, tousling his hair.

Within the space of a few minutes, four people were huddled around a fire sipping coffee inside a tent made of hand spun goat's hair. The tent itself hadn't been fully raised, their hosts explained, because they were only stopping to rest and wait out the storm. They had taken the bulk of the tent and unfolded it, pinned one edge to the ground in the direction of the wind, and raised the other end up on two poles, letting the excess material drape down on both sides to create a lean-to. The wind hit the lower portion and swept up over the top without blowing the shelter away. The five camels had been made to kneel around the shelter like a dust screen. The wind moaned, buffeting the walls of the tent for over an hour, and then stopped as suddenly as it had begun.

Mohamed stepped outside to find the landscape had entirely changed. No wonder they used the stars for direction. They certainly couldn't use landmarks. Nothing stayed the same. He took Layla by the hand and while their guides set about packing, wandered out into the desert. A billion times a billion stars speckled the nighttime sky, fascinating nebulas of green, blue, and pink, swirling in a cosmos with no discernable beginning or end, all declaring the glory of God. He felt like Ibrahim of old—*And he brought him forth abroad, and said, 'Look now toward heaven, and see the stars, if thou be able to number them.*

Mohamed squeezed Layla's hand, turning to explore her eyes. "You know what?" he said. "A lot of times angels are called stars in the Bible. I think every one of those is an angel watching over us. We're in good hands, Layla. God is going to make everything right. Layla didn't say anything, but she did lay her head against his chest, and with her arms around him, held him tight.

CHAPTER 36

*For you shall not go out with haste, nor by flight: for the Lord will go
before you and the God of Israel will be your reward. — Isaiah 52:12*

MOHAMED LET GO of Layla's hand and stepped back
to look up at the brownish pink walls of the seven story
cube with rows of vertical windows. The nondescript
building on Shari'a Ali Abdul Latif, looked more like a hotel than a
U.S. Consulate. If it weren't for the large satellite dish and antennas
on the roof, he wouldn't have guessed.

Their plane had only landed a half hour earlier, but in spite of
being up all night crossing the desert into Sudan, and then pushing
on another nine-hundred kilometers by plane to reach Khartoum,
and in spite of the fact that every muscle in his body cried out
for rest, rather than check into a hotel, as any sane person might,
Mohamed flagged down the first taxi he saw. "Please, we need to
get to the American embassy," he said, pushing a twenty into the
hand of the driver. He did not want to spend the night as an illegal
alien in a foreign country. He wanted to get Layla home.

A security guard approached and Mohamed extended his hand
through the gate surrendering thier passports. "We'd like to see
the ambassador," he said.

The man took the documents and stepped back into a small
cubicle. Mohamed watched as he flipped though their passports

and picked up a phone. A few seconds later he stepped back outside and unlocked the gate.

"Follow me please." The officer, a large black man in military uniform, escorted them down the walkway to the front of the building, using his access card to let them in.

A gentleman in a sharp looking business suit stood waiting on the other side of the door. He shook their hands cordially, initially welcoming them in English, and then in Arabic.

"My name is Stan Cobel. I'm assistant to Consular Affairs. How can I help you?"

"My name is Matthew Mulberry and this is my wife Layla," Mohamed said nodding at Layla, "and English is fine, please. We are Americans. We need to see the ambassador about receiving asylum."

"We don't have an ambassador, per se. Here he's called the Charge d'Affaires, and that would be Chester Fernman, but I'm afraid he doesn't receive unscheduled visits, and besides, you need to go through Consular Affairs. Our department handles lost or stolen passports, financial matters, pretty much anything that pertains to problems American citizens have while traveling in country." He narrowed his eyes slightly as though noticing for the first time their rumpled clothes and matted hair. "Why do you feel you need asylum?" he asked.

"I'd prefer to discuss that with the Charge d'Affaires."

The man shook his head. "Americans aren't well received in Sudan right now. We've had to send all non-essential personnel home so we're kind of understaffed. Didn't you read the travel advisory?"

"We don't want to be here. That's why we need to see the ambassador."

"I'm afraid it's impossible. It's not that Mr. Fernman wouldn't like to visit with every U.S. citizen that drops in, but his duties preclude it. He simply doesn't have the time. I suggest you take this up with Consular Affairs."

Mohamed pressed his lips together, looking to Layla for support, but she seemed dazed again, or perhaps just tired. Her eyes were droopy and unfocused. His wife had been raped, and he was accused of murder; and they'd traveled all night eating dust. He didn't care about the embargo placed on Sudan, he wasn't about to plead his case to a lower level bureaucrat. "I need to see the ambassador, or whatever it is you call him. Show him my passport and tell him to call Alexandria Baden."

"Alexan...the wife of the vice president?"

"That's the one. She'll vouch for me. Or have him call the FBI in San Francisco and talk to Agent Ambrose Barnes. It's extremely important. We're American citizens. We expect your full cooperation."

Layla squeezed his hand. He glanced over and saw her eyes imploring him to stay calm, but apparently the name dropping worked because Mr. Cobel opened their passports again and looked at the photos with renewed interest.

Stan snapped the passports closed and slapped them against his palm. "*Humm*, I can't promise anything, but if you'll wait just a minute, I'll see what I can do." He turned and walked away, the leather soles of his shoes echoing on the marble floor. He disappeared behind a closed door, leaving them alone in the lobby. Mohamed looked around. Two armed Marines in dress uniform guarded the door. Their rifles were held at their sides ready to spring into action. American and U.N. flags were stationed to their right and left.

Mr. Cobel was only gone a few minutes. He returned, holding out their passports. "Mr. Fernman regrets that he cannot see you today and has instructed me to refer you to Consular Affairs. I'm at your service. I'll be happy to assist you any way I can."

Mohamed inhaled slowly. "Please we only need a few minutes of his time," he said.

"I'm afraid that's impossible. He's been on the phone all day and is just rushing out to a dinner party. If you must see Mr.

Fernman, I'm afraid you'll have to come back tomorrow, but I already checked with his secretary and his meetings are scheduled pretty tight. Your only hope is that someone cancels, or a meeting gets cut short. As I said, you'd be better served to take your matter up with Consular Affairs."

Mohamed looked around. "Do you know a good hotel where we can stay?"

The man nodded. "Many of those who have business here stay at the Hilton. I've never been there, but I understand it has a nice view overlooking the Nile."

Mohamed extended his hand and thanked the man. The consulate was obviously engaged in matters of national security. It wasn't fair to expect him to drop everything to see a tourist. He apologized for being testy and explained that he hadn't slept in the past twenty-four hours. Taking Layla by the hand, he led her through the gauntlet of guards. One of the sentries leaned in to open the door. He heard a click as they stepped outside into the late evening sun and cringed a second time at the sound of the gates clanging shut behind them. The U.S. was locking them out, leaving them at the mercy of the Sudanese.

Layla gripped his arm, hanging on tight.

Mohamed waved his free hand to hail a cab, pulling Layla back as the taxi squealed to the curb. He opened the door and climbed in behind her, laying his head against the back of the seat with his eyes closed.

They rode through Khartoum in silence. Rush hour traffic glutted the streets. Men drove tuti carts pulled by donkeys. Store fronts crumbled, additional stalls of merchandise spilled onto the sidewalks, and Arabic graffiti was spray-painted everywhere. The man driving the taxi slammed on his brakes, pounded his horn and screamed a string of curses at a woman with a small herd of goats who dared to cross the road in front of his cab.

Mohamed didn't want to stay in Sudan, not even overnight. They had American passports with Egyptian visas, not Sudanese. They had entered the country illegally, and had no authorization to be there. If they were stopped for any reason they could be arrested and detained indefinitely, if not sent back to Egypt.

The cab pulled to the front of the hotel, rolling to a stop under a breezeway supported by three tall arches. Mohamed removed several U.S. bills from his wallet and handed them to his driver who smiled approvingly as he put them into the pouch he carried at his side.

The building looked fine from the outside. The sidewalks were bordered with hedges, and the manicured lawns decorated with palm trees. He helped Layla out, thinking positively about new beginnings. The bellman stepped outside to help with their bags, but backed up and held the door when he realized they didn't have any. The lobby was presentable, though with rattan furniture, looked less upscale than what he might expect of a Hilton. He approached the front desk. "How much for a room?" he asked nodding at the clerk behind the registration desk.

The man reached under the counter and brought out a sheet of paper. He was short, with hair that receded back to the middle of his crown. His glasses were rimmed in black plastic, and he wore a pencil-thin moustache. "Ah, you are in luck. I think we have one room available, ninth floor with a very nice view." The man slipped Mohamed a registration card to fill out.

Mohamed reached for the pen on the counter. "You didn't say how much."

"We have a prime location, as you will see from your room. This hotel alone offers the best view of the White and Blue Nile Rivers as the two become one. Most romantic, I think you will agree. A national treasure."

"How much?"

"The Bahr al Abyad, that which they call the White Nile because of the clay in its waters, flows here to Khartoum to meet the Blue Nile which flows from Lake Tana in Ethiopia. It is most glorious, this merging of the two into one."

Leaning on the counter to write, Mohamed rolled is eyes. "That's fine, but how much."

"For you, and because I have only one room which I would like to fill, three-hundred."

"I don't have any Dinar, only American."

"But, I meant American."

"Three hundred American a night, that's ridiculous." He turned to look at Layla but she had her back to him staring into the lobby. They'd never spent an evening in a nice hotel. He scowled at the clerk. Maybe it was worth it. A luxurious bed, a romantic view, with a little luck, it could turn into a pleasant evening—and he was too tired to think about looking anywhere else. He just hoped his mother's money would be enough to get them home, with a little left over to get them on their feet again.

The clerk blinked a few times and glanced over his shoulder as though searching for assistance. He brought his eyes around to look at Mohamed again. "For you, perhaps I can make it two-fifty, but this is the best I can do."

Mohamed signed the card and slid it across the counter to the man. "Please have a newspaper sent up to my room."

The man nodded. "Shokran, thank you. I'm certain you will enjoy your stay. Now I just need to see your passport and…"

"Passport? You don't need my passport. We're not traveling. We're just staying the night."

"I'm sorry, it is required we see your passport. We need proper identification."

Mohamed swallowed, small prickles of gooseflesh breaking out on his arms. He reached for his back pocket praying God would blind the man to the missing entry stamp and have him focus only on their photos.

The man took the passports and opened them, looking at Mohamed and Layla, who now stood beside her husband. "Thank you," he said, handing the passports back. "And here are your keys. Room 924. Please enjoy your stay."

It seemed strange riding the elevator up without luggage, almost like they were visitors instead of guests. The doors opened onto a hall with a carpet that needed cleaning.

"I hope the room is nicer than this," Layla said.

Mohamed felt her hand slipping into his as they walked down the dimly lit corridor. Several of the overhead lights were either burned out, or missing.

If he'd hoped for a suite, as he might have expected for the price, he was sorely disappointed. The room was old and dingy, and smelled of moth balls. Not only was it small—crammed with a double bed and a few pieces of marred furniture—it needed a good coat of paint. He tried to look on the bright side. At least it wasn't green and red like the room they'd stayed in while visiting Masud.

The air conditioner was on but Mohamed went to the window to let in fresh air. The smell was atrocious. A cobweb hung in the upper corner of the glass. On the street below a police car screamed by, its siren blaring. At least the promised view of the river was nice. He turned around.

Layla was slipping out of her clothes, pulling her dress over her head. He went to help, hoping for the right moment, but she turned away.

"No! I…I can't, not yet."

Mohamed backed up, his face sullen. "I'm trying to be patient, Layla, I really am."

"Let's not get into this, Mohamed, not tonight. I'm too tired. I just want to take a shower and go to bed."

"But…" he looked at his watch "…it's only seven o'clock."

Layla didn't answer. She took her dress and headed for the bathroom, shutting the door. He heard the click of the lock.

Mohamed gritted his teeth, his shoulders tensing as his hands balled into fists. He wanted to scream. Uthman hadn't just violated his wife, he'd cut out her heart. All that remained was an empty shell, a walking, emotionless zombie.

He dropped to his knees. *God, remove these thoughts from my mind. Please. She's hurting, I get that, I just don't know how to respond. Please help me, Lord—and please, God, get us out of here. Please!*

He got up and switched on the TV, dialing through the channels until he found a soccer match—Spain versus Italy—and fell back into a chair, watching but not really paying attention.

It was nearly an hour before Layla emerged from the bathroom with her hair wrapped in a towel, and when she did, she immediately slid under the covers and rolled over without a word.

Mohamed watched the TV a few more minutes, then turned it off and went to the bathroom himself. Layla had washed her clothes in the tub. They had been wrung out and stretched and hung up to dry. It was a good idea. Mohamed slipped his shoes off, and stepped into the shower fully clothed. He lathered his shirt and pants and then peeled them off. After rinsing and wringing them out, he washed himself.

Layla didn't move when he slipped into bed beside her. He lay on his back with his hands under his head watching a cobweb buffeted by the breeze of the air conditioner. He was exhausted, but he couldn't sleep. It was still light outside, and things weren't right between him and Layla. Another siren screamed by on the street below.

"I'm cold," Layla said. "Could you hold me?"

He rolled over and, slipping one hand under her pillow, wrapped her in his arms. They did not make love, but the warmth that passed between them was just as good. In some ways, it was better.

CHAPTER 37

Furthermore we glory in our tribulations, knowing tribulation creates perseverance, and perseverance good character, and character hope.
— *Romans 5:3-4*

MOHAMED LAY quietly in the predawn light trying not to disturb Layla, but unable to sleep. His eyes felt scratchy, his nerves tingling with an electric edge, his mind rampant with thoughts of what the day might bring. If they sent him back to stand trial, he wouldn't permit her to come. Baring a miracle, he was certain to be convicted. He would be sent straight to prison and then following a few futile appeals, be hung. He would not put her through that. She wouldn't like it, but he was determined to send her back to California where she'd be safe.

He tried to rest but sleep eluded him. He thought about the newspaper, the one he'd asked to have brought to his room. Opening his eyes, he glanced around. The walls were still shades of gray. He could see vague shapes and shadows, but there wasn't enough light to read.

His heart beat, *thud, thud, thudding,* in his chest. Then the silence was broken as the cry of the muezzin began blaring from loudspeakers atop a nearby minaret, the azan calling the faithful to prayer. He tossed the covers aside and went to the window. If he had to die, why couldn't it be for spreading the gospel? Why die for a crime he didn't commit?

Layla stirred. "Can't sleep?" she mumbled.

He turned and saw her stretching, her arms poking out from beneath the covers with fists clenched. "Come here and hold me." She opened her hands, reaching out, and then rolled over as he slipped into bed behind her, melting in the warmth of her skin. Her breathing was slow and steady. The smell of her hair and the soft beating of her heart soothed him, and within minutes, he accomplished what he'd been unable to do all night. He fell asleep.

The room was bathed in light by the time he awoke. He yawned and brought his wrist up to check his watch, then bolted upright.

"Layla, wake up, we have to get dressed."

"Hummmm?"

"Come on. We have fifteen minutes to get to the consulate before they open." Mohamed jumped up, dragging the bedding with him as he ducked into the bathroom to find his clothes.

"Hey! Not fair!" Layla scrambled for the blanket, but it was out of reach. She lay still for a moment, and then swung her legs around and sat up, gripping the edge of the mattress, but she didn't stand. Her hair was draped over her head hiding her features as she teetered, drowsy and lethargic, and after a few seconds, keeled over burying her face in the pillow again.

Mohamed came out of the bathroom tucking in his shirt.

"Habibty, Honey, come on, I want to be in the office first thing in case the ambassador has to reschedule one of his appointments." He took her elbow, gently lifting her but she pulled her arm free.

She sat up again, moaning, and with both hands pushed herself off the bed. She stood there wobbling on her feet.

Mohamed went to the bathroom to collect her things. He shook her blouse and skirt, fluffing out the wrinkles before handing them over—*thank God for permanent press.* He glanced at his watch, trying to be patient as she labored to dress. She hadn't brought any makeup, nor did she have a brush. She bent over double, combing through her hair with her fingers to loosen the tangles and snapped upright, flipping her hair over her shoulders.

"Okay, I'm ready," she said turning away from the mirror.

Mohamed looked at his watch, again. "Is it all right with you if we skip breakfast? Maybe we can grab a coffee and a bun to take with us, but it's getting late."

Layla nodded, waiting as he opened the door.

The newspaper he'd requested lay just outside. He considered taking it with him, but decided he'd have to read it later. He picked it up and tossed it on the bed.

"How was your sleep? Did you get a good night's rest?" he said as they sauntered down the hall.

"If you're asking if I slept well, the answer is, yes, like a rock, but if you're asking if I feel rested, no, it will take a lot of nights like that to catch up."

As the elevator took them down, she squeezed his arm, laying her head against his shoulder. The door opened and they stepped out into a morning bright with hope.

The Ambassador was already in his first meeting by the time they arrived. They weren't able to find a place that served coffee to go. They'd stood beside a vendor's cart hurriedly slurping the hot brew from ceramic mugs while their taxi waited at the curb.

Mr. Cobel met them in the lobby and apologized. Once again he urged Mohamed to accept the assistance of Consular Affairs, but Mohamed had discussed the idea with Layla on their way over. He didn't feel comfortable telling a junior diplomat he was wanted for murder. Mr Cobel ushered them to an unused office to wait, explaining that he had work to do, but that the Charge d'Affaires' had been informed that they were waiting and would let them know the minute something opened up.

Mohamed and Layla yawned and stretched, and settled into the boredom of watching grass grow. They counted the acoustic tiles, shot rubber bands at flies, and made chains out of paper clips. And every so often got up to stretch their legs. Mohamed read the State Department newsletter for the umpteenth time, now wishing he'd brought the newspaper, but that was hindsight. He explored the world map that was tacked to the wall, placing his hands over the Middle East and praying for every Muslim nation one at a time.

Around noon, Mr. Cobel dropped by to see if they wanted a sandwich, an offer they readily accepted, and for which they thanked him profusely. He disappeared for almost an hour before returning with a bag containing two falafels. Mohamed wolfed his down in a minute and turned to see if Layla would finish hers, but she did, licking her fingers in the absence of a napkin.

All in all, they sat for seven hours only to have Mr. Cobel come at the end of the day to inform them that they'd have to return tomorrow as the Charge d'Affaires had already left the building.

"Did he contact Alexandria Baden, or the FBI in San Francisco as I asked?"

Mr. Cobel shook his head. "I passed the information along, but I can't say what he did with it."

"What about you. You said this should be handled through your office. Can't you make the call?"

"I doubt the White House would put a call through to the vice president's wife from someone they don't know. I wouldn't get past the switchboard. And as for calling California," he looked at his watch, "with the time difference it's about seven a.m. there. I'm afraid your man wouldn't be in the office yet. You'll just have to wait until tomorrow and give it another try."

Mohamed took Layla's hand and nodded. "Alright, but please let the ambassador know that this is important. Tell him it's a matter of life or death."

"I'll do what I can."

That night they dined in the hotel surrounded by dark paneled walls and warm atmospheric lighting. Mohamed ordered roast chicken and Layla, steamed lamb on rice. She sat across from him, sipping soup and giggling at his recounting of their perilous trip across the desert.

It was worth staying an extra night just to see Layla smiling again. There was nothing to celebrate—they were still illegal aliens in a hostile country, still fugitives from the law, they could still be sent back—but she seemed almost buoyant. The candle, flickering on the table between them, cast a warn glow on her face, smoothing her worry lines and erasing the shadows under her eyes.

"So, did you enjoy your camel ride, little girl?"

"Me, I'm an old pro. You're the one who'd never been on a camel."

"I wish I had. I might have built up a few calluses. I was sore all day yesterday. I don't know how people ride those things. I couldn't get comfortable on the plane, or in the taxi, not even in the embassy. But I'm not complaining. Those men were good to us. I doubt my mother paid them to take us all the way to Wadi Halfa. Once we were across the border they could have left us beside the road to fend for ourselves."

"It wasn't just that. They took us right to the airstrip and made sure we boarded the plane."

"That's what I mean. Lucky for us we caught a flight out."

"I don't know what luck has to do with it. We've been in God's hands the whole way."

"Okay, bad choice of words, but you know what I mean."

"I'll tell you what lucky is. Lucky is how you're going to feel when we get back to the room tonight." Layla smiled playfully.

Mohamed's eyes narrowed, certain he'd misunderstood. He dropped his hand from the table looking around for the waiter. "I sure hope they bring our food soon. I'm starved."

For the third day in a row they met the same guard at the same gate and for the third time had their passports scrutinized. It was almost as if the man thought they went home and sent back clones, but Mohamed tried to be patient. The man was just doing his job.

For the third time the guard called someone inside to obtain permission for them to enter. And for the third time they were escorted into the foyer where they met Mr. Cobel in his pristine suit with crisp white shirt and tie, and for the third time Mohamed was embarrassed that they still wore their same grungy outfits. But what could he do? They hadn't had time to pack, and the Bedouins weren't looking to move people with luggage.

They were ushered into the same office, the one with a world map on the wall and a bust of George Washington on a pedestal in the corner. He was pretty sure the office wasn't assigned to anyone. There were tablets and pens and paperclips in the desk, but the files had been cleaned out, and there were no photos, nick-knacks, or other personal items on the credenza, not even a computer. The office had probably been vacated when the consulate was cleared of all non-essential personnel.

He'd finally had a chance to read his newspaper. It was filled with anti-Western rhetoric, making him glad he and Layla were of Egyptian background. Anti-American sentiment ran deep. The hotel clerk had seen their passports and knew they were U.S. citizens. He could tell someone, who might tell someone else, who might tell someone with a vendetta. He vowed to be less cavalier about traveling outside, but that only made it more urgent that they see the ambassador today.

It was just after noon and Mohamed was feeling his stomach rumble when Mr. Cobel marched in smiling. "If you come with me the Charge d'Affaires will see you now."

They rose from their seats, following him down a long corridor to an elevator as he continued talking over his shoulder. "Mr. Fernman apologizes for not being able to see you sooner, but it couldn't be helped. However, he's agreed to give up part of this lunch to see you today."

The space outside the office was large and filled with cubicles but they appeared to be empty. Mr. Cobel opened the wide double doors and ushered them inside. A man, tall and lean, with a face as gray as his hair, stood and extended his hand. He had a pair of reading glasses perched on the tip of his nose.

"I apologize for the delay," he said, releasing his grip on Mohamed's hand. "Please, have a seat. My aid tells me you've been waiting a few days. So, what can I do for you?"

Mohamed reached into his pocket, handing their passports to the attaché. "My wife and I are U.S. citizens," he began. "Recently we were traveling in Egypt and ran into a bit of trouble, not much different than what's going on here with respect to the hatred of all things American."

The ambassador eyed him suspiciously. He sat back in his chair with his hands folded in his lap, nodding. "Go on."

Mohamed relayed the events exactly as they happened. When he was through, the diplomat leaned forward with his elbows on his desk. "What you ask is difficult," he said. "The embassy isn't here to harbor fugitives."

"I'm only a fugitive because I'm a Christian. If I thought I could get a fair trial, I would gladly stay and fight. Right now they have evidence against me, but it's completely manufactured. My wife will tell you everything I say is true, but her testimony is all I've got, which they won't accept. Just help us get back to the states. I don't plan to duck my responsibility. But I need asylum until I can find someone who can follow the evidence and clear my name. I just want a level playing field, which means we need to fight this thing from U.S. soil."

The ambassador shook his head. "I'd like to help but our mandate strictly forbids us from becoming involved in regional affairs."

"So you're suggesting I go back and stand trial for a murder I didn't commit in a Muslim court with a Muslim judge. Look, this whole thing started because I was harboring converted Muslims. They'd put me in jail for that alone."

The diplomat spread his hands apart with his palms up. "It's not that I don't want to help, but I don't have authority in this matter. My hands are tied."

Mohamed took a deep breath. "All right, look, you need to talk to Alexandria Baden, the wife of the Vice President. Or failing that, call Agent Ambrose Barns at the San Francisco office of the FBI. I'm under their witness protection program."

Ambassador Fernman's face sucked into a pout. He began drumming his fingers on the desk. Scooting his chair back, he stood, looking at his watch. "I'm afraid that's all the time I have. I want to thank you for dropping by," he said, extending his hand.

"One call, maybe two, that's all I'm asking you to make."

"Go back to your hotel, Mr. Mulberry. I suggest you stay there until you hear from us. You're in a foreign country, once you exit these premises, you're no longer under U.S. protection. I would be careful not to break any laws. Mr. Cobel will show you out."

Mohamed stared out the window watching the early light of dawn spilling streams of red and blue into the Nile. It was the third night of his sojourn in Sudan, and his third night without sleep. He couldn't seem to quell the voices in his head.

Layla lay on her side curled in a fetal position, breathing deeply. He couldn't help feeling envious. The night had passed without word from the embassy. He wondered if Ambassador Fernman had even made the call. Surely Allie would vouch for him. She owed him. He'd saved her husband's life. The FBI was a bit more iffy. They might be inclined to cut their losses and let him hang. Washington was seven hours behind—he looked at his watch—which meant it was now ten in the evening, Washington time.

The ringing jolted him from his revere. Layla shot up groping for the phone. She fumbled with the receiver, handing it to him.

"Yes, this is Matthew Mulberry. What's that? Okay, I understand." He set the phone back in its cradle.

Layla stretched, rubbing her eyes. "Well, what did he say?"

"He said, 'pack your bags, you're going home.'"

CHAPTER 38

Three months later...

*And he said, "I have been very zealous for the LORD God of hosts...
and they seek to take my life. — 1 Kings 19:14*

THE ROOM—glibly called an evidence locker—was small
and dark, too dark to see clearly, and too small to allow
easy access. Hossame brushed against a shelf and turned
knocking a small box of teeth to the floor, scattering them in all
directions. He was too big to lean over and pick them up, and
there wasn't enough light to find them even if he wanted to. He
was looking for the knife that had killed Ubaid. It was stowed in
one of the boxes somewhere, but there were so many. "El shorta,
the big city police departments, they have budgets for replacing
lights, not the norta el shorta like us."

The light bulb had burned out several months ago, but for one
reason or another, Wessam, the man responsible for keeping and
cataloging evidence, seemed unwilling to replace it. And Hossame
sure wasn't about to do it. It wasn't his job to rifle through evidence,
that was for Wessam, and if Wessam wanted to work in the dark,
so be it. Where was Wessam? The man was never around when he
needed him.

The attorney waiting in his office wasn't a patient man. Lawyers
engaged by the Muslim Brotherhood seldom were. They were gathering the evidence they would need to hang Ostaz Mulberry. They

had the forensics report, but they wanted the murder weapon—
and they had a court order for its release.

He grabbed another box, moving things around to see if it
contained the knife but, no, it wasn't there. *Wessam, you idiot, where
are you?* He would have to tell the attorney to come back some other
time. What was the hurry anyway? Last he'd heard the American
government was fighting extradition. They were refusing to give
Matthew up.

It was insane. People were killed every day and no one cared,
but this time the Brotherhood was making it personal. He stepped
on a tooth and heard it crunch. *Drat.* He craned his head around
looking toward the door, and swept it under the shelf with his
foot. There was no reason to turn one lousy murder into an international incident, calling for protests around the world, riots in the
streets, and church burnings. It was absurd.

Hossame's protruding gut bumped the shelves, almost knocking
them over as he shuffled through the pistols and assault rifles, all
tagged and lined neatly in a row. Knifes were used more often
than guns. Over the years they'd collected too many to place on a
shelf. He continued combing through the boxes. *Ahhh*, now there's
a beauty. He held up a dagger with an oscillating blade, turning it
in the light that streamed through the open door behind him. The
tag read "al Karim." *Oh, that one.* The man had gone on a rampage
and killed his wife, her boyfriend, and his three children by slitting
their throats, and then sat around reading verses from the Koran
about the punishment meted out to those who were unfaithful
while watching them bleed to death. Made him glad he was an
atheist. He put the weapon back in the box.

The Muslim Brotherhood had appealed to the United Nations.
They were pressuring the U.S. to honor their extradition treaty. It
almost made him wish he'd arrested Ostaz Mulberry when he had
the chance. *Almost.* It might have been expedient, but expedience
didn't warrant putting an innocent man in jail. Uthman's story was
filled with inconsistencies, but with the fingerprints on the knife,

two supposed eyewitnesses, and religious prejudice stacked against him, Ostaz Mulberry didn't stand a chance.

Hossame spun around, his stomach bumping the shelves.

"What are you doing? No, no, no, you will mess up everything." Wessam rushed in taking the box from Hossame's hands. "Please, allow me. What is it you look for?"

"There's an attorney in my office insisting we surrender the weapon in the Mulberry investigation."

"Ah, you see, this is easy. All you must do is ask." Wessam squeezed by the burgeoning belly of the mabaneth and went to a desk. Sliding back the drawer, he removed a long bladed knife in a plastic bag and held it up. "I have kept this one aside, as the investigation is still open."

Hossame held out his hand. "I'll have the lawyer sign for it." He took the weapon and stepped back, but a box behind him made him stumble and he had to reach out to catch his balance, grasping at a wood pole that was leaning against the wall. A second later three shovels came crashing to the floor with a clatter.

"Hey, watch what you're doing."

The detective grunted as he stooped over to pick up the shovels, propping them against the wall as before, but as he reached for the third shovel, he noticed the blade of a fourth turned the other way with its handle hidden behind the desk. "Are these the shovels from the Taymur murder investigation?"

"Yes, that investigation is also still open so I keep them here."

"Didn't our forensics lab examine three shovels?"

"I believe so. Yes it did, I remember quite distinctly."

"Well there are four shovels here, see?" he grabbed Wessam's arm and pulled him over, pointing to a dark area on the floor. "Looks like there's one hidden behind your desk, which means there's a fourth shovel that hasn't been tested."

"But…"

"Relax, I'm not accusing you of anything. Just have it tested and apprise me of the results. And Wessam…"

"Yes, Ostaz El-Din"

"...Get a light. If it weren't so dark in here, you might have seen it." Hossame turned and walked out holding the knife that killed Ubaid in a plastic bag, muttering about the incompetence of his staff.

Mohamed paced back and forth, rubbing the goosebumps on his arms. The air was warm, though California was never as warm as Egypt, but it wasn't the temperature that gave him a chill, it was the newspapers splayed out on the floor in front of him. "What right do we have to give asylum to a man wanted for murder..." the Times quoted. "It is incumbent upon our government to honor the treaty established in 1874 between the governments of Egypt and the United States for the exchange of wanted criminals..." wrote the Tribune. "How can we call ourselves a just society when we withhold the right of justice from other nations..." opined the Chronicle. "Muslims around the world are enraged...Terrorist threats have been issued against American interests...Protests filled with anti American rhetoric...Violence has broken out in..." they all echoed. They made it sound like he was a threat to world peace.

Mohamed stopped reading and looked up as Layla entered the room.

"What are you doing?" she said. "Oh, don't read those; they'll only get you upset."

"You know I have to go back, Layla. The government may be protecting me now, but sooner or later they'll cave into public pressure. It's just a matter of time."

"Stop it! You're not going back. I won't allow it! *Ohhhh,* see your son doesn't want you to go either. I just felt him kick."

"Layla, you should be lying down. You know what the doctor said. You're spotting. You need to stay off your feet." Mohamed went over and gently took her arm, helping her to a chair.

"I'm all right, but you could get me something to drink. Really, Mohamed, your son needs you," she said as he disappeared around the corner. "You know you won't get a fair trial. The whole world's already found you guilty."

Mohamed returned with a glass of water and handed it to his wife. He knelt down beside her chair, laying his hand over her tummy. "First of all, we don't know we have a son..."

"I do."

"Okay, but that's based on a mother's intuition. Anyway, God will protect me."

Layla, grabbed Mohamed's hand, glaring at him. "God let Amin die! Martyrs die for the sake of the gospel every day, and I won't let you become one of them! I was just chatting with Sabah on-line. The atmosphere in Egypt is extremely volatile. A few churches have already been burned. It won't be long before someone gets killed."

"Don't you think I know that? You think I want to go back? Read the papers, Layla. The president will eventually cave in. He has too."

"But you saved his life."

"His, the vice president's and a whole bunch of senators and congressmen, but that's the point. He and the vice president know about it, but the rest of the world doesn't. It's all classified, and if it gets out, everyone will know I'm Mohamed not Matthew, and we don't want that. So that leaves the president having to deal with the media who see him as trying to protect a killer."

Tears appeared in Layla's eyes.

"It's going to be okay. God didn't bring us this far to abandon us now." He held her, letting her tears moisten his hands as he wiped them from her cheeks.

"I know," she said, but I'm scared, and it doesn't matter that I shouldn't be." She took a breath, the air fluttering in her chest. "I'm only human, Mohamed, know what I mean? I've prayed about it. I know God doesn't want me living in fear, but even Elijah felt this way, and I'm not some kind of super saint like him. Remember? He called down fire from heaven and destroyed the four-hundred prophets of Baal and then, when Jezebel threatened to have his head, ran off and hid in a cave. That's me, taking the coward's way…

"Layla don't…"

"No, hear me out. That's just like me. I know God called us to serve Him in Egypt, but I somehow can't get it in my head that He's going to protect us. God confronted Elijah in that cave. He said, 'what are you doing here, Elijah?' And over and over I hear this voice saying, 'What are you doing here, Layla?' And sometimes I just want to scream, 'Can't you see what's going on out there, Lord? If we go back they'll kill us,' but He just says, 'What are you doing here, Layla?'"

The doorbell *buzzzzed*. Mohamed reached over and used a thumb to smooth a tear from his wife's cheek. "I know, Layla. I'm not saying it's easy. Doing the right thing seldom is." He sighed and gave her a hug, then stood. "I'll see who it is."

They had installed cameras in the hall for added security but when he checked the monitor the passageway looked clear. He opened the door and there at his feet was a shoebox containing three short lengths of pipe, each capped at the end with lumps of soft clay. It was meant to look like a bomb, but no detonator or wires attached. A single 3 X 5 index card was inside. It had one word written on it in black felt pen. "JUSTICE!" it said.

"I'll be back in a minute," he called over his shoulder.

"Who is it?"

"No one. Just kids playing a prank, but while I'm up I need to get something from the car." Before Layla could respond, he stepped out and closed the door. He didn't want her seeing the box, not with the baby on the way. She was under enough stress.

The elevator opened. Two of his neighbors shuffled out but stopped abruptly, looking flustered. They turned the other way, ignoring him. That's why he needed a family, to lift him up and support him, even when times were hard. Families were supposed to love unconditionally.

He wanted a family more than anything—*his family*—a mother and father and children playing in the yard, *but why now?* He was putting on a good face, rejoicing with Layla, but the idea of leaving her with a child to raise on her own, troubled him. He wanted his child to have what he was deprived of—a home filled with loving, caring people. No, this was not the right time. *I never seem to know what You're doing God, I never seem to know…*

"*But we know that all things work together for good to those who love God, to those who are the called according to His purpose.*"

Quoting scripture wasn't going to help. Not now. He was already resolved in his decision. He had to see it through. He would take the box to the car and make sure it got to his friend, Ambrose Barnes, at the FBI.

Uthman glanced at the crowd of reporters. *This is good, very good, at least twenty, and all of them here to see me.* He'd already been introduced to representatives from *Al-Ahram, Cairo Live, the Cairo Times, Daily News Egypt, the Middle East Times* not to mention a man all the way from England who wrote for *Ikhwanweb* the London-based official web site of the Muslim Brotherhood.

He couldn't believe his good fortune, a lowly farm worker thrust into the world's spotlight. His eyes scanned the assembly, all of them milling about, anxious to hear what he had to say. He sat on a raised podium beside his colleagues from the Muslim Brotherhood, men who looked like sheiks with long robes and braided keffiyehs, though his own billowy turban sprouted from his head like a magnificent minaret outdoing them all.

The boys from the Brotherhood had become his new best friends, taking him under their wing, making sure he was sheltered and well fed. They were sponsoring this event. They had arranged the venue, called the news media together, and written his speech—but he, Uthman, was the one everyone came to see. He was the eyewitness. He alone had the power to bring the blasphemous Matthew Mulberry to justice.

This would be his finest hour. His photograph had been in the newspapers many times, but this was a first. This time there were television cameras. Foreign correspondents from America had come all the way to Asyut to hear him speak. Matthew Mulberry would live to regret the day he crossed Uthman Massri.

A man standing at the podium turned and waved him up. He stood, half expecting applause, but then realized this wasn't the right setting. That would come later at dinner parties thrown in his honor, after Oataz Mulberry was hanging at the end of a rope. He took his place in front of the microphone and shuffled his notes making sure for the umpteenth time they were in the right order.

Looking down, he began to read. "I am here to speak for someone who can no longer speak for himself. Ubaid…" The pack of reporters began to murmur and shift in their seats, interrupting his thoughts, causing him to lose his place. He looked up to find the cause of the commotion.

A Lada and a Land Rover pulled up behind the throng of news reporters, a major distraction causing everyone to turn their heads away. Uthman looked back at Sharifa ah-din, but he just shrugged.

The officers formed two lines and began pushing their way through the crowd one group coming up on either side of the stage. Uthman recognized the fat one. He was the mabaneth handling the investigation. He probably wanted to announce that they'd found more damming evidence against Ostaz Mulberry, but that wouldn't do. This was his show. He wasn't about to be upstaged by a local cop. He rushed over to head Hossame off at the steps.

Sharifa ah-din got up and joined them. Uthman started to speak but Sharifa raised his hand cutting him off and turned to address Hossame himself. "I'm not sure why you're here my brother, but we are trying to hold a press conference. I promise to give you my undivided attention as soon as we're finished."

Hossame took another step, using his weight to push Uthman aside as he acquired the platform. He looked at the Muslim leader. "That is most generous, Sharifa, but with my most humble apologies, we're not here to see you. We are here for the same reason you are. We want justice to be done."

"If you have something to say, call your own press conference," Uthman said.

Hossame reached into his pocket for a cigarette, ignoring the comment. He found a match and lit up, blowing a stream of blue smoke into the air.

Strobes popped in the audience, the atmosphere tense. Reporters sensed something big was about to happen.

"This is not a problem," Sharifa continued. "Please, I offer you my seat, and when Uthman is done, you may say whatever you wish. I ask only that you wait until…"

"I'm afraid that's not possible. I'm here to arrest Uthman."

"Me?"

Hossame looked at Uthman shaking his head. "The warrant was issued two days ago, but we didn't know where you were until one of my officers heard on the radio that you'd be speaking in a few minutes." He turned his attention back to Sharifa. "Thank you for assisting me with the arrest."

Uthman was backing away. At the last second, he reeled about but fell into the arms of two soldiers who had stepped onto the stage from the other side. They grabbed him, jerking his hands behind his back to place him in cuffs. Hossame walked over and stood facing Uthman. He looked up blowing smoke in the taller man's face. "Uthman Massri, I'm placing you under arrest for the murder of Amin Taymur."

Strobes popped and digital cameras recorded as Uthman was led away by the police. He tried to duck, suddenly not wanting to be photographed, but he was a star and everyone wanted his picture. There was no mistaking the excessive turban that sprouted from his head, or the beard that, as he stooped forward, almost touched the ground.

Hossame used his weight to push through the press of journalists, ignoring the microphones being thrust into his face.

"Can you comment on what just happened?"

"Why are you arresting the key witness for the prosecution?"

"Does this have anything to do with the church burning in Minya?"

He gripped Uthman's arm pulling him in close, his lips almost touching his prisoner's ear. "Smile, Uthman, it's your big day," he said.

CHAPTER 39

*From the Jews five times I received forty stripes minus one. Three times
I was beaten with rods; once I was stoned; three times I was shipwrecked;
a night and a day I have been in the deep; in journeys often, in perils of
waters, in perils of robbers, in perils of my own countrymen...*
— *II Corinthians 11: 24-26*

MOHAMED PACED back and forth looking down at the
crowd on the street below. More than a hundred people
were assembled, chanting "Hang from a tree, Mul-ber-
ry," and waving signs. "Hit the road, Jack, and don't come back."
They were a lynch mob waiting to see him hang. He moved away
from the window. There might be some crazy down there with a
gun. Or was that a lack of faith? Faith was the real issue, wasn't it?
He needed faith to do the right thing. Faith to believe God would
see him through—even if it meant leaving his wife.

"But look at Shadrach, Meshach, and Abednego, God saved
them out of the fire."

"And God allowed Paul to be beheaded." Layla retorted.

It was the mystery of God, that He should do His will in people's
lives, often keeping one while letting another go. Why were some
healed, while others died? Why was he himself saved, while Amin
perished? Why was his brother taken and he left here? Only God
knew.

"You can't go back!" Layla wrapped her arms around Mohamed, clinging to him, her tear streaked face pressed against his chest. "How can he do this to you? You saved his life."

"He doesn't have a choice. Right now, the whole world is against me. The president can't justify keeping me here, not with the leader of every nation crying out for justice to be done" Mohamed turned, breaking free of Layla's grip. He stepped back and held her at arms length, looking into her eyes. "I need you to be brave, Layla. I need you to be strong. You have to trust that God is in this. I need you praying for me every second of every day. God's not going to abandon us. He'll see this through to the end."

Layla threw off his hands, glaring at him. "I don't care. It's not right. Why would God let us escape only to send you back?" She stopped, looking at Mohamed, bringing a tissue to her nose. *Sniff.* "God didn't stop the mouth of the lions only to throw Daniel back into the den when the lions got hungry again."

"No, Layla. God's timing is perfect. Can't you see? If we'd stayed in Egypt, I would never have received a fair trial. They would have judged me as much for blasphemy as for murder. But now, with the international media reporting on the trial, and with the whole world watching, there's no way religion will come up. Egypt wants to maintain that it allows religious liberty, even if it's not true. And now that Uthman has been arrested for the murder of Amin, his testimony is tainted. The American government has promised to provide me with the finest legal counsel money can buy. I believe God's doing all this just to clear my name." He grimaced, hoping God would forgive the small lie.

Layla brought her hair around, twisting it into a rope. Her eyes were glassy. She *sniffed*, and reached for a tissue, wiping her nose. "But why don't they just drop the whole thing? They already know Uthman's a liar."

"It's not the same thing. Uthman's on trial for the murder of Amin. I'm accused of killing Ubaid. They're separate cases, though I'm still convinced Uthman killed them both. The trouble is, everything's been blown out of proportion. It's not about the murder anymore. It's about a U.S. president taking the law into his own hands. They're calling it an abuse of power, saying he granted me asylum for some personal agenda. The world wants to see me stand trial, and it's not going to rest until I do."

"But what if they convict…"

"They won't." Mohamed smiled, trying to convey confidence while praying his eyes wouldn't betray the uncertainty he felt. God had a purpose and a plan, but only God knew how that plan would work itself out.

There was a knock at the door, just three light taps. Mohamed knew it was Ambrose, though a faint knock was out of character for a man his size. "He's here, Layla. I have to go."

Layla took a deep breath, the air fluttering in her chest. She turned her head away, her hands continuing to knead her thick rope of hair.

Mohamed left the living room, walking briskly to the front door, keeping up a show of confidence as he let Ambrose in.

The government agent entered wearing a suit uncomfortably small on his thick chest and shoulders. He nodded at Mohamed and then at Layla. Without saying a word, he crossed the living room and went to the window, looking down on the throng of protestors and reporters assembled on the lawn in front of the building. There were crews from every major network and their local affiliates as well as crime reporters from both national and local newspapers. "The police are guarding the entrances keeping the media out, but we'll have to go though them to get to the car." He turned around looking at Mohamed. "You know I have to place you in handcuffs. I don't want to, but if I don't, some idiot reporter is going to say I gave you preferential treatment."

"I know. That's okay. You do your job."

Ambrose opened his jacket and unclipped a pair of manacles from his belt. "Could you please turn around and place your hands behind your back."

Layla ran over, grabbing his wrists. "No, I won't let you take him. I won't! He's innocent!" She reached around trying to push the FBI agent's hands away. "How can you do this? You know he's innocent. You're feeding him to the lions just to save the president's image. How can you do this? It's wrong."

Ambrose dropped his hands, pursing his lips to hold back words he'd promised not to say. He glanced at Mohamed who spun around to catch Layla.

"Layla, please, Ambrose is only doing his job. If he doesn't do it, someone else will. He asked for this assignment just so I wouldn't have to be carried off by a stranger. He's on our side, Layla." He let go of her hands. "Please let him do his job. Agent Barnes," Mohamed turned around placing his hands behind him, "just do what you have to do."

Layla stood back weeping as Ambrose snapped the cuffs around his wrists. They looked small in his meaty hands, almost like plastic toys. But the clicking sound was real. Mohamed was bound, ready to be dragged before Pilate, an innocent man falsely accused.

Layla lunged forward, grabbing her husband again. "You better come back, you hear me? You have a child to think about, a son who will need a father." She threw her arms around her husband's neck, tears gushing down her cheeks unrestrained. "Don't you disappoint me."

Mohamed leaned forward to kiss his wife, longing to return her embrace.

Ambrose gave them a moment, then took Mohamed by the elbow and tugged him forward, breaking off their goodbye.

"Pray for me Layla. Promise me you'll pray every day."

Layla's eyes looked to Ambrose again, pleading. "Please, I want to come."

"We've already been through all this, Layla," Mohamed said. "You know you can't. I'm being taken straight to the airport and put on a government plane. They're not allowing anyone near the airstrip. Not even the media. Just be grateful they let us have this time together. You have to be strong." He leaned forward and kissed her one last time on the cheek. "I love you, just remember that. And I love the child inside you. Make sure you tell him that every day until I return."

"You better be here when he's born," she said. Layla took a step back, wiping her cheeks with her palms and pulling her long hair around to the front. She tried to smile as though wanting to give him a picture to remember her by, but the effect was weak. She couldn't keep the moisture from clouding her eyes.

"You ready?" Ambrose said.

Mohamed nodded.

They stepped into the hall. Ambrose leaned in to close the door behind them.

They didn't see Layla as she fell to her knees sobbing. "Why God, why? Please bring him back God, I'm begging you, please bring him back."

His neighbors refrained from sticking their heads out to gawk at him as they brushed down the hall. He appreciated that.

Ambrose let go of his arm as they rode the elevator down, but took hold of it again as the doors opened. They went out the front entrance of the apartment building squeezing through the mass of reporters who jabbed microphones in his face while strobes popped and video cameras churned. Mohamed didn't answer the questions flung at him, nor did he try to duck or hide. He felt no guilt or shame. Some would interpret his confidence as arrogance, but he didn't care. Even if the whole world judged him guilty, he was innocent in the eyes of God. That's all that mattered.

Ambrose opened the door of the unmarked black sedan. Mohamed turned and glanced one last time at their apartment and saw Layla with her hands pressed flat against the picture window. Tears were streaming down her face. Her lips mouthed the silent words, *"I love youuuuuuu!"*

A few reporters were still throwing questions at him. He slid into the back. The door slammed cutting them off. Ambrose squeezed through the melee around to the other side and climbed in. Mohamed watched as the journalists scrambled to their vehicles while Ambrose put the car into drive and pulled away. Swinging his head around to look out the back window, Mohamed saw they were being followed by a half dozen news vans marked with television station logos. He brought his head around and caught Ambrose's eye in the review mirror.

"They'll only get as far as the airport security gate," Ambrose said, focusing on the road again. "I think you're a fool, you know. The president was ready to go to the mat for you. Soon as he learned that Uthman fellow was a liar and a murderer he knew you were innocent. He wasn't going to send you back."

Mohamed nodded. "Thanks for not saying anything. Layla would never forgive me if she knew this was my idea. Besides, it helps the president. Every week his popularity drops another few points and I can't be responsible for that, but I do appreciate his stand."

A van pulled up alongside. The side door slid open revealing a guy with a camera on a tripod, attempting to record their journey.

"Ignore him," Ambrose said, his eyes flicking to the rearview mirror and back again. "I just hope you're ready for what comes. You know you won't get a fair trial. The Attorney General's mobilized the best legal team he has, but our lead's already saying there's little hope. They'll make a pretense of listening to all the evidence, but nobody expects an acquittal. Egypt's under a lot of pressure from the Muslim world. They're just going through the motions for appearances sake."

"Yes, but now Uthman's credibility is..."

"Save it for your lawyer, Kid. He'll tell you what he already told us. They're two separate cases. The judge won't even allow your lawyer to bring Uthman's past up because it's prejudicial. Your case has to be argued on its own merits. You know I'm not a God fearing man, but if you escape the noose, I'll be the first to admit there's a God out there somewhere."

"Our God is able to deliver us out of your hand, but even if he doesn't, be it known unto you O king, we will not bow down."

"Huh?"

"Nothing. All men are destined to die sometime. I'd rather die for telling the truth than hiding from it. The apostle Paul was born into a pagan Roman society but became a Christian. He ended up getting tried by a Roman court where he refused to recant his faith and was beheaded, but at his trial he was able to witness to the truth. Maybe God wants me to testify before the world, too."

"And be beheaded?"

"Look Ambrose. I'm not doing this to become a martyr. I have no desire to die, though if I have to, I pray God will give me strength. The man Uthman killed, he died for what he believed. How can I do less? But this isn't about that, this is about saving my wife and child. You got that box. You saw the fake bomb. Did you get the latest letter I sent? They're going to kill me anyway. There's no avoiding it. You can put me in all the witness protection programs you want, but sooner or later they'll find me. My face is just too well known. I have to do this to protect my family. If I stand trial, they'll leave Layla alone, but if I don't, it won't be just me who dies, and I can't have that on my conscience."

Ambrose glanced at the letter lying on the seat of the car. It had been handed him that very morning.

"…We know that you, along with other agents of espionage organizations in the disguise of European and American pastors, are deceiving the Muslims and changing their religion and faith.

"You are standing against the Holy Organized Republic Islamic, and also to the billions of Islamic people. Be aware that in these days the power of the Islamic word is growing, it's army and economy's success have blinded the American and European governments, and have defeated and scared them.

"Very quickly all of Europe, America, Israel and all other satanic authorities of the world will be destroyed with the hands of

Islam, the only most holy religion will be increased and scattered throughout all the world and will lead the world."

The letter, signed by, "The Hezbollah Party, Army of the World's Imam" was much longer and spoke of bringing judgment upon Mohamed and his family.

Mohamed had received more than a dozen such letters, each one suggesting the world would be a better place without him. He'd been careful to always get to the mail before Layla. The threatening notes were immediately redirected to the FBI. His life was in danger, he could deal with that, but he wasn't about to let anyone hurt his wife—*greater love hath no man than he lay down his life for a friend*—He deserved to die, not Layla, he had his brother's blood on his hands—eye for eye, tooth for tooth, life for life.

"If I've been chosen to be a Martyr for my God, I'd rather do it proclaiming my innocence than while on the run," he continued. "Once I'm gone, I'm pretty sure they'll leave my family alone, but I want you to keep your promise and watch out for them."

Mohamed thought of a joke he once heard. A man asked how one should dress for their execution, and the answer was: "very slowly."

There was no avoiding it, now. They were running alongside a chain link fence that surrounded row after row of airplane hangers. One of those planes would carry him back to Egypt and, if Ambrose was right, to his death. His heart trembled in his chest. He prayed God would give him strength to say, as the Apostle Paul had said, "For me to live is Christ, and to die is gain."

The car rolled through a set of gates to the side of San Francisco International Airport. The guards checked Ambrose's I.D. and let them pass. There were no customs stations; no long lines for baggage check in. Mohamed twisted around to look out the rear window. The guards behind them halted the news vans, keeping them back. Ambrose pulled up next to a plane that already sat on the tarmac fuelled and ready. He got out and came around to the side door, opening it to help Mohamed out.

He took a deep breath, imbibing a strange blend of ocean brine and jet fuel wondering if he'd ever enjoy that scent again.

Mohamed woke to the smell of urine and human waste. The room was dark; the only light came through the small sliding window in the steel door, and it was closed. He tried to lift himself but his arms had no strength. He collapsed again. He had been there three days, or was it four? He could no longer keep track. It had to be at least three. Three full days and nights at the mercy of soldiers skilled in the art of inflicting pain. Three days without sleep. Three days without food. Three days of being beaten with telephone books. He knew what they were doing. They didn't want to bruise his flesh or leave marks that might show. Three days of being injected with drugs to make him confess. But he hadn't confessed, at least not to the murder. He couldn't. He'd done nothing wrong.

Why had they suddenly stopped the beating and let him sleep? The door creaked open on metal hinges. A man, or at least the silhouette of one, marched inside and stooped down setting a metal tray on the floor.

"Eat," the man said. "Today you will meet with a member of the American Red Cross. He will examine you. You will tell him you are being treated well. You understand? Now eat." The man turned and removed himself, heading back out the metal door through which he came, the sound of its closing reverberating through the cell.

Mohamed struggled to a sitting position. It didn't matter what he said, they were bound to see he was weak. All of a sudden the light above him snapped on. He raised his hand, squinting to shut out the brightness. A thin piece of bread and a bowl of watery bean soup sat in front of him. He reached out, but winced as pain shot through his arm. Rolling onto his knees, he brought his face down to the bowl and lapped until it was empty. The thin pita bread was harder to negotiate, his fingers weren't cooperating, but he managed to plop it into his mouth. He tried again to stand, stumbling backward into the wall. For the first time, he realized he was naked. The piles of feces scattered about the floor—were his.

The door opened, but this time two men entered. They each grabbed one of his arms and began dragging him down a hall where he was pushed into another room, one like the one he'd just been in—four scarred walls without windows and a drain in the floor that served as a latrine.

One of the men left the room for a moment and returned with a hose. The spigot erupted and Mohamed was hit with a torrent of water. He tried to raise his hands, fending off the assault, but it was no use. Wherever his hands went, the water went somewhere else. The stream was cold but fierce, and it stung his skin like fire. The hosing stopped and another man entered the room wearing rubber gloves and carrying a bucket. The man began to lather Mohamed with soap and a hard brush. The water was freezing and the bristles abrasive but Mohamed didn't resist. At some inexplicable level he appreciated the man's efforts to make him clean. When the man was through, he stepped away and the shower from the hose started again, rinsing him off.

The man with the bucket disappeared around the corner, followed by the man with the hose. A few seconds later he reappeared carrying a towel and a stack of clothes. He threw the pile on the ground. "Dry yourself and get dressed," he said.

Mohamed's visit with the representative from the Red Cross lasted all of about a minute. He was seated in a room in front of a table. There was no way for the man to see how weak he was. The man asked only three questions.

"Are you being treated well?"

Mohamed looked around. He didn't see any recording devices, but he was sure they were there. "Yes," he said.

"And are you being fed?"

"Yes."

The man nodded and wrote something down in his notebook. "Are you in need of medical attention?" he said, looking up.

"No."

The man wrote another note and got up, apparently satisfied Mohamed was in good hands. He slipped his notebook into his pocket and left the room.

The two who had cleaned him off, returned. They each took one of his arms and drug him down another long corridor. "It's time you got a little exercise," one of the men said as the other opened a door. Mohamed was shoved outside. He stumbled into an open yard as the door slammed closed behind him.

He stood wobbling on his feet, squinting to shut out the bright sun. The air smelled fresh, and he could feel the warmth of the sun on his face. He heard the twittering of a bird, perhaps building a nest. They were giving him a moment's rest, "Thank you Lor—" then a fist slammed into the side of his head, knocking him senseless. He went down, a melee of men engulfing him, pummeling him with their fists, kicking him in the groin, the face and ribs. He heard a voice he thought he recognized. Through the fray, he opened his eyes and saw Uthman standing back with his arms folded, smiling. The last thing he remembered before blacking out was the globe of Uthman's turban filling the sky like a giant white moon.

Layla stood in front of her television watching in horror as the image changed from the outside of a prison where dozens of people marched carrying banners and shouting surahs in Arabic, to the inside of a hospital. Now the picture showed a man laying in a bed. All but his eyes and mouth were wrapped in bandages and what little flesh was exposed was so black it defied the definition of skin. She didn't have to be a doctor to know what that tube coming out of his nose was for. Her husband was on a lung machine.

"...the warden has apologized for the mix up that resulted in Mr. Mulberry being released into the general population." The scene cut to the protesters outside the prison. The cameras went to a close up of a man screaming in Arabic with subtitles in English. "God has taken it upon Himself to punish the murderer for his crime." The scene switched again to the newsroom anchor desk. "We were not able to receive confirmation, but sources inside the hospital say Mulberry has a ruptured spleen and damaged kidneys, along with a concussion and internal bleeding. They're listing his chances of survival at less than fifty percent."

The doorbell rang but Layla didn't respond. She stood in front of the TV unmoving until whoever it was started banging so loud they could no longer be ignored. She went to the door, checking the video monitor. It was Ambrose.

Layla opened the door allowing him to enter, but he hesitated. He was looking beyond her into the room. She turned and saw he was eying the television.

"I'm sorry," he said. "I rushed over as soon as I heard. I wanted to catch you before you saw it that way."

She turned and with her hand still on the doorknob stood back sweeping her other hand toward the set. "I...I...that's Mo..." she sputtered. Her eyes rolled to the top of her head and she started to fall. Ambrose reached out, catching her before she hit the ground.

Ambrose kept his portable cherry flashing all the way to the hospital. His car wasn't equipped with a siren, but he had no trouble getting others to yield the right of way. Not slowing, he squealed around the corner and bounced up the driveway, sliding to a stop in front of the emergency entrance.

No one rushed out to meet him or to offer assistance as he bolted through the doors. "I need a wheelchair," he screamed at the first person he saw, but it proved to be a patient who said in return, "Sorry, I don't have one."

Ambrose jetted back outside and yanked the passenger door open, pulling Layla into his arms. A watery pomegranate colored liquid stained the seat. He whirled about and sped back inside, but this time he was met by a lady in a hospital uniform who took Layla's wrist and began a count. "What happened?" she said, trying to keep up with Ambrose as he hustled Layla inside.

"She passed out. I think she's miscarrying. I need to see a doctor, now! Where's a freaking wheelchair. I need a doctor!"

"Sir. I have to ask you to calm down. Sir! We'll take care of it. Is she your wife?" The woman turned raising her hand to wave at a young man in scrubs standing beside a rolling hospital bed.

"No, she's the wife of Matthew Mulberry."

The nurse's head snapped up. "*The* Matthew Mulberry?"

"Yes, that one." Ambrose placed Layla's unconscious body on the bed and reached into his inside coat pocket to produce a badge. "I'm agent Barnes with the FBI. This women is to get your best care, and I mean right now. She's part of an ongoing investigation. Are we clear?"

The nurse nodded, looking over at the man wearing hospital greens. "Get this woman to emergency, stat!"

Ambrose took a deep breath. "Thank you," he said. "And I need to talk to the doctor."

"That would be me," the woman said.

CHAPTER 40

I know a man in Christ who fourteen years ago, whether in the body I do not know, or whether out of the body I do not know, God knows—such a one was caught up to the third heaven. — II Corinthians 12:2

TO THE WORLD outside Mohamed appeared comatose, like the living dead, a body with breath, but no life—But inside, deep within that inner being of the subconscious, he was alive and well.

Sometimes his body would twitch, or jerk, as one does when caught in a dream. The nursing staff would chagrin, praying the spasm didn't mean he was on the road to recovery. Justice would be better served if he died, and saved the government the cost of a trial. His doctor, however, flown in by the U.S. State Department, was careful to see Mohamed received proper medical care.

Deep in his subliminal world Mohamed saw visions. Some were obscure in meaning, like seeing himself plucking figs from a tree in the middle of a dry lake, or seeing himself drowning, being sucked into a vortex of water with a life preserver just out of reach. Others seemed to have a spiritual connotation. He saw himself carrying a cross through the desert under a burning sun, with scorpions at his heals and birds dropping stones on his head, and then roaming the dark earth with a torch in hand searching for those who needed light. Today his body wrenched and shuddered at what he saw, his face contorted in pain.

He was climbing a flight of stairs, plodding up one step at a time. Two men attended him, one on his right, and one on his left, holding him by the arms, his hands securely tied behind his back. *Clunk, step, clunk, step,* he ascended moving ever closer to the noose strung from the gallows. He reached the top, sweat pouring from his brow, his heart hammering in his chest.

His body, lying on the bed, twitched, as his feet were positioned over the trapdoor. An ocean of people, stretching as far as the eye could see, had come to watch, shouting, raising their fists, cheering.

"Have you any last words?"

He swallowed, his tongue thick as a sponge. He nodded and sniffed, sucking in his breath. His lips trembled but his song rang out loud and clear.

> "Praise God from Whom all blessings flow,
> Praise Him all creatures here below,
> Praise Him above ye heavenly host,
> Praise Father, Son, and Holy Ghost."

A loud cry of boos, hisses, and catcalls rose from the crowd.

Then he was among them, shouting with the crowd, raising his fist at the man on the scaffold. He looked up and saw Uthman with a look of defiance in his eyes, just as they drew the rope around his neck. The mob screamed, "Crucify him, crucify him!" and he suddenly felt his hand drop to his side...*crucify?*

"Have you any last words?"

"La illaha illa Allah" There is no God but Allah. Uthman cried.

"No! Don't!" Mohamed began pushing into the crowd, elbowing his way through the masses, but it seemed useless; he had miles to go. He kept pushing, shoving, squeezing, refusing to give up until he broke through the line at the front. Uthman was still there. It wasn't too late. He launched himself up the stairs, his feet pounding with a *thud, thud, thud,* taking two and three steps at a time.

Uthman was waiting, standing on the scaffold, bound. He looked at Mohamed, his lips curling as he laughed. The executioner dropped a bag over Uthman's head and took a step back. The trapdoor under Uthman's feet swung loose and he fell. Below him the ground began to swirl, a cyclonic pit opening to reveal a cauldron of bubbling orange-red flames. Uthman, shrouded in black, slipped silently into the abyss.

Mohamed reached out. *"Noooooooooo!"*

A single low watt bulb, encased in a grill of wire mesh, was mounted to the ceiling, barely giving the mabaneth enough light to read. Hossame El-Din sat at a folding table, the bulge of his stomach preventing him from scooting closer. He reached for the folder, flopping it open, and felt the grit of the table's unwashed surface scraping against his knuckles. He pulled the file into his gut, trying to keep his coat from getting dirty. The walls were dingy, speckled with dried blood, and the cement floor smelled like a latrine.

The room was a small windowless enclosure commonly used for interrogation, and sometimes torture. It was designed to exact confessions from the guilty, but Hossame had no need to resort to such tactics. He removed a sheath of paper labeled "Deposition of Uthman Massri," and opened it to the first page, looking at the prisoner seated across from him.

"I'm here to make sure we have everything we need to prosecute Matthew Mulberry for the murder of Ubaid Sadan. You understand that this has nothing to do with your arrest for the murder of Amin Taymur. This regards the charges you have brought against Ostaz Mulberry. Should he live, he must still stand trial. I have been asked to confirm the information pertaining to our original interview. We must be absolutely certain we have all our facts straight before turning them over to the prosecuting attorney. Are we agreed on this?"

Uthman shrugged and gave a smile, his long beard coiling around his mouth. "Should Mulberry live to stand trial, yes, I agree."

"You further understand that this session is being recorded and may subsequently be used in court as evidence?"

Uthman flicked his fingers in front of him, waving Hossame on as though such a question didn't warrant an answer. "Of course."

Hossame nodded. He looked down at his notes. "You stated that you, Uthman Massri, along with two other persons, Ahmed al Atrash, and Ubaid Sadan were...what did you say?" Hossame turned back a few pages, "you were helping Ubaid bring in his sheep, is that right?"

"That is what I said, yes."

"Something troubles me about that. When we did our investigation, we didn't find any sheep. They were in another pasture about half a kilometer away. How do you explain this?"

Uthman looked up, his lips drawing into a frown as he stroked his beard, his eyes narrowing as though considering the relevance of the question. He shook his head. "I don't know, maybe we hadn't started yet, or maybe someone scattered the sheep after we left. What does it matter? Whether there were sheep, or no sheep, it doesn't change the fact that Mulberry murdered Ubaid. This I saw for myself."

Hossame scribbled a note and without looking up said, "All right, but you might want to think about how you're going to answer that question in court. A good defense lawyer would suggest you weren't there to gather the sheep at all, which begs the question as to why you were there. You don't want to give credence to Ostaz Matthew when he says you were holding his wife hostage. Now, in your original testimony you said he came in and accused you of killing Amin Taymur, and that he swore vengeance and lunged at you with a knife, but that Ubaid stepped in the way. Is that correct?"

"Yes, but I have already told you, I did not kill Amin. I am an innocent man. This I also told Ostaz Matthew, but he was like a madman, swinging his knife around, and when Ubaid tried to stop him, he stabbed him in the heart. It was only then that Ahmed and I were able to grab him and take the knife away. This is why my prints were also on the knife. But he was like a crazed man with seven times the strength of a normal man and he broke free and fled. We did not chase him because we wanted to help our friend Ubaid, but sadly, we could only watch him die."

"And how do you account for the wound in Ubaid's side."

"What do you mean?"

"You said Ostaz Matthew stabbed Ubaid in the heart and then you wrestled the knife from him. But there were two wounds. Ubaid was also stabbed in the side. That's the wound Ostaz Matthew claims he inflicted. He said when he left, Ubaid was still alive."

"But he wasn't. I was there when it happened. I saw Ubaid fall to the floor. If there were two wounds, it is because Matthew stabbed him twice. When the wound in the side didn't kill him he went for the heart. That much is obvious."

"And where was Matthew's wife when this happened? Because Ostaz Matthew says he caught you raping…"

Uthman slammed his fist on the table sending bits of grit bouncing into the air. "I did no such thing! This would be impossible because this woman was not even there."

"Then can you explain how she became pregnant by you?"

Uthman's eyes widened, his mouth, surrounded by a bush of hair, forming an O. "Pregnant? She is pregnant? I have a child?"

"No, I'm afraid not, but she did become pregnant. An agent of the American FBI thought the child might be yours, so when the woman miscarried, he ordered tests and the results confirmed you were the father." Hossame smiled. "Congratulations Dad, you just proved Matthew Mulberry was telling the truth."

"But…"

"I'm afraid, based on this new evidence, the charges against Ostaz Mulberry will be dropped."

"But…but I…you have the knife with his fingerprints. And Ahmed is also a witness."

"No, I already went to see Ahmed, and when I presented him with the facts, he changed his story. He now says he wasn't there when Ubaid died. He took your word for how it happened. He told me you and Ubaid had an earlier confrontation in which you were almost killed, and that you've slighted him ever since. And as for the fingerprints, as you just said, your fingerprints are also on the knife." Hossame stood, bumping the table as he gathered his things. "Seems you're going to stand trial for two murders."

Uthman sat back looking stunned, his face momentarily drooping but then the curls of his beard began to lift, wrapping around a smile. "This will not happen," he said, "I'm afraid your only witness against me is dead."

"I hope you're wrong about that. I'd hate to have to charge you with murder number three."

Hossame turned and started to walk away but stopped at the door looking back. "There's one thing I don't understand. Your God might, according to what you believe, forgive the murder of a blasphemer, but I don't think his mercy extends to those who kill fellow Muslims. You're going to hang for this. I certainly hope you can explain yourself." He rapped on the door with his knuckles and stood back swinging his belly out of the way as two officers entered.

Uthman's eyes widened as the same two guards that had delivered Matthew into his hands, now reached out to carry him away.

Ambrose lumbered down the hall, the same hall he had escorted Mohamed down after putting him in cuffs, but today he was the bearer of good news. The weight of his footfalls thudded on the carpet as he approached the door. He had only seen one news van in the parking lot, but others would follow. The court's findings had just been released. They'd want Layla's response.

He heard a buzzing inside as his thick finger jabbed the small white button a second time. *Buzzzzzzzzzz.* Maybe she wasn't even there. Folding his arms he stepped back and sighed. He should have called ahead. He'd just wasted forty minutes fighting traffic on a crowded freeway.

The door opened.

He started to smile, but it faded quickly. *Layla?* Her hair was piled on her head, frizzing out like a nest of twigs, and her eyes, darkened by rings, were hollow as caves. She was wearing her bathrobe like she had a bad cold, or hadn't slept in days. She used the tissue wadded in her hand to wipe her nose.

"You...you all right?" Ambrose stammered.

Layla's hand fell from the doorknob as she shuffled back into the room, leaving Ambrose to follow.

"No, I'm not all right," she said, flopping down into a chair. "How can I be all right when my husband's in a hospital not expected to live, and even if he does they'll probably hang him. And now his own wife has killed the one thing that might keep him going. Can you imagine how he's going to feel when he finds out his son is dead? He'll give up. And why not, he has nothing to live for." She sniffed into the tissue, and then blew her nose.

"He has you, Layla. I'm sure Mohamed wants to come home just to be with you."

"Me? The baby killer. I aborted his son."

"It wasn't an abortion. It was a miscarriage. You had nothing to do with it. It was the stress. You've studied medicine. I'm sure you know that."

Layla looked at him, blinking, her eyes filling with water. "That's easy for you to say. What am I going to tell him, Ambrose? What do you say to someone who's lost everything, and you've just stolen the one thing he had left. He was so happy I was pregnant." She straightened herself in her chair. "I don't know, maybe I'm just suffering postpartum depression. It's a cultural thing, you know? Egyptian women are expected to bare children. My mother-in-law was thrilled with the news. I haven't even called to tell her. I don't have the heart."

Ambrose shifted his weight from one foot to the other, the carpet creaking under his feet. He was a big man, long on brawn, short on sensitivity, well suited to the task of muscling bad guys, but mollycoddling emotions was out of his league. "Layla, you haven't taken anything from Mohamed. It wasn't his child. It was the child of the man who raped you."

Layla recoiled, shooting him a look. "What?"

"I had it checked out. You were impregnated by Uthman Massri. The timing was the same. You must have at least considered the possibility."

Layla stared at him, her eyes rimming as she swallowed. "But …there wasn't enough time, he… Mohamed was…we were both sure it couldn't be…"

"Then call it an act of God because that child was Uthman's. That's an undisputable fact."

Layla pulled herself up and began pacing. She whirled about to face Ambrose, an unspoken question on her lips.

Ambrose nodded. "He's still in a coma but he's responding to treatment. His doctor is hopeful he'll make a full recovery. As soon as he's able to travel, we'll bring him home."

"Home?"

"Yes, Layla, home. Our lawyer argued that Uthman raped you, which meant Mohamed was telling the truth, and the court agreed. All charges against him have been dropped. I'm surprised you haven't seen it on TV."

Layla glanced at her television set. "I…I…I haven't turned it on…not since…" Layla dabbed her cheeks with her tissue. "Oh, Ambrose, I could kiss you."

Ambrose raised his hands with his palms out, smiling sheepishly. "Easy, there girl. When Mohamed gets home, I still want to be his friend."

Then the lame shall leap like a deer, and the tongue of the dumb shall sing. — Isaiah 35:6

Mohamed grimaced, his mind churning with thought. It was like he was on the edge of consciousness, only a soap bubble veneer separating him from the real world, but he couldn't break through. Perhaps he didn't want to—because breaking through would mean facing what was on the other side. He felt his windpipe constrict when he conjured up an image of being hung. Or perhaps he knew he wasn't strong enough to face Uthman. He'd seen himself meeting with his accuser, offering forgiveness. They stood on opposite sides of a cell, but whether they were both behind bars, or one of them free, he couldn't tell. He just knew the real accuser was Satan. Uthman was a puppet in the devil's hands.

God had created man in his own image, some destined to commune with Him, others to rebel. Satan had risen up to exchange the goodness of God, Who gave men life, for the disobedience that brought only death.

But there were other things God had shown him, less troubling things. Pictures—*water spraying in a rainbow mist over fields of crops, rows of apartments with children squealing as they chased soccer balls through the yard, a church down by the Nile languishing in the orange warmth of a setting sun.* Internally, he shook his head trying to cast the images off. They were part of the ongoing dream, dark metaphors replaced with those of light—but they were of the farm *and*...and he was destined to hang, oh God give me strength...the music broke into his thoughts. He'd been hearing it for days, angels singing around the throne of God.

> My Jesus, I love Thee, I know Thou art mine;
> For Thee all the follies of sin I resign.
> My gracious Redeemer, my Savior art Thou;
> If ever I loved Thee, my Jesus, 'tis now.

It was the hymn they'd sung at Amin's funeral, and at the baptism. The words rang true...

> I love Thee because Thou has first loved me,
> And purchased my pardon on Calvary's tree.
> I love Thee for wearing the thorns on Thy brow;
> If ever I loved Thee, my Jesus, 'tis now.

because they spoke of a time before he knew Christ...

> I'll love Thee in life, I will love Thee in death,
> And praise Thee as long as Thou lendest me breath;
> And say when the death dew lies cold on my brow,
> If ever I loved Thee, my Jesus, 'tis now.

and after, when he would be called home to glory. He could hear himself mouthing the words, joining in the choir of heaven...

> In mansions of glory and endless delight,
> I'll ever adore Thee in heaven so bright;
> I'll sing with the glittering crown on my brow;
> If ever I loved Thee, my Jesus, 'tis now.

His eyes popped open. *"Layla?"*

She was leaning over him, holding his hand, singing sweet harmony, but her features were fuzzy. He blinked, clearing his vision.

"Oh, thank God!" She brought his hand up, kissing his fingers and pressing them to her cheek, washing them with her tears.

"You're…you're here?"

She nodded, kissing his fingers again. "I bought a ticket and caught the first flight out. I couldn't stay…not after…You were singing, Mohamed. In your sleep, you were singing!"

He swallowed, his throat raspy and sore. She was the one singing, he'd heard her voice—like that of an angel. He turned his head, glancing out the window, feeling a throbbing. He brought his other hand up and touched his forehead, pressing it with his fingers.

"You were wearing bandages, but they removed them after the swelling went down."

A hammer was pounding in his skull. He touched his lip, feeling the stitches. "Is…is there a mirror?"

Layla went to her purse and removed a small compact. Flicking it open, she passed it to him so he could see himself.

His face was a pulpy purple with stitches holding his lip together and several lacerations near his eye.

He snapped the compact closed, looking out the window.

"You were a prisoner when they brought you in so you had to be segregated. They put you in a room by yourself, and that gave me the freedom to sing and pray, and recite verses."

Mohamed nodded, then grimaced. "You think you could open that window. I'd like to feel the fresh air." He tried to sit up, but his chest exploded, a searing pain stabbing his groin. *Auggggggg.*

"Wait a minute. Let me help you." Layla slid her arm under his back, lifting, but he was too heavy. He tried to smile and reached up placing his hands around her waist—and then froze, looking perplexed.

"I lost the child," she said, turning away.

"What?"

"I miscarried." She kept her back to him and went to the window working the latch until she had it open. Then she paused, placing her hands on the sill. "It wasn't yours. They did a blood test and found the father was Uthman."

"Uthman? But you…"

She spun around, facing him again. "I know…I guess God had a different plan. The child was Uthman's proving I was… you know…" her eyes fell to her stomach, "…and that you were telling the truth," she said, looking up again. "So now he's been charged with the murder of both Ubaid and Amin, and you're a free man."

Mohamed propped himself on his elbows and took a deep breath. *Mmmmph.* He grit his teeth and pushed again, moving a few inches higher. "You mean?"

"Yes, as soon as you're well enough, you can go home."

"Home?"

"Back to your mother's, but we'll talk about that later. Right now you need to rest. Just know that God intervened and your lawyer was granted a motion to dismiss all charges." She returned to his side. "They won't admit it, but he thinks the government was happy to drop the case. It would have strained relations with the president if you were prosecuted, but the Brotherhood would have called for riots in the streets if you weren't. Proving your innocence was best for all concerned."

He looked out the window again, taking in the fresh air. The sky was turning pink. Somewhere the sun was setting over the Nile. Each day it would rise, and each day it would set, each day a new beginning, and each day a new end. Life and death, eternal opposites forever entwined, the yin and yang of good and evil, the polar extremes of Satan and God. The earth continued turning till the sun refracted off the window causing a prism of light to dance across the wall. Amin's light. God's light. God's love.

Mohamed rolled his head toward the door. He could hear them clomping down the hall—*his family*—filled with sorrows—*yes*—but also filled with hope. A troop of six people clambered into the room, chattering nonstop. They swarmed around his bed, four men and two women.

"Layla, you're here!"

"Oh Haj Matthew. You look terrible."

"It is good to see you, my son."

"We wanted to come sooner, but they wouldn't tell us where you were."

"Is it true they've dropped the charges?"

They were all chattering at once, talking over each other.

Mohamed glanced at Layla. She took his hand, smiling through her tears, and brought his fingers up again, holding them to her cheek as she began to sing: *"My Jesus I love thee…"* soft and slow at first but increasing in volume as one-by-one the others joined in until the room resounded with the ecstasy of an angelic choir—in which no voice could be heard singing louder—*than his own.*